molly booth

HYPERION

Los Angeles ✦ New York

First Edition, May 2018

10 9 8 7 6 5 4 3 2 1

FAC-020093-18089

Printed in the United States of America

This book is set in Avenir LT Std, Bembo MT Pro, Wingdings/Monotype; Bambusa Pro, Brandon Grotesque, Hey Comrade, Janda Elegant Handwriting, Larissa Handwriting, Marcello Handwriting, Museo, TT Berlinerins, Wanderlust/Fontspring

Designed by Whitney Manger

Library of Congress Cataloging-in-Publication Data

Names: Booth, Molly, author.

Title: Nothing happened / Molly Booth.

Description: First edition. • Los Angeles ; New York : Hyperion, 2018. •
   Summary: "Modern-day retelling of Shakespeare's Much Ado About Nothing
   taking place at an idyllic summer camp where the counselors have to cope
   with simmering drama"— Provided by publisher.

Identifiers: LCCN 2017034518 (print) • LCCN 2017045796 (ebook) • ISBN
   9781484758533 (ebook) • ISBN 9781484753026 (hardcover : alk. paper)

Subjects: • CYAC: Camps—Fiction. • Interpersonal relations—Fiction. •
   Love—Fiction. • Family life—Maine—Fiction. • Maine—Fiction.

Classification: LCC PZ7.1.B668 (ebook) • LCC PZ7.1.B668 Not 2018 (print) •
   DDC [Fic]—dc23

LC record available at https://lccn.loc.gov/2017034518

Reinforced binding

Visit www.hyperionteens.com

For Bonnie
whose insight and support flicker between
every word in this book

CHAPTER 1

Bee

I FOUGHT THE URGE to crumple the paper, shove it in my mouth, and eat it.

Flip-flops for the shower

Bucket for toiletries

Notebooks, pens, etc. will be available at the store

Why did my college's packing suggestions look so much like a list for summer camp?

Ugh. I wasn't supposed to have to deal with this for months. Packing. Moving. Boston.

"What's that?" My sister, Hana, peeked over my shoulder.

"Nothing!" I stuffed the list back in the envelope.

"If it's not about camp, you can look at it later," my mom said. We were all in the living room on our faded yellow floral sofa, huddled over the coffee table stacked high with mail. Our annual Leonato family spring camp paperworkfest! Every year, my parents picked a weekend in April—shortly after the application deadline—for us to organize our camp's employment for the coming summer. Counselor and activity leader applications; CITs.

I felt Hana's eyes watching me and my envelope with concern.

I knew my family was really going to miss me when I left—especially after this year, with everything Hana had gone through.

They didn't need to know how my stomach sank every time I thought about college.

Hana opened her mouth to say something, but I quickly cut her off—

"Good idea, I'll look at it later!" I resealed the envelope and hurled the entire packet behind me. It landed with a *smack!* somewhere in the dining room. Hana smiled. Sadness avoided, for now.

"Bee . . ." Mom's severe brow furrowed in my direction.

"What?" I said. "You told me to!"

"You could've broken something."

My dad carried in another gigantic armful of envelopes and dropped them in a pile on the floor. "That's it: next year, Camp Dogberry is going digital." Mom shot him a look. He gestured emphatically at the mountain of mail. "Nik, come *on*! Look at this! We're the opposite of eco-friendly. We're eco-mean."

Mom sighed. She abhorred technology. "I know you're right. As much as I hate to admit it. But, no"—she pointed a finger at my sister—"that does not mean you can use your phone at camp, Hana."

Hana turned red. We'd both gotten smartphones a few years ago, and ever since she'd been glued to hers.

"The no–cell phones rule is important," I said. "Don't forget the legend of *The Idiot CIT and the Bear.*"

"I don't think I remember that one." Dad grinned. "Bee, would you—"

"Maine is known for blueberries and bears," I began, in my narrator voice, standing up and taking my place in the living room archway. No sense in not being completely dramatic about this. "Camp Dogberry, in Messina, Maine, was practically bursting with blueberries. As for bears, rumors floated around camp. Largely because of one dangerous incident: *The Idiot CIT and . . . the Bear*."

"Dun-dun-duuuuuun," Dad added in.

"One summer, loooong ago, a young, dewy-eyed counselor-in-training was going for his early morning run, with headphones in." I mimed a slow jog, bobbing my head back and forth. "The headphones were plugged into his cell phone, on which he played *loud music*. This was his fatal mistake."

"Not quite fatal," Mom said, undermining my narrative.

"He set off around the coastline, blasting music into his ears instead of enjoying the harmonious sounds of nature. So loud were his tunes that he didn't hear rustling in the bushes. Thus, it came as quite a shock when a real live bear cub tumbled onto the path in front of him. Awww! he thought. A baby bear! How cute! I am clearly not in any danger!"

"Have we confirmed with the original source that this was his exact thought process?" Dad asked.

"The CIT stood transfixed by the adorableness of the bear cub. With the music still blasting into his ears, he was unaware of the approaching danger. Suddenly, he felt hot breath on the back of his neck. He froze." I froze. "He turned." I turned. "And directly behind him was an enormous black bear. A mama bear's job is to protect her kids, and she was afraid this clueless human was somehow going to hurt her baby bear. She didn't know the CIT was harmless. What would the CIT do now? What would you do? Because I guarantee, it's not this:

"The CIT grabbed two pine branches and waved them back and forth as he backed away, screaming, 'OLD MACDONALD HAD A FARM. EEEEYI EEEYI OOOOOH!!!'

"At this noise, Mama Bear stopped in her tracks, dumbfounded, and quite frankly, artistically offended. She realized that this creature was not dangerous, but totally ridiculous. She let the CIT turn around and run back to camp, where he did about five hundred jumping jacks to release his adrenaline, and then passed out on Monarch field.

"And that, kids," I finished, "is why we don't use cell phones at camp."

My family dutifully gave me a round of applause, to which I bowed deeply.

"Excellent performance as always, Bee," Dad said. "But I don't remember this cautionary tale making fun of the CIT quite so mercilessly. For instance, I don't think *idiot* is in the title."

"Okay, so I made some changes." I rolled my eyes and stepped over the table to drop down next to him again. "Stories evolve." I ignored the itchy guilt that crept up the backs of my arms. This story was funnier when the idiot CIT and I were still friends.

"Dad's right." Mom moved a handful of forms down the line. "We don't use the word *idiot* at camp. You know that."

"Obviously, I won't tell it like that *at camp*," I assured them.

"You can tell it however you want when you run the place." Dad smiled. "You can fill it with swears."

"I *am* running the place!"

"You're the assistant improv leader," Mom corrected. New title this year—it sounded so official. I loved it. Plus it meant I got to spend most of the camp day with our longtime improv leader, and one of my best camp friends, Raphael.

"Preeetty sure that means I'm a boss."

"Okay, boss, have a look at this application and let me know what you think." Mom passed me an envelope.

I bent back the metal fastener and slid out the packet of papers. The heading *Camp Dogberry Counselor Application* in our official green camp font, with little pine and dogwood trees on either side, greeted me. When my eyes landed on the applicant name, I had to fight another urge to crumple up the papers and shove them in my mouth. The staple would pose a problem, but I could spit it out like a cherry pit—

"What the hell?" I finally managed. I looked up right into Mom's eyes. Same eyes as Hana—big, light brown in the middle, dark brown on the edges. Like tree rings. Mom's usually reflected that firm, parental love, but now they were straight-up laughing at me.

"Seems promising, right?" She tried to keep from smirking. But not that hard. "Ben Rosenthal. He's applying for sports leader."

"Ben?!" Hana gasped.

"Do you think he's right for the job?" Mom asked.

Was this a joke? "Sure, unless we care about the sports program," I replied, still dazed.

"Wait, seriously, it's really him?" Hana hopped up and looked over my shoulder. I wanted to block her view, but my arms and hands didn't move when I told them to. "Ben? Ben's coming back?!" She squealed in my ear.

"I guess?" I handed her the application.

"Huzzah!" Dad clapped his big bear hands.

"But I thought last year was his *last year*?" Hana said, examining the application critically. I'd done the same thing, but it was definitely his handwriting—it looked like a chicken on a seesaw had filled it out.

"He certainly announced that many times," I growled. "What a dingus. I should've seen this coming."

Mom had moved on and was waving the next envelope. "Well, he's not the only one going back on his vow. Here's *Donald King* too."

"Both of them?" I demanded. "Unreal. They kept calling dibs on stuff last summer because it was their *last summer*. They got more breaks and chocolate and beer—" I stopped, quickly. Neither parent reacted, thank goodness.

Hana hopped over to Mom and grabbed the packet. "This is awesome!"

Truthfully, yes, I was excited that Donald was returning to camp. He always brought a special something to Camp Dogberry that no one else did. He was really cool—too cool—so he made everything at camp seem cool for the campers. And for the counselors, too.

"You're right, it's awesome," I said. "But what is *Ben* doing back at camp? Isn't he a doctor or something?"

"He's only been in college for a year!" Dad laughed.

"Well, it's pathetic." I shook my head. "He made this huge deal about 'moving on,' and now he's just, like, applied? Without saying anything?"

"What else would he say?" Mom asked.

That was a loaded question—one I was not prepared to answer.

"I don't know!" I sputtered. "He didn't call either of you, did he?"

Mom and Dad exchanged a glance. "Colleen might've mentioned something," Dad admitted. Colleen. Ben's mom.

Mom tapped his application. "And Ben might've called me a few weeks ago—"

"Seriously?!" I yelled.

"—to ask if applying for sports leader would be appropriate."

"He's a nice kid." Dad nodded.

"He is." Mom smiled back.

"I'm going to kill you both!" I threw up my hands. What were parents good for? I turned on Hana: "Did you know about this?"

"No!" she said quickly. "I haven't heard from him since he texted me on my birthday. . . ."

Ouch. I hadn't heard from Ben on *my* birthday. I looked down and scowled into my hands. Imagined his face on a grape. Squished the grape in my palm.

"But, Bee?" Hana's soft voice interrupted. "Isn't it better to have Ben back? Camp wouldn't be the same without him."

I looked up. She blinked at me. Hana acts all naive, but she's sneaky, that one. I shot her a death glare, extra death. Then I threw another application toward her.

"What about *you*, Hana? Would camp be the same without *Claudia*?"

She saw the name on the envelope and immediately dropped it like a hot marshmallow.

"Of course!" she said, voice screeching up an octave. "It's great they're *all* coming back!"

My parents looked at us both dubiously. Then Hana attempted her own version of a death glare. Her round eyes twitched. I laughed—it was like a stink eye from a baby seal. My sister was the cutest person alive, and glares didn't even work on her face.

"Ben, Donald, Claudia, and here's Margo!" Dad raised up another application. That broke up some tension: we all cheered for Margo. I already knew she was coming back, because we had one of those summer friendships that kept going the rest of the year.

"Excellent!" Dad smiled. "The Dogberry dream team. We're barely going to have to hire anyone new."

"I wouldn't be that heartbroken if, say, *Bobby* or *John* didn't come back," I muttered.

"That's not a very *teamwork* attitude," Mom chided.

Dad held up John's application. Crap. Well, he came with Donald.

"Okay." I nodded. "But more importantly, if *Ben* had miraculously got a life, would it really be that much of a loss?"

"All right." Mom sighed, running a hand along her right temple. "Bee, you have a couple months before camp starts, so work on losing that attitude. I can't take another summer like last year. You and Ben are friends."

"Not till it snows in July," I retorted. Friends. Friendly, friendly friends. "He's the biggest pain-in-the-butt friend I've ever had," I added. "And a seriously lazy employee." I cringed even as I said it. She was right, though—I needed to shut up. The bigger deal I made out of this, the worse the whole situation would be. And besides, it had been almost a year. When was I going to stop associating Ben with that one awkward night? I'd known him for six years before that. It made no sense, and it made me want to slap myself.

"You know Ben's got his strengths," Mom said. "Not everyone's good at getting up early."

"He *is* champion of Capture the Flag." Dad grinned at Mom. "Man. I really can't wait for camp to start."

"I'm starting to dread it." I stood up. "I need a break. I'll go into town and get us lunch."

"Pizza, please!" Dad brightened. "And can you stop at Reny's and grab us a pack of highlighters?"

"And clothespins," Mom added. We'd just hung up our laundry line.

"You got it!" I hurried toward the front door.

"I'll come with you!" Hana jumped up.

Argh. I wanted to be alone, but I didn't want to tell her no. She'd been a little clingy since my college acceptance letters. Look at me, I mentally muttered. Calling my sister clingy. This was Ben's fault. Before last summer, I never needed time alone to think. I did my best thinking *with* Hana. Now I had secrets.

"Parents—" I turned back to them as I pulled on my boots. "Let's not be hasty. I'm sure there are other qualified sports candidates."

"Bee, your promotion to assistant improv leader does not, I'm afraid, give you hiring and firing power." Mom waved me away. Insulting.

"Sorry, kiddo." Dad nodded. "Capture the Flag is my favorite part of camp, and Ben *is* Capture the Flag."

"I repeat: ugh."

I let the screen door slam on our way out. I usually looked forward to this time of the year. I felt the climbing anticipation—every form we filled out, every permit stamped and hire made, was another step toward starting day. Sun and sweat and laughter.

But this Ben thing pulled me up short; threw me.

Out the door, Hana had a mission. "Want to go look at the waves real quick?"

My sister loved all bodies of water, but particularly our waterfront, the pebbly edges of Messina Harbor. This coming summer would be her first as a full-fledged lifeguard and swim instructor, which meant she got to spend all day teaching campers to swim. And when she wasn't doing that, she'd be swimming just for herself. I'd known Hana since she was three and I was five, when my parents adopted me and brought me to the US from Ethiopia. They'd originally planned on adopting a baby, but when they got to the adoption center, I'd jumped into their laps and demanded a story, and that was the end of that. Luckily, it was a love-at-first-sight kind of deal for Hana and me. Being sisters was clearly our destiny.

I remember watching her in the pool, though, at our YMCA, and feeling slightly five-year-old suspicious. When I showed up, she could already dive and swim across the deep end.

These suspicions had not waned. I'd never been able to confirm Hana wasn't actually a mermaid.

"Sure, let's go."

We set off down the trail. I tried to shake off Ben, but my thoughts kept drifting back to him. Well, things around/adjacent to him. Sparklers and snowflakes. Grass blades and eyelashes.

"Are you okay?" Hana poked my side.

I smiled instantly. "I'm fine!"

"It *is* a little weird Donald and Ben are coming back," she ventured. "When they swore so many times they wouldn't."

"Yeah." I nodded. *Don't take the bait, Bee.* We walked the trail in silence for a few moments, while I fought my dangerously impulsive mouth. Hana checked her phone five times in a minute. She caught me looking at her and blushed.

"Maybe you're right," she admitted. "Maybe I am looking forward to seeing Claudia."

"Oh really?" I teased, relieved by the change of subject.

"Really," she admitted. "But I don't know if I'm over Christopher."

I bit my tongue. Come *on*! At least Claudia was someone new for Hana to obsess over. Not that jerkwad Christopher, who'd yanked her around all year, then dumped her, reducing my beautiful Hana to a phantom who could barely get out of bed.

"Okay," I said. "But what if this summer, we just did our own thing?"

"What?" I could already hear the defensiveness in her voice.

"I just mean . . ." I fought for the right words. "What if we just swim, and play improv games, do crafts, and hang out with Margo—"

I cut myself off with a sharp breath in. We had reached the part of the path where it divided into three separate trails: One led to the center of camp and our giant log cabin mess hall—Beaver Dam—and the sandy clearing out front with the flagpole. The second led to our swimming waterfront. Docks, buddy board, all that camp swim stuff.

And then there was the third option: a steep, scraggly path, hidden in the summer by ferns that were just starting to revive now. This little trail led up to Eagle's Nest, a clearing at the top of a hill hidden by trees, with a perfect view of the stars. AKA Nest, one of our counselor party spots.

Last Fourth of July, after our annual sparkler party, two of the counselors had stayed behind to clean up and had returned to their respective cabins just before morning meeting, causing wild intrigue and rumors to fly throughout camp.

That night.

"Bee," Hana's soft voice ventured.

"What?"

"Last summer . . . with you and Ben—"

"Oh my God." I groaned and stalked toward the water. "I've told you a hundred times: *nothing* happened."

CHAPTER 2

Hana

BEE WAS TERRIBLE at keeping secrets. She always cracked and spilled her guts. When we were little, if we did anything wrong, like take extra cookies or break a glass, I knew Bee would confess the second Mom walked in the room.

"Mom, I am *so* sorry, but we *betrayed* you *again*!" she would announce, bursting into tears. Eventually I figured out that if I wanted extra cookies, I had to keep my big sister in the dark.

So how had she kept this secret all year? I wished for the millionth time that she would confide in me. But I'd learned to let the question go, and for the millionth time, I did.

The sea felt gorgeous—wind danced across the water, flicking spray onto my face. Thick fog had rolled in, concealing the little island off our shore. I scooped some of the freezing ocean into my water bottle.

Bee stood on the swim dock, arms crossed, staring ahead into the haze. Her tall, dark silhouette almost disappeared into the mist. I wondered what song from *Les Mis* was playing in her head.

"Bee!" I called cheerfully. "Let's go get pizza!"

❧

After dinner, Bee announced she was done for the day, and she'd be in the den studying. My parents both looked at me pointedly—Bee's love of paperwork was legendary, and I knew they wanted me to follow, ask her what was wrong. But I just shrugged back at them; I knew she wanted to be left alone.

Instead I went up to my bedroom and poured this afternoon's saltwater into one of the glass vases on my windowsill. The bits of sand and plant swirled. This vase was halfway full now—it was my seventh. A long line of little vases, holding bouquets of waves.

My therapist, Louisa, and I had developed these "coping skills" to help with my depression. "Exercise" (swimming), "sleep schedule" (I'm not great at this), "school" (I kind of didn't do homework last fall), and "self care" (semi-insane craft projects).

My bedroom reflected the last one. A line of water vases, a stack of "adult & teen!" coloring books, and a shoe box full of tiny lucky origami stars, which I folded obsessively. I'd cleared out the camp art building, Painted Turtle, of all the rainbow origami paper. Still have to tell Mom about that.

When summer started, Donald and Ellen, our art leader, would give me new crafts to do. Tie-dye T-shirts, friendship bracelets, lumpy handmade candles . . . I could spend all day between the ocean and Painted Turtle. Just swimming and crafting.

And absolutely no Christopher.

I paused my social studies reading to check my phone.

No Christopher, even if I wanted him.

My ex . . . whatever. I guess I couldn't really call him an ex-boyfriend. We'd never been official. But he was still my ex-*something*.

I just needed to get through the next month and a half of school. Three more swim meets, three more papers, one guy I still couldn't shake. I mean, he mostly ignored me at school anyway, which was good. My therapist and I agreed it was good.

Except that I spent most of the school day waiting for him to accidentally make eye contact with me. I didn't tell Louisa that.

Suddenly, my phone lit up. Three texts in a row, all from Claudia.

No way. I had no idea they were coming back. Texting them now

Those idiots. What happened to "this is our LAST SUMMER"?!

TBH I'm excited though. That just made this summer even better

I smiled and quickly typed back.

Same!! I really can't wait

Claudia. Once we got going, we'd be up till two or three talking. It didn't matter what we talked about. I just liked this routine: I liked that someone else was awake that late, too; I liked that the later it got, the flirtier we'd get; I liked that every part of me would grow warmer, just for a few hours.

> Seriously. School needs to be over

> ☹ I know those feels. But we're so close!

> Yes. And then we'll be together

Together. That was such an incredible word. I melted reading it. Being apart made that word different. *Together* meant in the same place, her body in front of mine, and hearing her voice, soft and smoldering, like charcoal pencil strokes.

Claudia lived in Connecticut, hours away. We never saw each other, except for summers. All of this texting started a few months ago, during a weekend when Christopher had blown me off again. But it got more intense in the last couple months, when Chris and I had split. Well, he'd split from me. And I'd just wanted someone to talk to—and suddenly, she was there, in my messages, whenever I needed her.

And I'd felt that glow begin.

Sometimes I looked at pictures of her online and just stared, dumbfounded. Black hair streaked with gray and white strands, wiry arms, serious lips that grudgingly loosened into smiles. Could this beautiful person really be on the other end of these conversations? It didn't feel real.

Somewhere around eleven, Bee appeared in my doorway, catching me by surprise. She looked at the phone in my hands, said a tight "Good night, I love you," and then I heard a knob click.

I knew she was just worried about me, but it still hurt.

> Sometimes I wish my sister wasn't so judge-y

> Ha! It's not like she doesn't have secrets too.
> *Cough cough* Ben *cough cough*

We stayed up till three thirty, the longest we've ever talked. Claudia complained about her old, crappy group of friends. I told her about drama on our swim team. We whined about school and would it ever end? I think we both knew, even if we couldn't say it, what the end of the year meant:

The beginning of us. Maybe?

In between texts, I folded star after star, pinching my summer hopes into the paper points.

CHAPTER 3

$\mathcal{B}_{\varepsilon N}$

FOR THE LAST EIGHT YEARS, the end of June meant one thing—the beginning of Camp Dogberry. But Camp Dogberry meant a lot of things: wheezing in dusty cabins, no sleep, mosquito bites on sunburns, complete responsibility for a million children, the same food for two months straight, and boats. I hate boats.

Also, camp meant this one person, whose wicked laughter and glares I brought home at the end of summer. And like every June, I felt, like, so excited to see her. But I tried to squash those habitual feelings, told them to cool it. We hadn't so much as texted this entire year. Did she hate me? I had no idea where we stood anymore.

And *also* also, whatever, more importantly, Camp Dogberry meant my best friends and the best place in the entire world. Especially after spending a year trapped in the city of Boston, summer camp in Maine seemed like a rural paradise.

But this June wasn't supposed to be about camp. I'd made a solemn vow last year that it was my *last year*. I'd declared this, publicly, many times. I knew finding summer internships during college would be important, and any part of me that still clung to the idea of coming back was blown to smithereens that one night. After that

I'd just plain sworn off Camp Dogberry forever. Which was terrible, because I loved it.

Life was so complicated.

And there I was, year nine, waking up at fudge o'clock, rolling off the couch, grabbing a sleeping bag, kind of brushing my teeth, kissing my sisters' sleeping heads . . . then getting Layla a cup of water because she'd woken up when I'd kissed her sleeping head.

Finally, I wrote a note to my mom and left it on our new kitchen island.

"Ben! Look! Our own private island!" Mom had said, beaming, when we'd moved in the week before. I still wasn't used to her real smiles, but they automatically made me grin back.

I stumbled down the apartment building stairs, outside, and into Claudia's car.

The great thing about Claudia was that she understood I was not a human before ten a.m. I got in the car, we grunted at each other, she turned on the radio, and next thing, I woke up to the sound of tires crushing gravel as we pulled into the familiar Dogberry parking lot. Counselors' families and cars swarming, the smudged white check-in tent waiting to the left. I felt at home, but also like I might throw up.

"Ben, are we gonna get out or what?"

I startled, realizing that I'd been spacing out into the bushes in front of the car. When I looked at Claudia, I startled again at her new hair. For as long as I'd known her, Claudia'd had this long black sheet of hair. Now it was clipped short, shorter than mine. You could really see all her little white hairs peeking up throughout the black. She was the only seventeen-year-old I knew who actually had salt-and-pepper hair.

"Yeah, sorry, let's go."

Camp smelled like pine needles, saltwater, and good old dirt. It was a sunny morning, still chilly for June, but that was Maine for you, especially a little farther north. We grabbed our gear out of the trunk. A couple other cars were already there—I saw Donald's ridiculous green Mercedes and couldn't help smiling. It would be awesome to have everyone back together again, even if it felt like cheating adulthood.

"Oh hey." Claudia pointed ahead. "There's Hana."

Leonato Jr. held the check-in clipboard under the welcome tent. Her whole face lit up, and she waved us over. Claudia hesitated for just a second and fell behind me as we walked up. Jesus. Put Claudia in the path of a pretty girl, and she became a ball of idiot.

"Ben! Claudia! It's so good to see you!" Hana reached out for a hug. She must've had a growth spurt or something—she was nearly as tall as me now. Maybe a little taller?

"Hey, Hana!" I squeezed her back. "Did you grow or did I shrink?"

She laughed in my ear.

"Hey," Claudia mumbled behind us.

Hana pulled back and reached out tentatively to hug Claudia, who went in for an intense grip for one second, then let go immediately. Weirdo.

"I'm so glad you both came back this year!" Hana smiled, unflustered by Claudia's bizarro hug. "I thought you weren't going to?" That last part was directed at me. It only stung a little.

"Well, here I am!" I said cheerfully.

"Yeah—wasn't last summer your *last summer*, Ben?"

A voice stopped me cold. I tried to compose myself, but when I turned around, I still wasn't prepared for Bee Leonato. Fierce, beautiful, perfectly witty and weird. Always an inch or so taller than me, now even more so—her black hair was braided in intricate spirals that pulled into a faux-hawk on top of her head. Gold hoops hung from her ears, trembling in the force that buzzed around her.

Had I ever stood a chance?

Our gazes met. My eyelids fluttered rapidly, like I was looking into the sun. I forgot about replying and just focused on looking at my feet without falling over. My heart pounded into the dirt.

Bee didn't miss a beat. "Claudia!" She turned and gave her a quick smile and a non-awkward hug. "Great to see you."

"You too."

"So, Ben, what's up?" Bee tried again. "Are you here to drop off the girls? That's next week."

"What?" I fumbled. Another three seconds to prepare had not helped. Especially since her eyes were now fixed on me in their familiar glare. "No, I'm sports leader."

"Right . . ." Her glare slid over me. My stomach gulped. "You're sports leader this year. Even though you said you were done with this place, a *million* times."

"I . . . um . . ."

I glanced at Hana, for support, but she just blinked at me apologetically and pulled Claudia off to the side. Great.

So much for my hope that everything might be magically forgotten.

Bee was still staring at me, arms crossed. How was it she looked the same but everything was completely different? We should be catching up on the past year. I wanted to know where she was going to college. Plus I was full of news too—about the move, my sisters, Boston. I was bursting to tell her everything . . . but she kind of looked like she wanted to murder me.

"So yeah—" I tried—

"Why did you come back, Ben?" She had cut me off, her dark eyes clouding over, unsearchable.

"Family stuff." I lowered my voice. "We moved out. My mom and my sisters and me. It's complicated." Where did that come from? I'd sworn I wasn't going to tell anyone.

"Oh." Her glare softened the tiniest bit, and I instinctively leaned in closer. We could fix this. If I could just figure out the right thing to say—

"Bee, can we—"

"Beeeeeeee!" We both turned as Margo threw herself into Bee. I stepped back to shield myself from the hug explosion. Margo's hair sprang every which way, which was normal, but usually, it was a bright, fiery orange. Now it was a deep, shiny purple. Did Dogberry send out a memo that we all needed new hair this summer? After a full minute of squealing and jumping around, Margo finally noticed me.

"Ben! You're back!" She grinned, like this was just a little amusing.

"Hey, Margo."

We hugged, and then they went back to yelling in one another's faces. Bee and I were clearly done for now. Hana, while being squeezed by Margo, told Claudia and me that we could wait in Dam, where we'd all be meeting soon.

I hiked my orange duffel bag higher over my shoulder and led the way down the wide, shady dirt path, vaguely aware of Claudia trailing somewhere behind me.

My reunion with Bee was over, just like that. I'd been daydreaming about it for months, but in my dreams, I was a lot cooler, and Bee was a lot happier to see me.

We approached the biggest building at camp, an enormous pseudo–log cabin with a large porch and a flagpole area out front. Claudia tripped up the stairs. I wasn't the only one in a daze.

We pushed open the double screen doors; they shut with a comforting slam behind us. Rows of colorful tables and chairs, white twinkle lights wrapped around the rafters, the big welcoming window to the kitchen, the wafting smell of blueberry pancakes. Home.

"Hey! Nerds!" Donald called out as he sauntered across the hall and pulled each of us in for bro hugs.

"Hey man, how ya been?" I clapped his back.

Sunglasses, Afro, always the tie-dye shirts with designer jeans. Did he even own shorts? "Killin' it," he assured me. "It's good to see you."

He pushed his sunglasses back on his head. "Claudia, your hair's gone!"

"Really? I hadn't noticed," Claudia said sarcastically. Well, almost sarcastically—it had that awkwardness that kind of ruined the effect of sarcasm. I made a mental note: the hair thing was sensitive.

"Huh." Donald stared at her head for a moment before turning to me. "So, freshman year! How'd you do?"

"Oh, fine." I shrugged. "Good grades."

"Who cares? Do you have a girlfriend?" Donald pointed an eyebrow at me.

"I'm premed," I reminded him.

"So nobody wanted to fuck you?"

"I don't have time."

He snickered. "Please—virgins have tons of time on their hands."

I shoved him.

"Claudia?" He turned to her. Her entire upper half had disappeared into her duffel bag, rooting around for something.

"No, I don't have cash for a beer run," she answered from inside. I laughed.

"That too. But I was asking if you got a girlfriend this year."

Claudia pulled her head out, blushing. "Shut up. No." I laughed again. I really had missed Claudia. She reminded me of myself when I was twelve. Not that I would ever tell her that, since she was seventeen and a lot more muscular than twelve-year-old me. Or nineteen-year-old me.

"That makes three of us, then." Donald sighed and shook his head. "Single and back at summer camp. Pathetic."

"So nobody wanted to fuck you?" I asked innocently.

Claudia fist-bumped me. Donald laughed but then got serious and pushed both of us toward the corner of Dam with the drink machine—pretty much the only place at camp you were guaranteed privacy—glancing back over his shoulder. I looked in that direction: John, his half brother, with Connie and Bobby. They had formed a trio last summer.

"Actually, yeah, someone *did* want to fuck me," Donald whispered, under the buzz of the machine.

"Can I submit that to the camp newsletter?" I whispered back. Claudia smirked.

"But that guy"—Donald jerked a thumb in John's direction—"screwed it up for me."

"Screwed up the fucking," I summarized. Claudia laughed.

"Seriously!" Donald groaned quietly. "*Why* did my dad have to get that ingrate into Yale?"

Donald and John's dad was Josiah King, a New York senator. Their family was . . . complicated. Senator King had had an affair with John's mom and kept it quiet, but the whole thing blew up when the guys were in middle school, for reasons I never totally grasped. Nobody could really believe when Senator King had called the Leonatos last summer about John working here. John was an okay guy and okay at his job—but he and Donald did *not* get along.

Senator King had pulled strings to get *Donald* into Yale, too, but it probably wasn't a good idea to bring that up right now.

"Wait," Claudia whispered. "How could *John* get in the way of you having sex? That doesn't even make sense." I didn't voice aloud the image that question brought to mind.

"Well, because Yale sucks," Donald explained, like he was reviewing a pair of headphones online. "John and I were in the same dorm, on the same floor, so we knew a lot of the same people, went to the same parties."

"Right." Donald's college life sounded wildly different from mine. A month later, I was still recovering from finals and the one end-of-year party I had attempted to go to.

"So in the first few weeks, I was hanging out with this girl, Joanna, and man, she was *hot* and *cool*," Donald continued. "And we were so close, man. Like, so close. I got to third multiple times."

"Again, newsletter-worthy," I interjected. I was trying to keep it light—Claudia was a little younger than us, and as far as I knew, she'd never hooked up with anyone before.

"So we're supposed to go to this party together, right?" Donald's whisper became more of a hiss. "But she bails on me. And then the next night, she bails on me again. And then one of her friends tells one of *my* friends that Joanna told *her* that John told *everyone* that I'm a *virgin!*"

Claudia and I took a beat to react.

"Damn, Donald," I observed.

"But . . . aren't you?" Claudia asked him, at the exact same time.

"Yeah, but you don't *tell people* that at college!" Donald smacked his forehead. "At college you get to start over. People ask you how many girls you've been with, and you say, 'I don't know, I lost count.'"

"Smart." Claudia nodded.

I had to admit, I kind of wished I'd thought of that.

"So he told her that I'm a virgin, and she didn't want to be my first, so she ghosted me. Except that we kept bumping into each other in the bathroom and avoiding eye contact."

"What a jerk."

"Yeah, John's the worst," Donald said, glancing darkly over his shoulder.

"I meant Joanna," I said, lightly hitting his shoulder. "She didn't have to ghost you just because you'd never had sex."

"Uh, what's ghosting?" Claudia asked. "I'm getting some weird mental pictures right now."

"My only solace is that John's clearly not getting laid either," Donald said, completely ignoring both of us.

"Clearly." I yawned. "I'm going to get pancakes."

Just as I turned to go, Dam's doors banged open, and in walked Bee and Hana with Margo between them.

"Hey!" Bee called out. "Time to circle up!"

All the counselors gathered in the middle of the room, dutifully forming a large, misshapen circle. I glanced longingly at the breakfast bar one more time before falling in line.

Nik and Andy Leonato appeared at the head of the circle. Nik was our camp director. Technically Andy was the co-director, but Nik really ran the thing. She was short, tan, and intimidating, with an angular face and an impressive forehead. I used to be scared of her, and I still was a little bit, 'cause she was my boss. But I'd seen her soft side now too.

Where Nik was little and pointy, Andy was towering and doughy. He had a ton of curly hair and an impressive brown beard. I think I'd seen him frown maybe once in my life. Put it all together with his love of Jell-O, and it was totally obvious why a lot of campers called him Santa. Andy was a school nurse during the year, and he ran the Dogberry first-aid building, Black Bear.

"All right, kiddos!" Nik shouted. The hubbub died off immediately. "Welcome back to Dogberry, and welcome to our newest counselors—Dave, Doug, and Jen. As for you old-timers, it's good to see *all of you* back this summer."

Donald nudged me. I winced.

"We're in for another year of hard work, and our session numbers, miraculously, look good. Your cabin and age assignments are on the green lists going around, and the orange paper is the training schedule for the week. CITs and activity leaders will be here this weekend, and the first session starts Monday. Everyone needs to get certified, or recertified, in first aid and CPR. And if you need lifeguard or swim certs . . ."

Nik read off the list, and then Andy announced the activity leaders and assistants. Donald assisting in art, Margo in nature, and Bee in improv. We were the oldest counselors now. Totally weird.

Even weirder that I'd somehow landed sports leader, with Claudia as my assistant. I mean, Nik had told me to apply, but still. Even back when I thought I'd work at Camp Dogberry forever, I never thought I'd get promoted to leader before anyone else.

" . . . so now you have a few minutes to settle in," Nik finished. "We'll see you all in an hour at Monarch."

The games field. My office for the summer—so much better than my admin work-study job. I couldn't wait. The circle broke up with a happy racket, and Nik and Andy sauntered over to us.

"The mighty hath returned from war!" Andy clapped Donald and me on the back. "Glad you're back from college in one piece. How's Yale, Donald?"

"Failing everything."

"That's what we like to hear," Nik said, then looked at me. "How's BU, Ben?"

She knew. She'd talked to my mom last week. But I appreciated her not mentioning that. "It's good," I said. "Not Yale, so I'm doing well."

"Excellent." Nik nodded. "And it's still a great school. Bee applied there."

"Really? Where did she—"

"Claudia?" Andy leaned down and smiled at her.

She startled. "Uhh, I'm not in college yet?"

Andy smiled. "Great. Glad everyone's on top of their educations."

"Nik, the first-year counselors look so young," Donald whispered. "Are you sure they're not campers?"

"That's a sign you're getting old, Donald," Nik chided, "when you see the fifteen-year-olds as babies."

Andy chuckled.

Donald looked over his shoulder. "They *are* babies."

"Hana was a baby a second ago, and she's taller than me now!" I offered. "And since when is her hair all curly, like Andy's?"

Nik laughed. "Well, she is his daughter. Or that's what I told him, anyway."

Donald and Claudia cracked up. Nik grinned and kissed Andy's cheek. He raised his eyebrows at me, and they both retreated into the kitchen.

"I just meant," I mumbled, "I haven't seen her in a while, and it looks curlier now—"

"Why're you still talking, Ben?" Bee strolled over with Margo and Hana. "Nobody's listening."

"I . . . uh . . ."

"You know, Bee"—Donald leaned an elbow on her shoulder—"in some circles, Ben is actually smooth."

Everyone laughed. Thanks a lot, Donald.

"He's a city guy now," he continued. Please shut up. "He's got city game."

"Oh, is that so?" Bee turned back to me. "So . . . what? Did you get a *city* girlfriend?"

"Well, no," I sputtered. "I'm too busy studying."

"Oh, thank God." Bee smiled. "I'm so relieved for all the girls in Boston." Donald and Margo both laughed.

"So you've got a boyfriend?" I asked, before I could stop myself.

"No," she snorted. "I'd rather eat a handful of glass."

"Good!" Donald slung an arm around both of us. "So we're *all* pathetic and single. Maybe we can change that this summer."

"Some more pathetic than others," Bee singsonged, shooting a pointed look at me. "Some of us are actually single by *choice*."

"Whatever," I sighed. "Can you cut it out, Bee? I'm already so over this."

The group went awkwardly silent. Everyone glanced at Bee, waiting for her witty reply.

Bee's face fell, but her expression quickly morphed into a scowl. "Whatever, Ben. If you're over it, you shouldn't have come back."

The silence was less awkward this time. More hushed. Was this actually happening? Yes, that night—well, really the next day—had been the worst, but did that really mean we were done? Forever? I kept waiting for her to laugh, to take it back. But she didn't.

"Well, too late now." I grabbed my bag and headed over to the table to get my cabin assignment before anyone could notice how red my face was.

I was living in Snowshoe this year. Cool. There was an electrical outlet under the counselor bunk in that one. That was good. Forget Bee. Things were looking up. I headed out the door, and Donald and Claudia caught up with me. Neither one said a word about the train wreck they just witnessed, which was merciful of them. We went down toward the waterfront, where the path split for the cabins. Donald snatched my cabin assignment right out of my hands.

"Snowshoe. Nice. I'm in Coyote."

"Red Fox," Claudia sighed. "I wish I was over with you guys."

I was grateful they weren't bringing up what had just happened.

"Margo's in Moose," Donald continued, examining the list. "And Hana and Bee have the usual."

Bee and Hana shared a cabin every year—Little Bat. It was the nicest cabin, with two secret outlets, and built-in bunk beds. Plus it was closest to the big house, the Leonatos' year-round home, Big Bat. *And* the waterfront, Dam, and the nicest bathrooms.

"Seriously?" I just felt angry at everything right now. "They get that every year. It's total nepotism."

"Yeah." Donald started to head out. "At least you're not John. He's in Otter again. Serves him right."

"Whatever, he's a newer counselor," I replied. We'd all done our time in the crappy cabins farther out.

We parted ways at the split. Donald walked ahead while I paused at the waterfront and took it all in. The dock. The paddleboats and kayaks. Our little island.

That was the thing about summer camp. The job made sense: Wake up, set up the field, play sports all day, keep kids from killing each other. Try to eat and sleep in between. Sing songs, roast marshmallows, dress up in costumes, dominate Capture the Flag, sit on trial at Kangaroo Court.

It was pretty idyllic in every way. Or it had been, until last year.

As I set up my bunk, I came to a decision. If Bee wanted to be enemies, fine. But that didn't mean I had to fight back. I made a solemn vow, one I'd actually keep this time: no matter how I felt, I would not be involved in any camp drama this year. With my stepdad, Tim, and my mom's divorce, I'd had enough real drama to last a lifetime. This summer, no secrets, no fighting, and absolutely no *feelings*.

CHAPTER 4

Bee

"BEE, THAT WAS A little harsh," Margo said, once Ben had ducked out. "Can't you two bury whatever this fight is already? Have you even tried?"

"We're not in a fight," I retorted. "And I have to help with some food stuff. I'll see you in an hour?"

"Sure, darlin'." She shook her head, kissed my cheek, and grabbed Hana.

I ducked into the kitchen, found my way to the paper goods closet, and huddled on the floor. Shane, the cook, didn't see me. Or pretended not to see me. Thanks, Shane.

Ben hadn't even looked back. He'd just left Dam and disappeared forever. Well, probably disappeared into his cabin. And I'd have to see him in an hour anyway. I stood up, grabbed a stack of napkins, and started doling them into our little green table baskets.

Truthfully, I didn't know if I could handle this. His maddening, twinkly eyes and dusky-brown hair that flopped every which way. Something inside me still expected him to treat me like . . . like there was something between us. When there wasn't. Clearly. Margo was right—I needed to cool it, or they'd all start talking again. And plus, I didn't want Ben to think I actually cared.

Maybe that could've occurred to you a little earlier, Bee?

I kept forgetting what I was supposed to be doing, how I was supposed to feel. Like I was in a play, trying to play ten characters at once, with ten different sets of motivations. Where was Raphael when you needed an acting coach?

I made several trips back and forth from the kitchen, setting out the baskets on our blue-and-yellow picnic-style tables, imagining my character as an efficient lady with more important things to do than miss a boy.

The thing was, I did miss him—I missed my *friend*. Ben and I used to tell each other everything each summer. And sometimes we'd text each other funny links during the year. Not like Hana and Claudia, who couldn't go a day without texting each other. But Ben and I had a similar silly sense of humor. There were certain things I'd find online that I knew he would get and no one else would, so I'd send them, and the stuff he sent me *always* made me laugh. His texts were bright spots during the long weeks of studying and rehearsals. It made me feel . . . special, like he was always thinking of me, even when we weren't at camp.

This past year had been weird—looking at schools without talking to him. Picking a school without talking to him. Picking a school *in Boston* without talking to him.

He still didn't know.

As if he'd care. I was kidding myself if I thought *he'd* ever felt special because of *me*. To him, all we had ever been was that barely-a-friendship friendship. And what had happened last summer had killed even that pretty effectively.

WHAT HAPPENED: PART 1

Bee

EVERY FOURTH OF JULY, the whole camp goes to the nearby lighthouse to watch Messina's fireworks together. Then the counselors ditch the campers, put the CITs on watch, and meet at Nest. We call it the sparkler party.

This particular sparkler party progressed like usual: At first everyone was cripplingly awkward. Sometimes when you work with kids 24/7, you forget how to socialize without them. But then we remembered that alcohol helps with the awkward thing. I had a few beers, Ben had a few beers, and Donald had a few beers and proceeded to set three sparklers off at once in one hand and start screaming. Claudia calmly shook up a can and doused him. Margo videoed the whole thing.

Eventually, Donald insisted on Truth or Dare, which meant we all got to see Bobby streak across the clearing in the moonlight. While everyone was hooting at him, Ben and I stood next to each other, nearly silent in shock.

"Jesus Christ." He shook his head. "Why didn't we close our eyes?"

"I know," I whispered back. "I can't unsee that." He snickered, close to my ear. His breath made my skin prickle like saltwater. I tried to ignore it.

At the end of the night, the senior counselors packed up their blankets and headed back down the path. Like robots, everyone started to follow them. But I was still awake, and I realized the torch was being passed to us. Or, the sparkler bucket with blackened sticks. And blankets, and a warm cooler of floating beer cans, and cards everywhere. In grand tradition, we were being stuck with the cleanup.

"Hey, all—we need to get this cleared before we go." I crossed my arms.

"Aww, Bee," Donald groaned. "We're exhausted. We were up at six thirty."

"So was I!"

"Sweetums . . ." Margo drawled into a yawn. "We can take care of it tomorrow."

They didn't get it. My parents didn't mind counselor parties, but there was an unspoken agreement that we left no trace of them. We couldn't leave Nest like this overnight. What if they came up here early?

"Never mind." I shook my head. "I'll do it myself." Hana opened her mouth to protest, but I waved at her. "Get some sleep, babe."

"Are you sure?" Margo asked half-heartedly, already drifting backward, toward the edge of the trail. They thanked me again and filed down the path. I turned away and sighed to myself. *Whatever. You're always the one who gets it done.* Then I heard shuffling feet, and realized someone was still there, to my right, carefully collecting the scattered cards. My cheeks flushed, like they knew something I didn't.

"Ben, you don't have to help."

He shrugged, smiled. "Eh, I'm not that tired."

I grinned. "Me neither."

CHAPTER 5

John

FIFTEEN MINUTES AT CAMP, and I was already pissed.

The cabins were lined up along Camp Dogberry's shoreline, and for the second year in a row, I'd been tossed into the farthest one out, Otter. Cramped, ancient, devoid of electrical outlets, with no place to install your mosquito netting poles, which meant I had to duct tape them, and duct tape all the kids' poles too.

It was only my second year at camp, but I was *eighteen years old.* I'd just finished a year of *college.* Even one of the *first-year* counselors had a better cabin than me.

I collapsed onto the smelly mattress and sighed.

"Camp's not so bad, right, Johnny?" my mom had asked, anxiously, watching me pack last night.

"I like it there," I had assured her.

Camp Dogberry was one of King's stupid plans.

Last summer's press:

John Hernandez will be working at Camp Dogberry in Messina, Maine, with his brother, Donald King. "We're getting these city boys some fresh air!" Senator King said, to a friend at the ACLU benefit dinner.

I'd hated that my mom was letting him tell me how to spend

my summer, but then it had actually turned out okay. I had friends, there was a girl I liked, I made some money. Not a bad way to spend a couple months, but I did have to get past the whole it-was-a-sham-my-asshole-politician-father-put-together-for-his-own-image thing.

I hadn't planned on coming back this year, but then Donald had chickened out of his swanky internship, and my mom and I had gotten the call. Not like I had my own plans, like chilling for the summer at home with my mom in NYC. No, of course not. My entire state of being was waiting for instructions from King, obviously.

But at least I got to see Claudia again.

"This cabin's still the worst." Bobby swung the creaky door open, with Connie hovering just behind him. I got to see my weird Dogberry friends too, I guess.

"I know." I sighed and got up to unpack my stuff into the drawers under the counselor bed. "I don't get it. There's a new guy in Whitetail, and in Snowshoe with Ben, so why am I out here?"

"Did you ask Nik?" Connie, all legs and elbows, sat on one of the beds.

"Why bother? They're not gonna change it now."

"At least there's some privacy out here," she said. Privacy at camp? Not a thing. "So, guess what? I'm headed to Wash U in the fall."

Bobby, Connie, and I were all around the same age, but I graduated a year early, got into Yale a year early.

"Yeah? Congrats."

"Thanks." She smiled. "I'm pumped to go out west. Bobby's going to USM." She jerked a thumb at him. Bobby pretended to chug an imaginary beer. "So now you have to tell us," she continued. "What's college really like?"

"It's tough," I said. "I worked my ass off and still got a couple Bs."

"Not bad," Connie said.

"I don't care about your grades," Bobby clarified. "What's the party scene like?"

"Boring," I said firmly. "New Haven's nothing like the city."

"Aww, man," Bobby sympathized, even though he's from Maine, so he has no idea what I'm talking about.

"Yeah," I said. "And the *worst* part was that Donald lived on my floor." He was no doubt telling all his friends what a pain that had been, so I might as well tell mine.

"Seriously?!" Bobby laughed.

"Yeah, can you believe that?" I replied. "King's idea, I'm sure. They wanted to put us in the same room, but I got out of it." Actually, Donald had thrown a fit, but they didn't need to know that.

"That's such bullshit," Bobby groaned. "Can't your dad be cool for, like, five seconds of his life?"

"He's supporting the better health care bill—" Connie offered. Bobby threw my pillow at her.

"Yeah, so anyway," I said, swinging my legs around over the edge of the bed. "Donald shows up to campus with a truckload of stuff—"

"And another U-Haul for his ego?" Bobby asked.

"Nice." I reached over to slap his hand. "Yeah, and we're at the same boring parties, where he's bragging about all the girls he's slept with. And we have two classes together, and he doesn't even acknowledge me. Looks right through me. I couldn't take it anymore."

"What did you do?" Connie leaned forward.

"There was this girl he was hooking up with, and I told one of her friends that Donald was a virgin."

"*What?!*" Bobby shouted, cracking up. "*Dude!*"

"Oh my God!" Connie squealed in laughter.

"I know, and she *dumped* his ass."

"*Dude!!*" They both lost it. I grinned at the ceiling.

"So, then, you two are kind of even now, right?" Connie said, sounding hopeful. "So maybe you can just relax this summer?"

I wanted to point out that King and his family had pulled so much shit that nothing I did could even come close to leveling the playing field. But being a drama queen was Donald's thing, not mine.

"Sure," I said instead. "Relax and hook up with Claudia. She got even hotter this year."

"You mean balder?" Connie snickered.

"Jealous?" Bobby raised his eyebrows at her.

"As if."

"Short hair is a thing," I explained patiently. "Tons of girls have that cut in New York."

Connie looked doubtful. These Mainers, man.

"It looks pretty good," Bobby offered. "Her neck is, like, really elegant." He winked at me. I laughed. This effing kid.

"Dear lord," Connie groaned.

"The point is, I'm totally asking her out this summer."

"Hell yeah!" Bobby high-fived me. "I'm totally hooking up with Margo again this year."

"Oh excellent." Connie rolled her eyes. "So she's going to act like it's not happening, and you can spend another summer whining about it?"

"She's got you there." I smiled. I had to admit, Margo was definitely the dude of that hookup situation.

Bobby sighed. "I mean, I'd rather not keep it a secret and sneak around all the time," he acknowledged. "But at least I'm getting some." He pointed at Connie. "Who are *you* going to hook up with?"

Connie turned red. "Like you care."

"You're right," Bobby said happily. "I don't care."

She got up and smacked the back of his head. "Come on, guys. We're supposed to meet at Monarch."

As we left the cabin, I felt almost a fondness for the creak in the creaky door. It felt good to be back at camp but have friends this time. Even these two.

At CPR training, I made sure to get paired up with Claudia. I cracked a joke about how all the breathing dummies were white, and she laughed. Unlike the rest of Dogberry, I felt so chill with her. We'd been thrown together to teach the knot-tying elective last year, and she'd been so cool about it. Just handed me a rope and showed me knot after knot, almost silently. Even though she was friends with Donald, I never felt judged around her. That's why I liked her.

That, and her intense gaze—the way she looked at me, like I needed to be untangled. Her eyes were what most people would call honey-colored, but with Claudia, it was more like fierce bronze. Fierceness doesn't come from an easy life, and I knew, I felt, that we got each other. Knot after knot, I'd fallen for that bronze gaze. But I didn't have the balls last summer, and I didn't think I'd ever see her again.

Now I had another shot, and no way in hell I wasn't going to take it.

CHAPTER 6

Vanessa

COUNTDOWN TO CAMP: four days.

Which was good, because my sisters were driving me absolutely up the wall. Like I was clinging to the ceiling.

"It's *my* night to sleep on the top bunk!" Ava insisted.

"But you always take Smooshie up there with you!!" cried Layla, cat lover.

"Two bedrooms is what I can afford right now, but we'll find somewhere bigger when we can," my mom had explained apologetically, biting her lip, when we'd first seen the new place. I'd looked at the small white box-shaped room, with one window, too high at the back.

"Totally!" I'd agreed, smiling. "Not a problem, Mama." Immediately, my nose had started burning in that fuzzy, pre-cry way. When she'd turned around, I'd wiped the tears out of my eyes. Ben had seen and quickly given my shoulder a squeeze. Sigh. I knew better than to complain. Ben had to sleep on the couch. But still, it was pretty clear then that this rooming situation was going to cost me my sanity.

I wasn't wrong. Writing in my journal, I became aware of deadly silence. I looked up from my bed: Ava and Layla were rigging some kind of cat pulley–system. Smooshie watched, naively curious.

"Hide," I whispered to him.

Sharing a small room with seven-year-old twins made a cabin with patchy mosquito netting sound like a fancy hotel.

A knock came at the door—

"Vanessa, phone call!" My mom poked her head in, smiling. The way she said it, I already knew it wasn't my dad.

I jumped off the bed, grabbed the cordless from her, and ran out onto our teeny back porch.

"Hello?"

"Hey, Ness, how's it going?"

"Ben! Do you really want to know? The girls are bouncing off the walls, and Smooshie's about to die in a tragic elevator accident."

"Our place doesn't have an elevator."

"It does now."

"Oh good." He laughed.

"How's camp?"

"Orientation's fine," he said. "We did some team building stuff on the ropes course today. And I double checked for you—Sophia and Wallace are both on the CIT list, for the whole summer, just like you."

"Yes!! Thanks, bro." My best camp friends. They'd both said they were coming back, but you never knew.

"No problem. Yeah, so, we did CPR, which you'll do on Sunday, and first aid—"

"Cool, cool," I said. "But what's the camp *news*?" Not that I didn't care about CPR, but, like, c'mon. There had to be more important stuff happening at Camp Dogberry. There always was.

"Let me think." I could hear him running his hand down his face. "All right. Claudia got a real short haircut."

"She *did*?"

"Yeah, it looks pretty cool."

"Oh. Well, that's good. Anything else? Who's my counselor?"

"I don't want to spoil everything—you'll be here in a few days, and you can do all the gossiping you want."

That was a lot of gossiping. "Reaaaaally, Ben?" I whined. "You can't even tell me, like, one more thing?"

"Fine."

"Yay!"

"Andy got a new car. It's a blue hatchback."

I groaned. "I hate you."

"And I love you." He laughed. "I have to go to lunch. Hang in there with the girls."

"I'll try."

"How's Mom?"

"She really likes it here." I smiled. "I think it makes her happy." I didn't think, I knew. She'd told Aunt Deb on the phone, like, five times.

"Good. See you in a few days. Call if you need anything, but unless it's an emergency I have to wait to—"

"Call at the end of the day. I know."

We said our good-byes, and he hung up. I secretly wished he could've stayed until I left for camp too. It had been awesome to have Ben with us for a whole month—I'd missed him so much during the year, when he was at college. The new apartment had felt better with him here.

I brushed my bangs back, tried to think positively. Maybe it was a little cramped, but at least we'd moved out of Aunt Deb's. And no matter what, it was still better than *home* home, living with Dad. I didn't miss him hovering around like a storm cloud in scuffed-up loafers.

I took a deep breath and went back inside, read my camp packing list for the four hundredth time, using it as my calming mantra.

Watershoes optional, watershoes optional, watershoes optional.

CHAPTER 7

$\mathcal{B}\varepsilon\mathcal{N}$

I THREW A STACK of plastic mats out onto the one patch of pavement at Camp Dogberry: the foursquare court. Claudia turned the hose on them, spraying away the layers of dust and grime built up over a year in the sports shed. Training week had passed quickly, in a blur of CPR, child psych overviews, and so. Much. Cleaning. The CITs and other leaders were coming tomorrow, which meant the campers would be here in two days. That was kind of terrifying.

Except that meant I'd get to see my Vanessa tomorrow. It'd only been a week, but I missed all three of my sisters.

Claudia and I had also been prepping Monarch this week. Repainting the white soccer lines, setting up the volleyball/ badminton net in its patch of sand, and writing lists of games that worked last year and games that didn't: notably, Dodgeball had been a disaster—the kids didn't like the confines of organized teams, because they wanted to whip the squishy balls at whoever they wanted to (their friends and secret crushes). Thus, Sproutball was born, which was every-kid-for-themselves, free-for-all chaos. It was a new addition, but I liked it almost as much as Mashed Potato War or Capture the Flag. And I got to plan all of it now. Aces.

When I thought about that, I seriously couldn't wait for camp to start.

But.

All week, as I sorted the balls (soccer, volley, beach, squishy, etc.), I felt more and more pathetic. Here I was, back at this camp where I'd been since fifth grade, planning to pit children against one another in Sproutball death matches. Part of me wished I could've gotten an internship, like all my other premed classmates. But then I wouldn't have been able to help Mom move—most internships don't start *you know, whenever you're done moving.*

"Done," Claudia said, winding up the hose. "We should spread these bases out to dry in the grass."

I followed her lead, and then we spread ourselves out to dry too. The grass was still pointy and hard from its first summer cutting. It poked through my shirt and athletic shorts like needles. It wasn't a particularly pleasant sensation, but I found it comforting. That's how the grass was at the start of camp. Soon the whole field would be torn up.

"Can I ask you something?"

I kept my eyes closed. "Yeah, sure."

"What do you think about Hana?"

Something in Claudia's voice made me nervous.

"Hana's the best," I said. "She's a good kid."

I heard Claudia roll over, felt her look at me, and ignored it. "She's pretty, right?"

"Not like Bee," I mused, then quickly realized what I'd said. "I mean, yeah, whatever. I can't think of the Leonato girls like that. I've known Hana since she was, like, eight or something." That should shut Claudia up.

"Well, I think I'm in love with her."

I sat up so I could stare down at her. "What?!"

Claudia turned red, all the way up to her sticky-out ears. "I said I think I'm—"

"No, don't say it again," I pleaded. "Unsay it. Right now."

"What?" she asked, confused. "No—I'm in love with her."

I'd forgotten that though Claudia didn't speak often, when she did, she didn't know how to do the shutting up part. It was one of her talents.

I scrambled to my feet. "You've just ruined the entire summer!"

Claudia looked baffled. "But—"

"Who's ruined the summer? I'll kill 'em!"

We both jumped: Donald had appeared on the field, sunglasses on, hands and forearms splattered with paint, sucking a purple freezer pop.

"Claudia! Kill Claudia!" I demanded, pointing at her. "She's 'in love'! Or something."

Claudia stood, defensively, and turned a shade of red I hadn't realized was humanly possible. I felt bad, for a split second, but then I envisioned all the drama and gossiping and PDA that would happen as a result of this. I hated when camp became high school. Like what had happened last summer—or hadn't happened (whatever Bee wanted)—*that* had been totally high school.

"She's in love?" Donald smiled, his teeth a violent shade of grape. "With Hana?"

Claudia narrowed her eyes. "How did you know?"

"Oh my God!" I stumbled a few yards away and threw myself back onto the field, facedown in the pointy grass this time. "This is a nightmare."

"C'mon, Ben." Donald gently kicked me. "This is adorable, man. What's better than two of our favorite people getting together?"

"No," I said into the dirt. "It's a disaster. Plus, who tosses the word *love* around like that? What happened to *like*?"

"I know what I feel," Claudia said indignantly. "We've been talking all year—"

"Just because *you've* sworn off dating women," Donald chided me, "doesn't mean Claudia has to."

I stood up. The prickly grass had won. "I just don't want to waste my time *dating*. I'm premed."

"We *know*." Claudia sprayed me with the hose. Donald cheered.

"You guys are such jerks." I took off my soaked shirt and started down the path toward Dam. They followed, not drenched.

"We're the jerks?" Donald laughed, with kind of a snap. "Claudia just told you something personal, and you had, like, the worst possible reaction."

I glanced behind me at Claudia, who was staring pointedly at the ground. Oh, crap.

"God, you're right." I stopped in the middle of the trail, wringing water out of my shirt. "I'm sorry, Claud."

"It's cool." She shrugged. But it clearly wasn't.

"It's just . . . romance, or whatever, creates drama." I slid a hand over my face. "I think we'd all be better off just staying friends."

"We *are* being friends!" Donald shoved me. "We're going to help Claudia, our *friend*, get the girl!"

"*See!*" I protested. "Games! Drama! You're doing it right now! You're like the drama activity leader!"

"I kind of like that!" Donald smiled. Then he started rubbing his palms together—never a good sign—and focused on Claudia. "So, first party tonight. What are you gonna do?"

I bit my cheek and pulled my wet shirt back on.

"Umm . . ." Claudia thought for a moment. "Go for a little while, feel awkward, drink, and leave?"

"No! Well, probably." Donald led the way up to the veranda outside the dining hall. He jumped up onto the banister. "But you're also going to make a move! Tell her how you feel!"

"Oh." Claudia shook her head. "Yeah, no. I don't think I can do that. I wouldn't know how to . . . what to say."

"That's true, she's pretty bad at that," I added, hoping to squash this idea.

"What if I told her for you?" Donald hopped down in front of Claudia.

"You?"

"Yes!" Donald clapped. "I'll pull Hana aside at the party, one-on-one, and tell her that—"

I glanced around: "Maybe we should shut up about this outside of the—"

"Hey, all." Nik, our *camp director* at our *place of work* (who also happened to be *Hana's mom*) had appeared at the top of the stairs. Exactly what I was afraid of. Donald was being so unprofessional it was ridiculous.

Claudia backed into the corner, like a terrified wild animal. A flickering feeling of déjà vu hit me. Didn't I feel extra terrified of Nik last summer? Guess I didn't anymore. . . .

"You all coming in for lunch?" Nik asked.

"Sure, yeah."

"Absolutely, in a minute." Donald smiled.

"Great." She opened the door and called into the dining hall, "Donald, Ben, and Claudia are coming in a minute! They have to talk about all of you first!" She tuned back and beamed at us.

Claudia looked like she was going to be sick.

"Um . . . thanks?" I said to Nik.

"Sure thing." She cackled, clearly delighted with herself, and held the door open. Donald threw an arm around Claudia and steered her into Dam. I let them go and took a somewhat private moment on the veranda to deeply regret my choice to return this summer.

WHAT HAPPENED: PART 2

Ben

OKAY, IF I'M BEING real, I did not stay behind just to help Bee clean up. I mean, yeah, that was the right thing to do. But also, I had this idea.

A year and a half before, Bee and I had kissed. In January, under a half moon, snow falling all around us like a terrible movie. And I'd wanted to kiss her again ever since. And it was my *last summer* at camp, so I had to go for it.

The going for it, however, proved harder than I'd anticipated. We'd cleaned up slowly, circling each other, picking up sparklers and trash in muggy silence. I thought about asking Bee to hang out on her own, just for a sec, so I could do a quick run down to the cabins and wake up Donald for advice.

After a few more silent minutes, I couldn't take it anymore. The awkward, burning sensation that I was thoroughly screwing this up. So I did exactly what I felt like doing—I collapsed facedown in the middle of the clearing, on a forgotten, scratchy picnic blanket.

My own breath bounced back and hit me in the face repeatedly. As long as she didn't notice, I could stay there, slightly suffocating, forever.

Good move, I told myself. *Until you figure out what to do, don't do* anything.

Then I heard a laugh—her laugh. Cackling, like Nik's, but sweet, like a really nice witch. Suddenly, I felt a weight drop onto the blanket next to me. I turned my head and opened my eyes. She'd sat down. Aces.

"I thought you weren't tired?"

I couldn't see her face—just her legs. That felt creepy, so I quickly sat up too. She passed me a warm beer.

"Definitely not tired," I replied. "It's just so hot out."

"Yeah, it's really gross." She opened her beer, the noise thunderous, and took a long sip. I waited for *Come on, dingus, we need to get back to work.* Nothing. Weird.

I looked down at the beer in my hand, and a thought hit me in the gut like a kick ball: *She has the same idea. Of how this could go. Maybe?*

"So, do you think . . ." she began, and my breath caught. ". . . that Margo and Bobby are going to hook up again this year?"

"What?" I sputtered, spitting out a little bit of my beer. She laughed at me again.

"Margo and Bobby." She sipped from her can and stretched out her legs. I tried not to stare at them. But then, if I didn't look at them at all, would she think I didn't like her legs?

"Were they flirting tonight?" One part of my brain somehow kept on top of the conversation.

"Uhhh, duh!" She rolled her eyes. "Didn't you notice?" I used this question as an excuse to properly look at her: hair tied up in an elegant knot, the moonlight illuminating her skin, her eyes— widening, prompting me, indicating my incompetence.

I tried to clear my mind enough to answer. "Yeah, I mean, I really mostly noticed Bobby's ass?"

She laughed. That was three. "Right, yeah, that was pretty spectacular. I bet Donald'll do a beautiful impressionist collage of that sprint someday."

"Titled 'Truth or Dick'?"

We both cracked up.

"Anyway, that was Margo's dare," she continued. "Not a coincidence."

"And you don't like the whole Margo-Bobby thing?" I guessed. I knew she wasn't Bobby's biggest fan.

She sipped her beer, wrinkling her nose. "Bobby's immature. But they kept hooking up last year anyway, so . . . maybe they're meant to be or something."

Aha! I had something to say about that. "*Meant to be* is kind of a bullshit concept," I declared.

"Oh?" She turned to face me, brown eyes pinning mine. I almost lost my words again.

"Yeah." I looked at the blanket so I could talk. "Because we're not *meant to be* with just one person."

"Huh," she replied. I felt her go cold—then it dawned on me what I'd just said.

"I didn't mean it like that!" I said quickly. Back up, Ben. "I meant *fate* doesn't exist, we have free will, so how can anyone be *meant to be*?" I said the last part as more of a demand. Whoops.

Bee sipped her beer again. I'd said too much. Maybe I was ruining the mood. Eventually, she murmured: "I guess I didn't really think about it like that."

"Right?!" I turned to her excitedly. "I didn't either. But it's total bullshit. Because you can choose: you can be with someone, or you can leave them. It's not already written out for you. None of it is."

A bead of sweat trickled down her neck. I wanted to lick it. Ew no, no I didn't. What the hell was wrong with me?

I waited for another response, but again, didn't get one. I looked away.

Maybe, I thought, you're not supposed to tell a girl that you think fate is bullshit on the same night that you badly want to kiss her.

CHAPTER 8

Bee

"MUSHROOM FAIRY!" Margo said sternly. "Get in here, darlin'!"

The jet-black baby pygmy goat stared back at her with his bizarre rectangular pupils. Then he looked away and kept eating. Margo might sound no-nonsense, but she looked downright charming standing there with her purple pigtails and knee-high rubber boots.

"Bee, can you give him a nudge?" Margo held open the shed door, blocking the opening with her leg so the other four kids wouldn't escape.

"Probably have to do more than nudge." I eyed him.

Margo spent most of her time here, at Salamander, the dusky green nature building, complete with accompanying goat shed. It was her favorite place at camp. As soon as Margo arrived every summer, my parents relinquished animal care to her. We had turtles, lizards, a pair of rats, and a new crop of baby goats each year, in addition to whatever our grandma-like nature leader, Doc, would show up with tomorrow.

I grabbed Mushroom Fairy's collar and led him up to the door. "*How* did he grow an extra set of horns?"

Farmer Amy, who'd lent us the goats for the summer, had removed their little baby goat horns that spring, but Mushroom Fairy's had freakishly begun to grow in again.

"He's clearly the alpha," Margo said, shoving his bum into the shed. "And destined for greatness."

We grabbed pitchforks and started mucking out the goat pen, big shovelfuls of hay and poop. I was always thankful that when the CITs and campers arrived, we'd divide up the chores.

It had been a slow afternoon, for the first time all week. We'd been recertified, I'd gone over every inch of CIT paperwork, and we'd had the diversity and "camp-appropriate" talks with Dad. Now we were almost ready for campers. One more weekend of spending way too much time around Ben, and then the kids would get here, and it would be so hectic I would hardly notice him. Right now he was, well . . . noticeable. Twinkly and floppy. I hated the sight of his adorable bare chest at the waterfront.

"So, island party tonight?" Margo asked, casually flinging muck into the fertilizer bin.

Right, I also had to survive the *island party with Ben.*

I dug my fork into the muck with my boot. "Donald's collecting the booze money. I still don't know how he's going to get it."

"Yeah, he's kind of booze magical," Margo said. She passed me a heap of straw, and we started laying it down on the less poop-y dirt.

Margo tossed a handful behind her. "So, can we talk about my boobs?"

I laughed. "Sure, what's up with your boobs?"

We deposited our pitchforks in the bucket and made our way to the side of the building to wash our hands in the squeaky outdoor sink.

"Have you not noticed?" She gestured to her chest, soapy water drops flicking onto her shirt.

"I've noticed you have boobs," I admitted. "Is there something in particular you're referring to?"

"Is there something in particular?" Margo flung her hands down, exasperated. "Bee, they're *huge*! They just like, *popped* at the end of the school year. I bet Max is *really* regretting dumping me now."

Awww. Margo'd had her first boyfriend this year, but he'd broken up with her a couple months ago.

"If Max is regretting dumping you for that reason, he's a jackass."

"Well, he *is* a jackass." She laughed. It teetered off into what she'd call a big ol' sigh.

Poor babe. I struggled for the right words to say. I almost wanted to tell her I knew how she felt—but something stopped me. I couldn't . . . It was just easier if nobody knew. Instead, I slung an arm around her and pulled her into Salamander. Once inside, Margo grabbed a chunk of lettuce from the mini-fridge and started tenderly feeding the turtles. I sat at one of the old soft wooden tables, etched with claw marks.

"Okay," I said. "So what was it you were going to say about your boobage?"

"Well—"

The door flew open. Margo scowled and turned pink all at once—maybe she was expecting one of the guys, but it was just Connie.

"Hey!" Connie kind of shouted.

"Hey," Margo and I chorused.

"Have you guys seen Donald?" she asked. "I'm trying to find him to . . . get him cash. I've heard he's making a run after dinner."

"He's probably in Turtle," Margo replied. Her face was returning to normal, her freckles slowly reappearing.

"Or illegally napping," I added. "I'd check his cabin, too."

"Okay, thanks, guys," Connie said. "You excited for the party tonight?" She slid onto the bench next to me.

Margo and I exchanged glances. Connie DeAngelo had been at Camp Dogberry for years—she'd done her CIT training here and everything. She was so cute: tall, dark tan skin, shiny black hair. She was nice, kind of friendly, but *just so awkward* sometimes. A few summers back she and Bobby led a hiking trip and returned best friends, and then they glommed on to John last year.

"Not really." I made a face. "I heard Donald's getting tequila."

"Is he?" Margo's face lit up.

"Yuck." Connie stuck out her tongue and stood up. "Well, that'll be fun—adding tequila to the Donald mess. That won't backfire at all."

I'd kind of been phoning it in, but at that, I turned and blinked at her. "Donald mess? What?"

"Yeah, huh?" Margo looked at her, bewildered, then at me. I shrugged. Connie paused, leaning her right elbow up against the doorway, but, like, all wrong. It just kind of stuck into the wood. It looked super uncomfortable, and I wanted to tell her and her elbow to chill out.

"You know . . . that rumor going around camp?" she said, but her voice sounded less certain. "The one about how Donald likes Hana?"

"Hana?" I asked. "Ha!"

"No way." Margo's eyes went wide. "Who told you that?"

"Ellie," Connie said. "She heard Ben, Donald, and Claudia

talking outside Dam at lunch. Donald said he was going to make a move on Hana tonight. At the island party?"

Ellie, a second-year counselor. Not the best source, but . . . Mom had made this funny comment at lunch, about how those three were standing outside talking about us. I'd assumed she'd made it to embarrass them. What if they actually were talking about us?

Donald liked *Hana*?! Hana was a baby! What the hell?

But it's not like he'd tell you, a voice reasoned in my head. *And Hana doesn't look like a baby anymore. . . .* But really? Donald liking my little *sister*?

Suddenly, I realized Connie was nervously glancing between Margo and me. I tried to come up with something to say that didn't give away how disturbing this was. "Uhh, well . . ."

"*Bee*, we should muck out the goats before dinner," Margo said quickly, saving me. "See you later, Connie?"

"Sure." She nodded. "See you. Um, sorry?" She and her strange elbow stance disappeared from the doorway.

Margo immediately sprang across the room to me. "What is *going on*?"

"I don't know." I shook my head. "But I think we need to tell Hana."

CHAPTER 9

Hana

AT DINNER, EVERYONE BUZZED about the island party. The beer, the fire pit, the s'mores . . . all I could think about was the moonlight. Claudia in the moonlight, specifically. And her text this afternoon.

> I can't wait to be together tonight

> Same ☺

I had to believe we were speaking in code. There were times that I began to doubt and felt a little unsure—Christopher had spoken in code, too, but like a code nobody, like none of my friends, could crack. I'd known Claudia longer, so my gut told me to trust her. Although my gut had told me to trust Christopher, too. . . .

She sat toward the other end of the table at dinner, every so often glancing in my direction in a way she thought was sneaky. Her shorter hair brought out her cheekbones and made her look older.

And hotter. This entire week had been torture. I'd crushed on her last year, but I knew how to kiss now, and I wanted to kiss *her*.

"Hana!" Bee poked my shoulder. I looked up, dazed.

Margo poked my other shoulder. "Dinner's over. Let's go get ready."

"Definitely!" I smiled, stood up, scraped my leftover food, almost the whole plate, into the compost bucket.

"Girls!" On our way out, Mom and Dad called us over to their table in the corner. Margo recognized a family conference and went over to wait by the door.

"So, morning meeting is tomorrow at eight," Mom said in a lowered voice. They were both polishing off bowls of red Jell-O with whipped cream, a Camp Dogberry special.

"Might wanna make that nine," Bee suggested. "Or noon?"

I nudged her.

"Noon?" Dad looked alarmed, which was not normal for him. It looked weird on his face. "If you're *staying up* so late that you can't get up before noon, we have a problem."

"Relax!" Bee laughed and waved a hand at him. "I was joking. Ten is fine."

"Eight thirty," Mom pointed her spoon at Bee.

"Nine thirty."

"Nine."

"Done." They nodded solemnly—their version of a handshake.

"And be careful." Mom's brow wrinkled into her worry lines. "I don't want anyone getting *rowdy* and pushing someone into the water."

"Well, *we* don't get *rowdy*," Bee reminded them. "But I can make no promises about pushing people into the water."

"I'm not worried." Dad stood up and shoved his chair in. "If Ben drowns, we'd know immediately who to blame. I think you're smarter than that, Bee."

"Am I?"

Our parents started walking toward the dish pit, but Mom stopped and lowered her voice even further. "Call us if you need help." She held up her walkie-talkie. "We'll leave this on. I expect you"—this was mostly directed at Bee—"to keep the madness to a minimum. And be watchful for the first-year counselors, please."

"Of course." Bee was suddenly serious.

"I can help too."

We both jumped and turned around. Ben had been hovering nearby, hands behind his back, looking eager. Bee eyed him for a moment, then turned back to my mom.

"Yeah, don't worry, *I* got this."

"Thanks, Ben." Mom squeezed his shoulder as she walked past him. Bee wasn't going to like that. "And, Bee, if Ben's boat capsizes . . ."

Bee threw up her hands. "Ben's *really bad* at boats!"

"Not *that* bad," he protested, but Bee was already walking away. I shot Ben what I hoped was a supportive smile, then caught up to her.

After changing and grabbing our supplies, Bee, Margo, and I went to the bathroom for the girl cabins, Opossum. I'd changed into a white eyelet tank top and khaki shorts, nicer than anything I could wear during a normal camp day. Margo wore a blue halter top with leggings, and Bee hadn't changed anything: she still wore her ripped jean shorts and green camp T-shirt. Once in the bathroom, she slipped on a pair of large gold wind-chimey earrings. That's all it took for my sister to go from camp to party.

"Hair?" she asked.

I looked in the mirror. I had some zits and flyaways. Not all of us could look so flawless with zero effort.

"Half up, half down, with a braid!" Margo called, from her position at the sink. She was doing eyeliner calligraphy—little wing tips. It looked really dramatic with her pale complexion and loose, dark violet curls.

"Sounds good." I nodded.

Bee sat me down on a stool and carefully moved her fingers through my hair, which had started curling out of of nowhere this year. I still didn't really know how to wrangle it. I felt lucky to have Bee and Margo figuring it out.

Bee gave me a little scalp massage, and it felt so good, I closed my eyes, relaxed, and let myself think about the space between Claudia's ear and her neck.

"So, dearest, there's something we should tell you." Margo's voice floated in.

"Now?" Bee whispered.

"What is it?" I was still mostly thinking about ear-neck situations.

"Well . . . the thing is . . ." Margo's voice came closer. "Donald likes you."

"What?" My eyelids sprang open. Margo cringed in the mirror.

"Don't move!" Bee corrected my head forward again. My sister was somehow still concentrating on my hair! "Margo, maybe this wasn't the best time."

"Sorry, but when did you want to tell her? Five seconds before we got there?" Margo bit her lip and eyed me warily. "It's true, Hana darlin'. Donald likes you."

I watched the sunburn drain right out of my face. "No way. Did he say something?"

"No. Connie told us this afternoon," Bee said, still working on the back of my head. "She thought we already knew."

"Apparently, Ellie heard Ben, Donald, and Claudia talking about it outside Dam at lunch today," Margo confirmed. "I asked Ellie about it at dinner, and she said it was true."

Bee tied off the braid in my hair. "Done!"

The top half was pulled back so you could see my face, and the bottom curls fell down around my shoulders. It looked really cute, but I couldn't enjoy it, because Donald? *Donald?!* It didn't make sense. He was like an older brother.

"So . . . do you like him?"

I turned to Margo. "No, of course not."

"Didn't think so." She sounded a little relieved. "So what are you going to do?"

"What do you mean?" I said, not comprehending most of this.

"Oh, that's the other part." Bee grimaced. "The rumor is he's going to tell you he likes you tonight—"

"Tell me!" My stomach plummeted. What would I say to him? Donald, who I'd known forever? Maybe I could tell him I was gay. But that was a lie—I was bisexual or pansexual. I didn't know for sure, but I knew I didn't just like one gender. I could tell him I had a boyfriend—but that was a lie too. And if Claudia heard that . . .

"I don't think I should go." I felt tears well up in my eyes.

"No, you have to go!" Margo turned away from Bee's cheeks.

"Hana." Bee waved Margo's brush away and put her hands on my shoulders, looked straight into my eyes. I relaxed a little. "If Donald likes you, and you don't like him, it's okay to tell him that."

"But—"

"I know he's our friend, and he's great, but you can't control how you feel," Bee continued.

"Totally." Margo came over and slipped an arm around my waist. "And I'm pretty sure you feel things for a certain salt-and-pepper babe."

"And wasn't tonight kind of, like"—Bee smiled at me gently—"kind of a big night?"

I smiled, my ears burning a little. "Well, yeah . . . maybe. But what if Claudia knows that Donald likes me?"

"It doesn't matter how many people like you, it matters who *you like back*." Bee hugged me.

"Real." Margo nodded.

Bee pulled back. "So if Donald confesses his love, just tell him you like someone else! We can't let dramatic boys ruin the evening."

"Okay." I smiled and wiped the beginnings of tears off my lower lids. I checked my eyeliner. Waterproof—I was good.

"Besides . . ." Margo had slipped back in front of the mirror and was applying bright red-orange lipstick. "I could probably be persuaded to comfort Donald."

Bee rolled her eyes. "Could you really?"

We all laughed.

We finished up like everything was normal. I took some deep breaths while Margo fussed over Bee, finishing up dusting some shimmery powder on her cheeks.

As we walked down to the dock, I tried to calm down and push away thoughts of what might or might not happen. *You can't control or predict what comes next*, my therapist's voice reminded me. *Just take it moment to moment.*

CHAPTER 10

Ben

THAT NIGHT, AS THE sun disappeared into the tree line, we fitted on our headlamps and headed down to the docks. As we got closer to the waterfront, something buzzed in the air. Probably Claudia's nerves. She and Donald had been scheming all through dinner. I wished there was some kind of anti-drama product I could use—like bug spray, but for feelings.

With some help from the others, we pulled a handful of paddle-boats off the rusty racks. Kayaks were faster, but much harder to steer drunk, and Donald was counting on everyone being hammered for the trip back.

We sat on the dock, dangling our feet over the water, waiting for Bee and co. Everyone but Claudia, who paced up and down, her footsteps rattling and clanging against the metal slats. I checked my watch. *Who's late now, Bee?*

Claudia's pacing made me antsy. I got up and pulled aside Dave, Doug, and Jen, our new first-year counselors, to talk about the one beer per hour rule. I'd now been to enough unmonitored drinking parties (one) at college to understand why it was important.

"And drink water. We don't want any of you throwing up," I

explained. "Throwing up from drinking is not actually cool. It just makes you smell bad and feel like shit the next day."

They nodded at me, eyes wide. This was their first party, their first summer as real counselors. The CITs weren't here yet, but even if they had been, they wouldn't have been included. "Babies" were never invited out after sunset.

Finally, just as Claudia looked like she might explode, Bee, Hana, and Margo arrived, carrying backpacks I hoped held marshmallows and chocolate. I saw Claudia freeze. I guessed *not* out of excitement at the possibility of s'mores.

"What're you all standing around for?" Bee called out.

"We got the boats, Your Highness!" Donald called back.

They leaped out onto the dock. Margo and Hana were all dressed up, but Bee just looked . . . Beeish. I couldn't look anywhere else, so I attempted to look everywhere else. Water. Trees. Boats. Donald. Awkward eye contact with Doug. Whoops.

"You're late!" Donald announced. "Let's go! I wanna get drunk!" The younger counselors giggled nervously.

"Not *drunk*." Bee walked up and pointed her flashlight at him. "Just buzzed." Donald batted the light away.

"Listen, Bee," he said, climbing into a paddleboat and motioning for me and Claudia to follow. "You need to learn how to drink, for school. Don't worry—Ben and I can teach you."

Claudia hopped in the front next to Donald. I paused. Logically, I knew these paddleboats were sturdy. I'd ridden in them every year and supervised other kids riding in them every year, for seven years. Nobody'd ever drowned off a paddleboat. But God, in the dark, gently bobbing in the water, they just looked straight out of a nautical horror movie. The "trustworthy" boat would randomly spring a leak, and a shark would be waiting, right under the surface, in five feet of water—

"Thanks for the offer, Donald." I woke up to Bee's voice, sounding annoyed, standing right next to me. "But I think I know how to drink."

She'd crossed her arms. Donald grinned at her, which made me want to punch him.

"Not like us," he insisted, looking at me. "We're gonna get hammered, like a real party. Right, Ben?"

Bee raised her eyebrows at Donald, then me. I looked away quickly, before I turned to stone.

"Um, yeah," I agreed. "Long week. Let's get hammered."

Bee looked almost disgusted as she strode over to her own boat. Hana followed, but Margo stopped to whisper, "Hey, teach me to drink?" She winked.

"You got it!" Donald whooped. "Let's get fucked up!" She laughed and jumped in the back of Bee's boat. Almost everyone was seated now. I needed to get in before they noticed I wasn't and started in on me. With as little a hop as humanly possible, I lowered myself into the back seat. The boat wobbled slightly to the right, but hardly made a splash. My sneakers planted on the slimy plastic. Success.

Once settled, I glanced around—it seemed like nobody'd seen my awkward entrance. But then I felt someone staring: of course, directly across, Bee sat in the front seat of her boat, facing me, eyes laughing. She'd seen the whole thing.

Just as I saw her, something bumped our boat, and I almost screamed.

"Where's your yacht, bro?" John asked from the boat that had just grazed ours.

"Hey, bro." Donald whipped around. "Fuck off."

"Can we get that again for a sound bite, Senator?" Bobby quipped, as they moved along past us. They cracked up at their own hilariousness.

"Bastard," Donald muttered.

Bee's right, I thought. All we need now is this fun bunch to get drunk.

"Whatever, let's go," Donald decided, and we sped off into the moonlight. And by that I mean we slowly paddled away from the dock like a school of geriatric turtles.

I watched the silhouette of Bee's faux-hawk against the navy-blue sky, just starting to sparkle with stars.

Maybe we just needed more moonlight. Maybe that could fix everything.

CHAPTER 11

Claudia

IT TOOK TWENTY MINUTES to get the fire going, but in the meantime, we got a show: Ben and Bee attempting to start it together.

"Shouldn't we be building a pyramid?"

"Are you seriously using a lighter?"

"That kindling is green."

"Back up. Do you want to burn your eyebrows off?"

I thought about helping, but their arguing actually produced a well-constructed campfire.

The island is small, maybe less than half a mile across, and in the middle, there's a fire pit with log benches circled around. I sat across from Hana, too nervous to attempt sitting next to her. The fire popped, the stars came out, and Donald passed out beers like it was Halloween and we were trick-or-treaters. Bee let him, and then situated the beer cooler in the clumps of bayberry bushes behind us.

"Stop being paranoid!" Donald laughed. "The police are not going to show up on the tiniest island *ever* in northern *Maine* and card us."

That got a laugh from the group. But I kind of understood it. Bee was the camp directors' kid. She needed to set a good example. Of hiding the alcohol.

Once everyone was settled in around the fire, and the bug spray had been passed around, Bee opened a beer for herself and raised up the can.

"To Camp Dogberry, the most beautiful place in the world."

A murmur of agreement.

"To old friends returning, new CITs coming—"

"Our fresh crop of servants," Donald interjected, to a round of cheers.

"And our beloved campers, soon to be here, to make us want to give up and torch the place."

Another cheer.

"And to summer." She paused, to look up at the sky. Then she grinned at Hana. "*This* summer."

A toast of cans smacking into each other.

Bee was right. We only had one summer. Who knew what would happen after that?

Across the fire, I watched Margo whisper something to Hana. She smiled in reply. Hana didn't laugh a lot, not unless she was really comfortable. She mostly smiled. Tonight, her dark curly hair was pulled back from her face and hovered loosely on her shoulders. Her skin was already starting to tan from hours on the water this week. I wanted to run my fingers down her arms, then catch her hands at the bottom.

"Hey, Claudia, can you pass me a beer?"

I looked up. John. I grabbed him a beer from the cooler and another for myself. I opened mine and drank half in one go. I needed to calm down.

Hana, so pretty. So perfect. Calm down.

"Claudia?"

I looked up again. John was still there.

"Did you get your beer?" I asked, checking around me. "I gave it to you, right?" Who knows what I'd done with it.

"Yeah." He stared at me for a second and then walked away. Weird. Bee passed around a bag of marshmallows, and I found a stick and roasted one, on autopilot.

Hana sat across the fire, carefully rotating two at a time. I wanted to be sitting over there, talking to her. I felt like it was an attainable goal, but how to get from here to there?

Donald. Wasn't he supposed to be helping me? He was talking to Ben. I reached forward and tapped his shoulder. His shoulder was so much bigger than mine. I needed to work out more.

Donald turned away from his conversation with Ben to look at me.

"Yeah?" he asked.

I widened my eyes. Bat signal.

But he just raised his eyebrows back, like he somehow did not recognize the bat signal. Shit.

"No, umm . . can you umm . . . go talk to . . ."

Expressionless, he watched me fumble. Maybe he'd forgotten about the entire plan. God, it was so annoying to bring it up again. *Stop it, Claudia.* Then Donald suddenly cracked a smile and shoved my arm.

"I'm just kidding, Claud, I got this."

He hopped up and sauntered his way around the fire pit, like I never could. I am rarely, *rarely* attracted to dudes, but Donald was so good looking it hurt. Dark, smooth skin; Afro; and a loud, infectious smile. Teased you all the time. He was unstoppable. And it wasn't just me—he had that effect on the younger counselors, CITs, even the campers. They swooned over him.

John might be like that too, I thought, if Donald wasn't around. He was kind of good looking, too—smooth, tan skin, buzzed hair on the sides, black curls on top. But he had none of Donald's confidence.

As I watched Donald approach Hana, I felt my legs start to shake, knees almost knocking.

What if, on this moonlit walk, Donald charmed the hell out of Hana? He *did* say Hana was really cute, and he had offered to talk to her . . . and how could you not like a guy like Donald?

But I noticed Hana's smile faltered, just a little, when Donald offered her a hand. She glanced at Margo, who glanced at Bee, who nodded at Hana, encouragingly. What the hell? Were they all secretly shipping them, and nobody'd told me?

Wait, didn't I *want* Donald to talk to Hana?

Donald laughed, made some joke, and Hana looked a little less terrified. As they disappeared from the firelight onto the trail, he slung an arm around her, in a friendly kind of way, like he'd done to me or Ben or Bee a thousand times.

Okay. Calm down. It's Donald we're talking about. He's got your back.

I took a breath, switched gears. A walk-around couldn't take more than fifteen minutes. After a year of waiting to see her again, of hanging suspended between text messages, I could make it fifteen minutes. No problem.

The group had dispersed some. I noticed Connie and John wandering onto the trail. Maybe they were an item too. And a few younger counselors were missing. Ooo freakin' la la.

"Claudia, that's your third beer in, like, twenty minutes."

I looked up. Ben stood over me. I hadn't even realized I'd opened another one, but there it was, half-finished in my hands.

"Slow down, yeah?" He sat down next to me. "And if you don't stop staring longingly at the trail, I *will* vote you off the island."

"You don't have the power to do that," I countered. "And I'm taller than you now." I'd grown a couple inches, and now I totally looked down at shorty Ben.

He snorted. "Just wait till Capture the Flag. We'll kick your asses."

"Not this year," I vowed.

It must've come out really serious, because Ben cracked up, which admittedly made me smile and forget about Donald/Hana for half a second. But then it came back—I glanced at the trail entrance again, wondering where they were on it. Ben started talking about something, school maybe, but I couldn't really hear him. I jiggled my leg. Then the other leg.

"I'm gonna pee." I stood up. I needed to move, and conveniently, when Ben had pointed out I'd had three beers, I'd suddenly felt them in my bladder.

Ben sighed and went to go sit with Rachel and Doug. He was friendlier to the younger counselors than the rest of us were. Guess it was all those little sisters he carted around. I was pretty grateful to be an only kid, even if that made the gay thing more intense with my parents. Sometimes I found myself wishing I had a nuisance older brother, the kind that always got detention.

I wandered onto the trail, and then off it a ways. As I went to unzip my shorts, someone's voice scared the crap out of me.

"Whoa, whoa!"

I jumped—to my right, in a bayberry bush, Bobby.

"Dude!" I yelled.

"Sorry!" he yelled back. "I was looking for somewhere to take a leak."

"*I'm* leaking here," I protested. Whelp. I was definitely drunk.

Bobby laughed. "Right, sorry, man." He waved his hands in apology and started to walk toward the trail, still talking. "With all the hookups, it's hard to find a spare tree."

"Sure." Wait. I turned. "Who's hooking up?"

"Dave and Jen."

Oh. First years. Who cared about them?

"And Doug and Ellie . . . and Donald and Hana . . ."

I immediately didn't have to pee anymore. Or maybe I'd peed myself. I wasn't sure. Everything had gone numb.

"Donald and Hana?"

Bobby paused at the edge of the trail and yawned. "Yeah. I heard him asking her out. And then—you know where that big rock is on the other shore? I saw them over there."

He didn't say it, but we both knew that was the *kissing rock*. What the hell was happening? My face felt hot as a sunburn. Something boiled in my stomach, like I might puke.

"Cool," I heard myself say. And then I pushed past, our shoulders thunking into each other.

"Hey, are you—"

I ignored him. I rifled through my options: I had to get back to the campfire. Act normal, grab another drink if Ben would let me. I couldn't paddle back and disappear. People would notice.

Don't explode, Claudia, don't explode.

Donald and Hana, his fingers in her hair, his lips on her lips—

I stopped on the trail. I couldn't go back there. I was still too hot. My insides churned. I reached up to a smaller, low-lying branch on the nearest tree, and tore it off, stepped one leg up onto a stump, and split the branch over my knee. It hurt, but I felt a little better.

I wrapped my arms around my stomach, trying to hold myself in place.

The ocean roared to my left. Hana was the water, and I'd been pulled under. As I was sinking, she'd made me forget the rest of the world.

And now I'd never be hers.

Well, who wanted that, anyway? I could barely remember the Claudia who did.

"Claudia?"

It was just Ben, with his dopey, concerned face. He had a beer in his hand. I wanted another beer.

"Are you okay?" he asked, walking up.

When I didn't respond right away, he poked my foot with his.

"Did something happen? You look like crap."

"Thanks," I bit out. A shiver went through me. It was cold. I'd worn a ribbed tank top because I thought Hana would like how it looked.

Ben didn't say anything, but he shuffled off his sweatshirt and held it out. I took it, fought it on. He sipped his beer, waiting.

"Donald's kissing Hana," I whispered finally.

"Wait, that's what this is about?"

I hated the laughter in his voice.

"It's *true*." Hot tears blurred my vision. "They're down on the kissing rock."

Ben actually laughed at that. "Okay. And Bee's making out with Dave in a paddleboat?"

"Seriously," I said.

"Did you actually see them making out?"

"No. But everyone else has."

"Okay." Ben sighed, like I was a seven-year-old camper throwing a tantrum. "Do you really think Donald would do that to you?"

Drunk thoughts swam through my brain.

"All Donald wants is to get laid."

"True," Ben replied, too calmly. "But he's a good friend. Bros before . . . you know, whatever. I wouldn't believe this till I saw it."

"Fine." I said. "So I'll go see it."

CHAPTER 12

Bee

WHERE HAD EVERYONE GONE?

It had been twenty minutes at least, and Margo and I had watched all of our friends vanish, in varying degrees of drunk and huffy.

As I bit into a crinkly golden marshmallow, a scene flashed in my mind: Hana rejecting Donald, him bursting into tears, and Hana, unsure what to do, then awkwardly comforting him. Or maybe he was shouting and being a dick. Either way, I'd let this go on long enough.

"Don't you think melted chocolate kind of looks like poop?" Margo giggled at her s'more.

"I need to pee," I announced, and stood up.

The crowd around the fire startled and looked up at me. Was I that loud?

"I need to go with her," Margo also announced, with a hiccup.

"Ooookay," Ellie offered.

We grabbed our beers and stumbled over the logs toward the trail. It was a good thing we were senior and kind of in charge, because otherwise we'd have been real weirdos.

"So are we looking for Hana and Donald?" Margo whispered to

me, once we got on the trail. Luckily, the Maine sky had turned out tonight. The stars were breathtaking, if you weren't worried your sister was currently getting Nice Guyed somewhere underneath them.

"We're not *looking* for them," I whispered. "But we're not *not* looking for them."

"Goooootcha."

"I also do have to pee."

"Me too!!" Margo giggled.

I wobbled, just a little. Two beers in. I really wasn't good at holding my drinks. Both metaphorically and physically—I tripped and dumped a splash of beer into the dirt. Margo steadied me, and we found an adequate pee clearing in the shallow woods. As I peed, hugging a tree, I contemplated how, if it was daylight, definitely harbor boats could see us.

We hopped back on the trail, and I led the way in the opposite direction of the fire. Maybe now I was officially on the Hana hunt.

"Did you see Ben?" I whispered to Margo as we walked.

"Where?" She turned around. Had she been sneaking extra drinks? Maybe to impress Donald and his drunk boasting.

"No, not here." I rolled my eyes. "At the campfire earlier. He was talking to *Janine*." It came out darker than I intended.

"No!" Margo almost yelled. Margo and I both have loud voices normally. Give us a couple beers, and we're belting a duet. "But isn't Janine, like, *fifteen*?!"

I shushed and pulled her closer. "She *is*. But they were totally talking, for, like, half an hour." She'd shoved him playfully and everything. But if I'd told Margo all of that, she'd know I'd been watching them, and not exactly 100 percent listening to her rehash her break up with Mike.

"Whoa," Margo whispered. She reached an arm around my waist to steady herself. "But, like . . . maybe he was just talking to her. You know, Ben talks to a lot of people."

Super astute. This girl was hammered. "Or maybe," I whispered, "Ben's trying to date someone on his maturity level."

Margo giggled. "Noooo. I don't believe it. Maybe she's just got a crush on him, and he's being nice. Ben's really nice."

"Marf," I replied. Which wasn't a word, but it was how I felt.

We'd almost looped halfway around the island by then, with no sight of Hana or Donald. We even stopped to check the kissing rock, but nothing. As we made our way back to the main trail, Margo's arm over my shoulder, she asked me:

"Hey, Bee, have you asked them yet? Why they came back? Donald and Ben, I mean."

I hesitated. Somewhere in my brain a warning signal flashed: SECRET, SECRET, SECRET. Right. Ben's family moved. *You will not say that*, I briefed myself. *You will say something else.*

"I bet Donald's dad made him come back," I fake speculated. "So that he and John still look buddy-buddy."

"Oooh." Margo nodded. "That makes sense."

"Yeah, and then Ben just followed, like a lost puppy."

Margo liked this. "You think so?" She smiled. "Ben kind of does look like a puppy."

"Oh yeah." I steered us around a fallen tree in the path. "Ben wouldn't have had the guts to come back alone."

"Well, I probably wouldn't come back without you or Hana," Margo said. "Who'd want to be stuck here without our friends?" She swung her arm down and grabbed my hand, which made it easier to walk on the uneven path. We stopped to check another make-out spot, the kissing cove, and kind of walked in on Doug and Dave. Whoops.

"So sorry, guys!" I called back. Margo was just a giggle now. There was nothing else left of her.

Privately, I felt a teeny stab of jealousy. I remembered when I felt like Hana did, and clearly like Doug and Dave did. Like something exciting might happen at one of these parties, something that might change the next day.

Things were better this way, though. Friends were better. Just friends.

"How do you feel about it?" Margo asked.

"About what?" We were nearly to the other side again. Maybe Donald and Hana were already back at the campfire.

"About Ben coming back?"

It took everything in my physical power not to stop in my tracks. I mean, I knew Margo suspected . . . but did she actually know something? Had Ben talked to Donald and Claudia, and they'd talked to her?

"I wish he wasn't here," I said quickly. When I said it, I realized it was really true. If only he'd stayed away, like he was supposed to. Then maybe I could finally get rid of these feelings, these memories. "He's just—"

A snap in the bushes cut me off. I could see a shadow looming. Someone was there.

Margo and I looked at each other. The shadow from the bush had a suspiciously floppy-haired head. Was Ben eavesdropping on us? Margo's laughing face confirmed that she'd had the same thought. Her chin quivered from the effort of not giggling. I threw up my hands.

"Anyway," I said, much louder than before. "What a great summer it would've been *without Ben*."

"What?" Margo's eyes went wide. She hadn't picked up on the plan I'd just sent her telepathically: smoke Ben out.

"Yeah, I was *really* looking forward to it." I sighed. "I mean, the last thing we need around here are *childish* employees."

Margo still didn't get it. "But what have you really got against him?" she demanded. "He sleeps late sometimes—"

"And is so disorganized, never remembers anything—"

"Well, yeah, but he always figures out the lessons in the *moment*—"

"He makes my life harder," I said. "He's immature, he follows Donald around like a puppy, he's obnoxious and spineless, and never says what he's thinking."

"What?" Margo sounded confused, but I was barely paying attention.

The bush was practically shaking with anger. Any second now Ben would jump out and yell at me. I couldn't wait.

"Okay, okay," Margo's voice got soft. She laid a hand on my shoulder. "I get it. You guys don't . . . get along anymore. I mean, I still don't get *why*, but . . ."

Too close, too close! Suddenly, I really hoped that *wasn't* Ben in the bushes. I backpedaled so fast the boat nearly turned over.

"Let's just get back to the campfire." I looped my arm through hers. "I think we missed them."

"Okay." Margo looked over her shoulder. I pulled her forward but snuck a glance back myself. The bush looked like it knew my secrets. Fuck you, bush.

WHAT HAPPENED: PART 3

Bee

IT WAS FINALLY ALL happening: Ben and me. We were up far past our bedtimes, on purpose. And he'd stayed behind to help me, and now we were sitting on a blanket together, happily drinking warm beers. And we were laughing, and tipsy, and some kind of energy coiled in the space between us. Maybe just static from the scratchy blanket, but it felt like more.

But then he'd started ranting about how "fate is bullshit," and I started to get the idea this was maybe not as romantic as I had begun to let myself think.

"Ben, what are you *really* trying to say?" I asked. "Like, you don't believe in relationships, or what?" *Wow!* That sounded a lot bolder than I felt. Thanks, beer. He was dancing around something, and I wanted him to spit it out. No more dancing. Just spitting.

"Okay, fine." He let out a big rush of breath before continuing. "It's nothing like that. It's like . . . my mom."

"Your mom?" We were jumping all over the place.

"Yeah," he murmured. "My mom, and my stepdad, Tim. He's an

asshole. He screams at my mom. And me. Not at the girls, anymore. Not since last winter."

"Last winter?"

"When we showed up at your house."

I swallowed. We'd never talked about that night.

He sighed again. "But yeah, Tim's not my mom's soulmate. He's just a shitty guy. This wasn't *meant* to happen to my mom, it just did."

I waited for more, but he only scrunched up his face and rubbed his nose. The clearing went silent. That was the end of the confession. I'd known things weren't perfect in Ben's home, he'd alluded to it before, but he'd never laid it out for me like that, in plain terms.

I thought about him at home, with Nessie, Ava, and Layla. I thought about all of these years struggling to protect them. About how he'd never really dated anyone.

"I'm so, so sorry, Ben," I said, trying not to let my voice catch. This wasn't about me.

"Thanks," he said softly. "My mom's making a plan, so . . ."

"Can I do anything to help?"

"Well, I mean, your parents have helped a lot already. Nik took my mom to a group, and she's got a job now."

I nodded, slowly putting everything together. That made sense. Mom never told me why their family had shown up that night, but after, that spring, I sometimes heard her whispering to Dad about seeing Colleen, Ben's mom. And sometimes she'd gone over "to visit" two hours away.

"That sounds like them," I whispered.

"Yeah." He nodded. "They're good people. Camp Dogberry's always been the best place to escape."

I felt my eyes widen. Of course. Since fifth grade, Ben had come here, every summer, for the whole summer.

Suddenly, I turned to face him. He copied me, but before he could ask why, I reached forward, wrapping my arms around his shoulders. He felt so much bigger than I thought he would. Slowly, his arms circled my waist. My chin hovered awkwardly, but then I relaxed and rested it between his neck and shoulder. We were locked, chests pressing up against each other.

After a few moments, we both pulled back, but paused with our faces close.

His brown eyes twinkled, his nose an inch from mine, his lips—

"Do you think . . ." he began, his breath alighting on my skin. "Do you think at some point tonight we're going to kiss?"

CHAPTER 13

John

I HAD ONE MISSION for the island party: ask Claudia to hang out. Slow, yes, but I *liked* Claudia. I didn't want this to be a drunk hookup that got awkward in the morning.

Down at the waterfront, everyone waited for the rest of the ringers to show up. Claudia wore a black tank top, shorts, and high-top sneakers. She looked chic as fuck.

Once we got to the island, I had to admit, it felt good to be outside, partying around a fire, instead of cramped into a sorority house or dorm room or apartment. Some part of me filed it away—I could tell my New York friends about drinking under the stars, like it had been romantic, and then I'd tell them about the girl.

It was hard to get close to Claudia at one of these things. She and Ben were Donald's lackies. I didn't hold that against her though, because everyone thought Donald shat gold. I guess that's what happens when you're insanely rich your entire life.

Donald finally disappeared. This is it, I thought.

Drinking makes me nervous, but you have to drink at a party. I had a couple beers, and then jitters crept into my legs. I steadied myself and walked over to Claudia and asked for a beer. She seemed out of it though, annoyed, and I chickened out and sat back down.

"Where're your balls now?" Bobby snickered.

"Wanna go for a walk?" Connie asked.

I glanced at Claudia. Ben had swooped back in. So why not? We ditched Bobby and hopped on the trail. Connie peered around at the bushes and trees.

"Do you see Donald and Hana?" she asked.

"Who cares?" Gross. My older brother making a move on a vulnerable sixteen-year-old. Pathetic, but unsurprising. Like father, like son.

"I don't think she's going to go out with him," she continued. "If it makes you feel better. Bee and Margo got really weird when I told them about it earlier."

I nodded. That actually did make me feel better. Shot down by a high schooler was good ammo for the fall, if Donald pulled any crap at Yale. I wouldn't even have to make it up.

About halfway around the trail, we spotted Bobby.

"Guys!" He ran up in the dark.

"Not a guy," Connie grumbled.

"Claudia," Bobby said, breathless. Dude was not in shape. "I bumped into Claudia, and then I saw her head down to the rocks."

"She's alone?"

"Definitely. We almost peed on each other."

Connie and I looked at each other.

"Accidentally," Bobby clarified.

"Gotcha."

"Make your move, dude!" He punched my shoulder.

Fuck. He was right. This was my moment. Man up.

"Thanks." I clapped his shoulder and took off in Claudia's direction. My heart drummed in my chest, my ears. I rounded a corner, pushed through a couple bushes and out into moonlight, and then I saw her, down on the flat "kissing rock" (camp was so cringeworthy) overlooking the harbor. She sat with her knees pulled into her chest. She'd put on a camp sweatshirt.

"Hey! Claudia!" I jumped down the small, steep trail.

She turned her head. "Oh, John, hey."

She made no move to stand up, so I sat down next to her.

"What's up?"

She stared out at the water.

"Sucky night," she said, finally.

"That . . . sucks," I said. Not the smoothest.

"Yeah," she sighed. "I'm just trying to cool down."

I glanced at her. She wasn't lying. Her jaw clenched tightly. Something was really pissing her off. This was why I liked Claudia—she was real, like a real person. Not like other girls, who pretend like everything's fine, and then flip out at you.

"Sorry," I said, scooted a little closer. I reached into my pocket, pulled out a set of strings. "Knots?"

She looked at my outstretched hand and actually smiled. "Yeah, thanks." She grabbed the black strings and began folding them, pushing, pulling until she had a fish hook. Straightforward, perfectly done.

"This helps," she said. But not enough. Her jawline still looked like the Hulk. "So how's your night?"

I thought about it. "Fine," I said. "But I did want to ask you a question."

"Okay, shoot," she said. She started on a monkey's paw.

"Do you want to, like, hang out sometime?"

She paused. "Like, how?"

A fair, vague question. She was good. I tried: "Like, on the week-end? Not at camp?" I hoped she got the message. I couldn't go fur-ther than that without feeling like I was handing her a bat to bust my nuts.

"Do you mean like a date?" she asked, still staring at the string. I was super affronted. That sounded so old school. *Date*. It was pretty cute, though.

"Like, *hanging out*," I clarified.

She paused again, then nodded. Phew. Hard part over with. But then came something worse: silence. Not actual silence, because the small waves broke softly on the rocks in front of us. I counted waves instead of seconds: One . . . two . . . three . . .

"I'll think about it," she said finally.

"Really?" I said.

Someone else's voice jumped out. "Hey, friends, what's going on?"

Claudia freaked and shoved the rope back into my hands.

CHAPTER 14

Ben

I WATCHED BEE AND Margo go, then stepped out of the bush, prickled and dazed.

Bee. Talking to Margo. About me. Behind my back.

Well, technically, in front of a bush, but whatever.

Cool. Real cool. I loved parties.

I kicked a pebble. Camp Dogberry was really something else. You stop to pee and get to hear all your worst qualities listed systematically. Bee's words echoed all tinny in my head: *childish, disorganized, immature, obnoxious, spineless, puppy-like.*

I wish he wasn't here.

I shivered. So, the moment with the boats, the bantering over starting the fire . . . I was a moron. None of that meant anything. I breathed in and out.

It's fine. *You knew she didn't like you, Ben, you just let yourself get carried away for an hour.* That's nothing after getting carried away every summer for eight years.

I would walk back to the campfire, but from the other direction. I didn't want Bee to think I'd overheard their conversation.

Or did I?

I stood there in the dark, unable to decide.

Goddamn it. Immature? A terrible employee? I mean, I was late to morning meeting a lot. And yeah, I was never great at planning ahead. And sometimes I forgot things, like deodorant or my sleeping bag. And okay, one summer I forgot pants. Just all my pants.

Did she really think I'd just do whatever Donald did?

Well, you did feel like you could reapply once Donald told you he was coming back.

Fuck you, self, it was also because of the move.

Did you even really want an internship, or were you just afraid you wouldn't get one?

You totally are *spineless.*

Shuuuuuut uuuuuuup.

I'd changed. Didn't she know I'd done a whole year at college? I'd never missed a class, had aced my work, and spent every waking hour studying. Not that she'd heard about any of that, I guess. Because we weren't friends anymore.

It shouldn't have been that big of a surprise that she felt this way. I knew things were bad between us. I knew that I might've done something wrong that night. The problem was, I didn't know what it was.

Or maybe this was how she'd felt all along. I mean, from that conversation, it *sounded* like Margo didn't know anything about that night last summer, and Bee and Margo were close. So the only logical explanation was that Bee super regretted what had happened, and she was horrifically embarrassed, and she didn't want anyone to know.

I was so sick of guessing. Would I ever actually know the truth?

Whatever the case, clearly, she hated me, and she never wanted to kiss me again, maybe she never had. I shouldn't have come back here, with the harbor and the trails and the drama and the stars so gorgeous they almost reminded me of Bee.

When I got back to the campfire none of my friends were there. I grabbed another beer and sat down to discuss Capture the Flag strategies with Dave. I laid out a tentative plan for this year.

"Isn't that against the rules?" he whispered, concerned.

"Do you want to play by the rules, or do you want to win?" I whispered back darkly.

He looked confused. "Both?"

"Wrong. Answer."

"We're *baaaaack*, losers!" Donald had appeared on the other side of the fire. As my eyes adjusted, Margo and Hana materialized next to him. Where was Claudia? And—

"Where's Bee?" I called out. Shit. This second beer had gone straight to my mouth.

"She's coming!" Margo assured me, with a giddy smile.

I shook my head, stood up, and walked across the campfire area. Like I figured, Donald wasn't holding Hana's hand, so it looked to me like Claudia was just being her usual paranoid self. Not that she didn't have good reasons, but this was camp, not school, and nobody here was looking to make her miserable. That settled in my mind, I made a decision.

"I think I wanna go," I said.

"What?" Donald laughed. "Absolutely not."

"I'm tired," I explained, as if that had ever been a good enough reason for Donald. When I said it, Margo looked at me, then away quickly. Had she seen me on the way back? Did she know I'd heard their conversation?

"You're not tired." Donald shook his head. "It's, like, ten thirty. Why do you want to go?"

"Look, I just don't want to deal with Bee right—"

"The feeling's mutual."

I turned around, and there she was, illuminated by the fire, casting a ten-foot shadow, the flames' light shimmering across her cheekbones. *Goddamn it.*

Focus, Ben, she just trashed you.

CHAPTER 15

Bee

SO I *HAD* BRUISED Ben's ego. Serves him right, I thought, for snooping on our conversation. I couldn't help it—my gaze flickered over to him, and his eyes flashed hurt back at me.

Whatever.

"Donald"—I turned and addressed him—"you asked me to get Claudia." I stepped aside and revealed Claudia, who was scowling powerfully. "I found her sitting on the rocks, sulking." I left out *with John*. Something weird was going on there, but we'd left him and his buddies on the trail. No need to make any of this more complicated.

"Oh, come on!" Claudia cried, startling all of us. "I was not sulking!"

"You were hunched over on the rocks," I pointed out. "And you had a big pouty face on."

"Can everyone just leave me alone?" she asked loudly. "I just want to get off the island." Had everyone had too much to drink? Wasn't Ben supposed to be keeping track of this? Incompetent.

Hana bit her lip and glanced at me.

"Me too," Ben interjected. "I want to go to bed." He stood not quite upright, leaning to the left. So much for teaching me how to drink.

"All right, all right." Donald tried to put an arm around Claudia, but she shrugged him off. Tipsy was not a good look on her. I glanced at Hana, whose forehead pinched in worry. All the other counselors watched us like we were onstage. Which, I guess, we kind of were up here, front lit by the fire.

"Maybe bed isn't a bad idea," I said quickly. "Ben, can you take Claudia—"

"Got it." Ben nodded at me and strode toward her. I guess he wasn't so incompetent, under direct orders. I felt warmth spread in my cheeks, but it wasn't the beer or the fire. It was that feeling that I could count on Ben, even when we were at odds, in moments like these.

"No, no, no, no, no, no. No." We froze. Donald pushed Ben away from Claudia. "No sleep till *kissing!*"

Our audience erupted in laughter. Ben threw up his hands. Margo giggled so hard she sputtered her sip of beer. But one of us still wasn't having it.

"Who's kissing, Donald?" Claudia snapped.

"*You're* doing the kissing, dummy." Donald rolled his eyes and held out his free hand to her. Claudia didn't move.

"I don't think she wants to kiss you," Margo whispered loudly. More laughter, including Margo, cracking up at her own joke. I shushed her.

"I don't want to kiss her, either," Donald whispered loudly back. "She's going to kiss"—he pointed to my sister—"*Hana.*"

At Hana's name, Claudia's whole body changed. Her arms uncrossed, her jaw unclenched. She panicked, looking at Donald quickly, then Hana, who braved a small smile. Donald dropped his beer in the dirt, *thunk*. He grabbed Hana's hand first, then Claudia's, and brought them together.

"Hi," Hana whispered. I swooned at the cuteness, just a little.

"It's official: You two totally like each other! You both told me!!" Donald proclaimed giddily. "Now, kiss! Or something."

Hana stood there, hand clasped in Claudia's, her smile soft and hopeful. Claudia, meanwhile, looked like she'd been punched in the brain.

"Kiss! Kiss! Kiss!" Donald started a chant, Margo immediately caught it, and soon everyone was chanting and clapping. The strangest repeat-after-me song ever. Claudia looked up, suddenly realizing what was happening, and stared at the mass of chanting weirdos with absolute terror. Hana registered Claudia's alarm, and the bubble popped. She went from thrilled to seriously uncomfortable in a snap.

I grabbed them both and ushered them toward the trail, away from the fire, to an "Aaaaww!" from the disappointed chanters. The new couple both looked at me, dazed, waiting for instruction.

"The kissing rock"—I nodded down the trail—"has a really lovely view of the harbor."

"Ooooh." Hana smiled.

She glanced shyly at Claudia, who nodded in reply, still looking like a moose in headlights.

"Thanks, Bee," Hana said, and without another word or look, took Claudia's hand and led her down the trail.

"No problem!" I called after, and watched them float off into the darkness. A couple whistles and hoots came from the campfire behind me, but it didn't seem like they could hear it. I'd never seen Hana look at someone like she'd looked at Claudia. Well, I'd never seen her look at someone that way and have them looking back. Their connection sparked visibly in the dark air.

Without warning, tears welled in my eyes.

"You gonna keep creeping on your sister?" Donald shouted to me.

I pulled down my sweatshirt sleeve, wiped at my eyes, and walked back to the campfire.

"It's just nice to see something actually working out," I said, and sat down directly across from Ben.

CHAPTER 16

Hana

IT DIDN'T REALLY MATTER that the rock had a nice view. The only thing that mattered was the kissing part.

Kissing Claudia was like ascending a flight of stairs that seem to go on forever — every height you reach, you realize there's more. It kind of hurts, but you keep going because you know, you feel, that there's something magical at the top.

Claudia

Kissing Hana was everything I'd ever wanted.

Hana

Our lips touched, again, and again, and again. Sometimes for a few seconds, sometimes barely brushing. My head reeled, softly. I stroked her cheek, her neck, under her ears. One of her arms wrapped around my waist, and it fit perfectly.

Claudia

I glanced up toward the trail, the fire pit in the distance. I tried not to worry about if anyone could see us. Because this incredible, beautiful person was kissing me like her life depended on it, and I'd never kissed like this before.

I wondered if she had.

Hana

Lips, hands, lips, eyes, skin. Claudia, Claudia, Claudia.

Claudia

Eventually, I pulled back. When I did, she looked confused, and kind of dizzy. I tried not to smile at how cute she was.

"We should probably go back up," I whispered. My fingers tentatively reached out to touch her cheek. She brought her hand up, placed it on top of mine, and closed her eyes. I didn't know what to do.

Hana

I closed my eyes, took a breath, pulled myself together. I really wanted to keep falling apart, with her, in this new way.

"If we have to." I sighed and looked at her. She smiled. Her smile was so genuine. I felt like I knew everything behind that smile. I realized I trusted it.

I took her hand in mine as we stood up. We made our way back to the fire pit. Right before we got within earshot of the rest of them, I whispered, "To be continued?"

Claudia

Hana asking *me* that was a joke. But I nodded at her. "To be continued."

Would I really get to touch her again? Would I get to keep

touching her? Was this summer going to be the best summer of my entire life?

When we sat back down, I could've sworn the fire danced just a little higher.

CHAPTER 17

Bee

"ANOTHER HAPPY COUPLE, brought together by *me*!" Donald crowed.

"You're praaaactically cupid!" Margo singsonged.

I rolled my eyes but laughed, too. It was late—we were on our way down to the dock for departure. Claudia and Hana were walking slightly ahead of the group, so blissfully into each other that they couldn't hear the group of tipsy, tired counselors fumbling behind them.

"*Another* couple?" Ben asked Donald. "Pretty sure this is your first success. Unless you count Kangaroo Court."

Kangaroo Court was our mock trial performance game at Camp Dogberry. Raphael, our improv teacher and my favorite person ever, ran it. We let the campers put the counselors "on trial" for silly things, like not wearing enough sunscreen (Margo), or singing loudly and badly in the shower every morning (Donald).

Raphael also liked to perform fake weddings at Kangaroo Court. He married Mom and Dad last year, and Donald had convinced him to marry Francis and Sam, a couple of older counselors, a few years ago.

"Well, first of all, I *do* count Kangaroo Court," Donald said over his shoulder. "But I have a *real* couple success rate, too." He turned, and flashed his flashlight into Ben's eyes.

"Hey! Ow! What?"

"You and Bee, four years ago, second-year CITs?"

I snorted.

"That *really* doesn't count," Ben said. Why did that make me want to smack him?

"Oh, that magical summer," Donald sighed. "When you two couldn't get enough of each other."

"Ooooh! Right!" Margo wrapped an arm around me. Then something horrific dawned on her: "Hey, did you guys kiiiss? Were you *first kisses*??"

Ack. "No," I said firmly. "We didn't do anything. It was just one of Donald's stupid schemes."

"But . . ." Margo's face screwed up in tipsy thought. "You *were* his girlfriend, right?"

"She was," Ben interjected, glancing over his shoulder at us. "For three entire days." I glared at him. "And we slow danced," he continued. "At the dance party that year."

"Ooooh!" Margo giggled. "Scandalous!"

I couldn't believe Ben. I took a breath and reminded myself that I promised my parents I wasn't going to murder him.

Buuut you only said you wouldn't drown him, I realized. *You could still murder him in other ways.*

"If I remember correctly, I dumped you *during* that slow dance." I settled for death by humiliation.

"Right," he agreed, too easily. "For being *childish, obnoxious,* and *spineless.*"

Crap. My own words from earlier echoed back at me. Ridiculous, eavesdropping Ben. My eyes rolled and my cheeks burned all at once.

Great, Bee, you brought this completely on yourself, vis-à-vis the most absurd boy in the world.

"But hey," he continued. "I don't think that actually counts, either—can you even dump someone if you weren't technically dating them?"

"You totally can." Donald sighed and shook his head. "She's got you there, bro."

"Hey, Ben." Margo reached out a hand. "You just found out you were dumped four years ago. Do you need anything? Ice cream? A hug?"

And now we were laughing again. I couldn't decide if I was fine with all of this, or if I wanted to set myself on fire. And because this was still an enormous joke, everyone quickly grabbed paddleboats and left me with two options: 1. Hop in the moping boat, John's vessel, or 2. Enjoy a paddle for two with Ben.

"Jerks!" Ben shouted at the other four, as they pulled away from the dock.

I stomped into the front seat. "Let's just get this over with."

He looked at my outstretched hand, sighed, and took it. Shaking violently, he stepped forward, then collapsed awkwardly next to me.

"Thanks," he muttered, righting himself.

"No problem."

As we chugged away from the dock, my right hand buzzed on the steering handle. I told it to stop. It kind of listened. I felt Ben to my right, maybe looking at me. A small silence passed over us, and I almost felt something reset in my chest. The boat, the water, the island, what if last summer had all been a dream—

But by the time we reached the Dogberry shore, we were arguing again.

"Capture the Flag is *always* at the end of the week," Ben complained.

"I know," I said as I steered us toward the hazy outline of the beach. "But it's always a nightmare to do that the same morning the session checks out."

"So what are you suggesting?"

"I'm not *suggesting* anything. It's a done deal," I said. "My parents asked me to set the events schedule for the summer, and I did. Capture the Flag is on a Wednesday." I hopped out of the boat into the knee-deep water and pulled the boat in closer.

"But I'm the sports leader!" he complained, still sitting in the passenger seat. "Shouldn't I get a say in this?"

"Capture the Flag isn't a sport," I snapped. "Can you get out of the boat, please?" He grumbled and climbed, very slowly, onto the dock. I was regretting any and all of this. Tonight, the last week, last summer, every summer leading up to that . . .

All the counselors had pulled in and were helping each other stow their boats back on the racks. Margo and Donald helped with ours. John and co. had already disappeared. The younger counselors wandered off toward their cabins, promising they'd hydrate. I looked for Hana and Claudia, and saw them lingering in the water. Was it possible to enjoy kissing with your feet that cold?

Slowly, I became aware that Ben was still muttering about Capture the Flag, sort of directed at me. I decided to ignore it on purpose now.

"You know." Donald came up behind me and swung an arm around my shoulders. "It kind of seems like you two aren't in love anymore."

That brought Ben up short. He shoved his hands in his pockets.

"Tragedy." I laughed. "I guess I'll give up. I'll never love again." Kind of pleased with how that sounded so over it. I was. I was so over it.

"Never?" Donald turned to me, his face close to mine. Alcohol breath. I inched back a little.

"Please," I sighed, in spite of myself. "The potential dudes at my school were the worst. Maybe I'll have better luck in college."

I thought I could feel Ben's eyes on the back of my neck. I turned to glare—

"Well, what about me?" Donald asked.

"Ha!" I snorted. But when I looked at Donald, he wasn't laughing. By the yellow light of the buddy board, I could see him watching my face intently. Wait, was he serious? I couldn't tell, and I'd already laughed. Shit. Shit. As Raphael would say, *commit.*

I laughed again and shoved him away. "No way, Donald. You're too fancy for me—I couldn't go to those big black-tie senator events every weekend. I'd end up stabbing someone in the eye with my salad fork."

There was an awkward pause, in which I freaked out that I'd erred to the point of no return. Who was listening to us? Ben? Crap.

But then Donald cracked his familiar smile. He clapped his hands, hooting. "I'd like to see that!"

"I didn't say I wouldn't be stabbing *you,*" I pointed out.

"Damn, Bee!" He reeled, laughing. I couldn't tell if his reaction was genuine or overkill.

"Sorry, not sorry," I said, shooting him a smile.

"No apologies, please." Donald shook his head. "Happy to be roasted by your wit."

"That's why we love Bee!" Margo popped in between us and slipped her hand through mine and squeezed. "She's the wittiest, silliest Queen of the North. Plus, she's a Libra."

I squeezed back. "You and your *astronomy*."

"What, it's true!" Margo insisted. "The stars don't lie—your planet is Venus, hon, and you're beautiful, just, and super sarcastic."

"How scientific." I laughed. "Well, my birth mom *did* warn the adoption center that I was 'born under a dancing star.'"

Immediately, the group around me went silent, pity hanging in the air, and I cursed myself. Sometimes I forgot how people acted about my childhood and adoption, even my close friends.

Everyone panicked. Donald looked at Margo, who looked at me, then glanced at Ben, who took a step forward—and suddenly, bringing a great wave of relief, Hana was at my side.

"I've always thought that star must've had some serious dancing skills."

"You know it!" I laughed, too loudly. Hana held out a hand, I twirled into her, and she dipped me. Everyone laughed a slightly hysterical laugh, glad the awkward was over. For them, anyway.

"Now, unlike you jerks," I said, standing up, "I have to be awake to help Mom and Dad set up before morning meeting. So I'm going to bed."

They whined about me skipping the after-party, but I yeah-yeahed, kissed Margo's cheek good night, and started back to Little Bat. Halfway there, I heard small footsteps running to catch up behind me, and Hana's soft voice:

"Bee! Are you okay?"

My little baby seal. I pulled her in.

"I'm A-OK. Now tell me everything!!"

CHAPTER 18

Ben

THE BALLS OF MY feet tried to push me forward, to run after Hana and Bee. My ears rung, and my chest burned from wanting to so much. I was dying to go after them, to apologize, and make sure Bee was okay. Everyone had acted so weird. But considering everything that had happened tonight, and I guess the last year, I was pretty sure I wouldn't be welcome.

I turned and trudged after the other three instead, toward Donald's cabin for the "after-party."

"I'm such an idiot," I heard Donald say as I caught up. "And Bee's *such* a queen." Was he an idiot for a dumb joke? Or for actually trying to ask Bee out?

"Agreed to both." Margo patted his shoulder. "The queen bee among us workers."

"Yeah, but she's changing the day of Capture the Flag," I said with a scowl.

"Which makes sense," Claudia said over her shoulder. Seemed she'd recovered enough from kissing to speak. "We're always scrambling afterward to get everyone packed up."

"But ending a session on Capture the Flag always leaves the

kids super pumped about camp, and all the great times they had,"
I complained. "Even if they were homesick and miserable the whole
week."

"Like Dale." Donald nodded.

"That's not a bad point," Margo offered.

"Besides, I'd already planned a kick ball tournament for that
Wednesday."

"No offense," Claudia said. Yay. "But considering your disorganized track record, Bee probably didn't suspect you'd planned
anything."

I groaned. "Well, she could've asked!"

We'd arrived at Donald's cabin. He flicked on the porch light,
nearly blinding me. Donald looked hungover already—Claudia had
all the kissing energy to eat up the alcohol.

"Well, dude, she's had it in for you since last summer," Donald
pointed out. "But I can't imagine she changed the camp schedule just
to spite you."

"Can't you?" I demanded. "She hates me now! She thinks I
shouldn't even be at camp. Even though I *run the sports program*, I'm,
like, a hopeless kid to her."

Margo shifted, arms hugging her stomach. "Umm, Ben . . ."

I looked around and realized everyone was staring at me. Probably
waiting for the downer to leave so they could party.

"Sorry, guys." I sighed. "I'm going to bed." I was getting out of
line, and I didn't want to make Bee's stinging opinion of me stick
with the rest of my friends.

"Night," Claudia called after me. I waved in her direction. I
couldn't *really* be mad at her for falling in love with Hana. But if
tonight was any indicator, I'd been totally justified in my rant about

drama. Or was nobody else disturbed by Claudia's earlier flash trans-formation into a possessive, paranoid snapping turtle?

Whatever. All's well and all that.

I walked back to the waterfront, just past my cabin. I grabbed a few flat stones, skipped them on the top of the little waves. From here, I could see Little Bat's windows glowing in the dark.

And I could almost see my younger self, staying up late with the Leonato girls, playing Uno, drinking bug juice till our teeth were stained red.

Why had I tried? How had I messed this up so badly?

Why had I come back?

WHAT HAPPENED: PART 4

Ben

SO I ASKED HER if we were going to kiss, and she laughed right in my face. Classic. And then I laughed too. What an asshat thing to say. *You barf your heart out about your family, and she was nice to you, so what, now you get to make out with her?*

"Ben!" she managed to say, through the giggling. "What in the world—"

"Sorry, sorry." I waved my hands. "That was uncalled for."

She bumped her shoulder against mine, still laughing.

"But I mean," I ventured, "it is my *last summer.* . . ."

She landed a thorough smack in the middle of my chest.

"Well deserved." I nodded. "Sorry, I'm buzzed."

"I'm buzzed too," she pointed out. "And *I'm* not proposing ideas completely devoid of any sense."

"That's fair." *Devoid of any sense.* Right. I collapsed again, falling back onto the blanket. This was *really* why I never dated anyone, I thought. Because I am the most awkward human being alive, and any attempts I made to be otherwise were pointless.

"But I am going to lie down too," Bee announced. I looked over, but suddenly, she was there already, her head resting on my arm.

"Can I use you as a pillow?" she asked all nonchalant. "I'm a little sleepy now."

"Sure." I could barely believe it, but then she snuggled up into my armpit. I stared into the sky, praying silently to the Maine stars that my deodorant had lasted. I scooped my hand up and around her shoulder. And then, like magic, I was lying on a blanket, with my arm wrapped around Bee Leonato, the greatest girl in the universe. Breathing in tandem, our bodies slowly syncing. I could've lain there with her forever. The leaves above us could've changed, the snow could've buried us, I wouldn't have cared—we'd just thaw out in the spring.

"I have one," Bee said.

"One what?" I murmured.

"A personal confession."

That woke me up. "Okay, go!"

"Well . . ." she began. I tried to look at her, but I couldn't without moving, which would probably ruin everything. "When I was five years old," she continued, "when my mom and dad brought me to the US, it was obviously a big adjustment. I didn't know English when I first came, just basic phrases, and they only knew some basic Amharic. So I liked everybody and all that, but it didn't feel like home."

"That makes sense." Maine was nothing like Ethiopia. Even I knew that.

"During that time, I thought a lot about running away . . ."

I knew the feeling.

". . . I think partly for the adventure of it. I'm not sure." She paused. "But anyway, the day I decided to actually do it, I told both my parents."

I laughed, thinking of little Bee, the honest rebel. I could sense her smiling next to me.

"I know, right?" She laughed, too. "And Mom said, 'Okay, I don't want you to go, but if you're going to, we should pack you a bag first.' So they packed my backpack with my clothes and my toothbrush. They put on my puffy coat and sent me into the woods behind Big Bat. And as I left, Mom said, 'Bee, before you get too far, check the front pocket of your backpack.' So a few steps in I did, because I was convinced it was candy."

I couldn't help laughing again, and then I gave her shoulder a small squeeze. I didn't plan it, it just happened naturally. Instinctually. Did I have good instincts? I think she liked it, because for a moment, she stayed closer, in the squeeze, her head farther up my shoulder.

"Anyway." She relaxed. "It wasn't candy. It was a note from my parents, which was at first a bit of a letdown. But then I read it. It said: 'Bee, we love you, please don't go.' Simple English," she explained.

"Right," I whispered.

"And every time I decided to run away, which was a lot in that first year, they'd pack my backpack and put a note in the front. And eventually I named it the Bee-Don't-Go Bag. And then I stopped wanting to run away."

"Bee-Don't-Go Bag," I repeated, dumbstruck.

"Mmmhmm."

I'd seen framed photos of little Bee at the Leonatos'. Braids, shining cheeks, that huge grin, one arm planted firmly around little Hana, always. I'd envied her perfect family, getting to live at Camp Dogberry all year long. Here, it was safe. I never really thought about how maybe it hadn't always felt like that to her. I pictured Nik and

Andy, dutifully packing a backpack for her, and then waiting for her to return. Hoping the next time that she wouldn't feel she had to go. . . .

. . .

"Ben?"

. . . . . .

"Ben, are you crying?"

"No. I mean, I can't help it."

She laughed and sat up. My shoulder felt cold. I sat up too, and rubbed at my nose, trying to wipe off all the gross happening on my face. I must be pretty wimpy and disgusting to her, I thought.

"But, uh." I wiped my hands on my shorts. "That was such a beautiful story." I finally looked at her again. Our eyes met. And I realized she really didn't think I was disgusting.

"Aww." She smiled. "Well, you're the only one outside my family who knows it. This probably goes without saying but—"

"Never. What happens at Nest stays at Nest."

"I promise too." She put her hand on top of mine.

We were looking at each other like that again. Like when I'd asked if we were going to kiss. I forced myself to hold steady—I wanted us to keep looking at each other like that, to stay in one of these moments, because inside them, there was this tiny possibility of something.

Like it might actually happen.

CHAPTER 19

Hana

AFTER FIFTEEN MINUTES OF sister talk, Bee yawned enormously and said she was going to sleep. I ducked out to go to Donald's, and as I walked away from Little Bat, I stopped in my tracks: Bee might've been faking the yawn.

I turned back to look at our cabin—a flashlight lit one of the windows. I wondered if I should go back and make sure she wasn't being upset on her own. I'd been so wrapped up in Claudia (literally) that I'd only caught the end of the adoption conversation. Once we were alone, she'd given me a quick rundown, at my urging, and mentioned something about Donald "making a joke" about asking her out, and then things getting weird. When I tried to ask more, she'd insisted we talk about the whole Claudia-and-I-kissing situation instead.

On my way to Donald's, I filled my water bottle up with the shallow water, just at the spot Claudia and I had lingered. It had been amazing to me we hadn't been electrocuted. I swear, I had felt sparks between our lips. I bottled up the memories with the water, and screwed the lid on tightly—later, I'd empty it all into one of the vases in my bedroom.

Coyote's screen door fell sharply on the frame behind me.

"Hana!" Donald looked up, delighted, as I stepped inside. Coyote was a cavernous cabin—twelve beds, *two* lights. Every Dogberry cabin had camper signatures all over the walls and bedposts, written in permanent ink, but only Coyote had signatures in every color. Donald always brought a pack of rainbow Sharpies.

Steady rap music played on Donald's laptop on the floor. Margo and Donald sat on his counselor's bed on the back wall, a bottle of something between them. Above his bed, Donald had pinned up the big collage he'd made last year: a coyote's face, with enormous yellow eyes, constructed out of tiny newspaper and magazine clippings.

Claudia hovered next to the door, wearing boxer shorts and a not-loose-enough-fitting gray T-shirt.

I needed to sit down.

"Hey." I smiled and slid onto the bed opposite Donald's. Claudia immediately sat down next to me. I felt my smile widen. "I couldn't sleep."

"Kind of glad." Claudia nudged me with her shoulder.

"Excellent!" Donald proclaimed. "Welcome to the exclusive after-party!"

"Where's Ben?" I asked.

Donald shook his head. "He went to bed."

Margo made an "eek" face. "I don't know how he's going to fall asleep over all that angry muttering coming out of his mouth."

"I think he'd been chewed up enough by Bee," Claudia offered. I winced.

"Well, they chewed up each other. . . ." I trailed off.

Donald smirked, and Margo giggled.

"Umm, never mind." Claudia blinked at me, her honey eyes laughing. She held up her left arm, and I scooted in under her shoulder. Her hand kind of flopped over the side of my arm. It was sort of awkward, but that didn't make it any less magical.

"No!" Donald shouted. "*Do* mind, because we have an idea."

"Mmm!" Margo agreed, smiling a little too wide. "And we need your advice." These two were going to be real gross in the morning.

"Oh?"

"Yeah," Claudia sighed. "Donald wants to do another setup."

"*You two* can hardly complain." Donald pointed a finger at her, at *us*.

I let out a giggle; Claudia shivered. I put a hand on her leg to steady her. More teeny shocks. How many body parts could we touch before lightning struck?

"Okay, who's getting set up?" I asked. "Margo and Bobby? Officially?"

"Ew, no!" Margo said quickly. "*Bee.*"

I looked at Donald. "With who?"

You?

The last few years, I'd noticed Donald around Bee. Donald was always funny, always on top of it, but around Bee, there was this tiny falter, this small hitch in his game. He always pushed through like it hadn't happened, but I'd got the sense he felt something for her. I'd never mentioned it to Bee, because it was pretty clear to me she didn't feel that way about him.

Which was partly why that whole Donald-liked-me rumor had been super weird today. Thank goodness it had been nothing.

If Donald's feelings had been hinted at before, I was pretty sure they'd been confirmed tonight. Even if he'd played it off as a joke, and then put his foot in his mouth.

"We're setting her up with *Benjamin*!" Donald declared, raising his bottle. "Those two have been into each other since . . . seventh grade?"

"Years!" Margo yelled in agreement. "They're my OTP."

We laughed. I guessed they were my One True Pairing too. I'd always thought they were going to get together.

"Right," Donald nodded. "And we *know* something happened between them last summer."

All eyes turned to me. I held up both hands. "I don't know anything," I assured them. I felt guilty even confirming that piece of non-information.

"And she wouldn't tell us if she did." Margo toasted the bottle at me.

I smiled at her. "No, I wouldn't."

"But something *did* happen!" Margo continued. "It's so obvious. They've been acting weird ever since last year's sparkler party."

I watched Donald's face. Was that the tiniest flinch ever, or a blink?

"Well, they've always made fun of each other," Claudia said.

"Oh, come on," Margo said. "It wasn't like this before. Before it was friendly. Or *flirting*."

"That's true," I said. "They were friends." I turned to Claudia. "Good friends."

"And this could be Ben's last shot!" Donald hopped off the bed in excitement, held out his arms wide. A presentation was beginning. "Bee's gonna get scooped up by some hottie this fall."

"Totally." Margo nodded. "She's already joined, like, nine clubs."

I felt a pang. Had she?

Donald laughed and pointed at Margo. "Exactly. She's a hot nerd, and there's gonna be a line of guys banging down her door. So Ben's got one last shot, this summer."

I wasn't a fan of discussing Bee's love life behind her back, but Donald was probably right. Bee was going to have her pick of guys at college. My mom had sometimes said this to Bee, when she'd bemoaned her dating options at Messina High. Unlike me, she'd never even sort of dated anyone at MHS. But in Boston, that big, looming skyline in my head, she'd have so many options. Odds were she'd meet at least one guy she might actually want to spend time with.

Maybe this *was* Ben's last shot.

"Well," I managed. Claudia gave my shoulder a squeeze. She'd figured out what to do with her floppy hand. I loved this.

Donald clapped at me. "Hana's on board. Claudia?"

"I don't know what I'm agreeing to yet."

"Good point." He climbed back on the bed, put one arm around Margo, and leaned in. He motioned for Claudia and me to come over. We glanced at each other, quickly acknowledging neither one of us wanted to move, and then we did. We crowded around Donald on his squishy, orange sleeping bag.

"I have a plan," he whispered.

"Of course you do," Margo said, tipping over onto his shoulder.

I should've guessed. He was on a roll. He'd been so proud earlier, taking me for a walk, little by little revealing that Claudia liked me, while at the same time making sure I liked her back before he did. I'd been so terrified that *he* liked me, the entire thing had worked perfectly.

"What's the plan?" I asked him.

"We're going to *trick them* into admitting they like each other!"

Donald said triumphantly. "You and I," he said to Claudia, "will set up Ben so that he overhears us saying that Bee likes him but won't tell him. And then *you two*"—he gestured to me and Margo—"will do the same thing with Bee. Reversed."

Margo squealed and hit my arm excitedly.

"I actually like that idea." Claudia raised her eyebrows. "It's like Battleship."

I smiled, but I wasn't so sure. I wasn't going to bring it up again, for fear of more speculation, but we *didn't* know what had happened between them last summer. We didn't know what we would be getting in the middle of. What if it was serious?

But wouldn't Bee have told me if it was?

"I'm a genius." Donald twirled his pointer fingers.

"But, *genius*," Margo whispered, "what comes after that? After they hear they like each other?"

"Yeah, how do they get together?" Claudia asked.

"Aha! That's the best part!" Donald bounced on the bed. "They have to figure it out, and *we* get to watch!"

Claudia lit up. "Okay, that's good. But what if they don't figure it out?"

"Oh, they will." Margo nodded. "Eventually. Probably. Hana, what do you think?"

Three pairs of eyes on me.

I wanted Bee to be happy. And right now, when she and Ben weren't busy shouting at each other, they were ignoring each other. Something had happened, and she wouldn't even talk to me about it, but I could tell she was still upset by whatever it was. I wanted to fix that for her. Maybe this would.

"Let's do it," I said, finally.

"We have the sisterly blessing!" Donald whooped. "Let's start this week, so they're paired up for the sparkler party."

Margo shook her head. "Darlin', you're one part schemer, one part disgusting romantic."

"Darlin'," he twanged back, "I've never claimed otherwise. And now you all get to share in my glory!" Donald grinned. "Because we'll *all* be the camp cupids this summer. And this will be our ultimate victory, in the name of *love*!"

Claudia, Margo, and I looked at one another, wide-eyed. Donald had finally lost it. I grabbed his water bottle from the floor and tossed it to him.

"Bro"—Claudia moved toward the door with me—"go to sleep."

We slammed out into the night air, and Margo followed a few moments after.

"I tucked him in," she whispered.

On the trail back, Margo couldn't stop giggling about our plan, and her giggles combined with the night peepers made a soothing, happy soundtrack for our walk.

At Little Bat, she turned to us and said, "Well, I'll leave before this gets awkward," and bounced away.

"Good night!" I shouted after her.

"Thanks for not making it awkward!" Claudia called half-heartedly.

In the dark, I couldn't quite see Claudia's face. But I could feel her hands, and then her lips, her breath. I could feel her. I wanted her. My mind pulsed, begging this night to never end.

But eventually, the kisses got longer and sleepier. One more kiss on my cheek. A whisper:

"To be continued."

Forever, I thought.

I watched her leave, striding back to her own cabin, her shoulders slightly hunched. This adorable, awkward, perfect human was mine.

I stayed outside for just a few more moments, and then, as if just for me, the moon peeked out from behind the clouds, lighting up the world in a blue crush. I stood on Little Bat's porch, listening to the peepers and the waves, still feeling Claudia's lips on mine, aching for them for one more second. I wouldn't need to make any paper stars tonight. I was already filled up with my own.

A light caught the corner of my left eye. I turned to see Margo and her flashlight, popping up back down the other side of the trail, near the boys' cabins. The *exclusive* exclusive after-party. I wondered how any of them could even stay awake. I'd just been kissed within an inch of my life, and I'd never been so happy to snuggle down into my sleeping bag. It was easier to fall asleep when you were happy.

CHAPTER 20

Vanessa

COUNTDOWN TO CAMP: *zero* days, one hour.

I had been waiting *my entire life* for this. Well, umm, about five years. But that's still a long time. Fine. I had been waiting *more than a third of my life* for this.

My mom found Camp Dogberry when I was eight, and she'd sent us here every year since. My sisters came for the first time last year, but they'd been to camp to pick us up and drop us off so many times it was a tradition for them too. We all loved camp. The food was great, the cabins were cozy (especially Little Bat—and it has a skylight roof), and I wasn't one of those campers who got homesick. In the past, it had been this big escape, but I still got to be with Ben. So it was perfect.

Mom woke me up with a finger to her lips. She pointed to the girls—they were still asleep. She whispered she'd gotten a babysitter for the morning so we could drive up to camp alone together.

"And get breakfast?"

"Yes, we'll get breakfast."

I quickly showered and threw on the first-day outfit I'd prepared: well-worn red Camp Dogberry T-shirt, so I looked official, running shorts and Keen hiking sandals. I said good-bye to Smooshie. I felt bad I couldn't say good-bye to Ava and Layla, but they were sleeping like logs. Snoring logs. I hoped I didn't have eight-year-olds in my group.

We put my big bag out in the car. It was heavy, but I was positive I hadn't forgotten anything. *And* I'd brought an extra pair of Ben's pants, just in case.

Mom and I talked about everything at the diner, even though we'd talked about all of it for the last week straight. Which counselor and cabin I wanted, which campers I hoped were coming back, what they'd name the goats this year. I told Mom the story of Capture the Flag two years ago again—the one where Ben had defeated Claudia with a gorilla suit.

We finished breakfast and got back in the car. As we passed the town line, I felt an itty-bitty pang of sadness. We'd just moved here. Even after the month at Aunt Deb's, I still wasn't used to walking around a home freely, no longer waiting for a bomb to go off, a burst of ringing anger.

Dishes! Money! Your mother! Your brother! You people!

I winced. How long would it take to forget all of that?

Camp. Think camp.

Countdown: thirty minutes.

I'd wanted to be a camp counselor since that first summer. The counselors were so cool. They were all best friends, and they got to stay up late and decide which games we were going to play, which art projects we were going to do. I wanted so badly to be a part of that.

Ben always said it wasn't as glamorous a job as it looked, but I think he just told me that so I wouldn't be jealous. Now I didn't have to be jealous anymore, because this year I'd get to spend the entire summer at camp as a counselor-in-training. CIT. I loved saying the acronym out loud. It felt professional.

We roared up I-95, and the trees and bushes got wilder and wilder the farther north we went. Mom chatted on the way up about the girls, and how they'd be there in a week so I didn't have to miss them too much.

"Can't wait!" I said. I knew in my heart that was true, it's just my heart was kind of full of other things at the moment. Like my cabin assignment and being on staff with my favorite counselors.

Countdown to being a first-year counselor: 1 year, 364 days.

"Nessie, are you going to get out of the car?"

We were here!!

Warm, sunny Camp Dogberry, which always felt warmer than the rest of Maine. I opened the door and breathed in that camp air: boat grunge, saltwater, animal poop, and rising bread. I hopped out of the car, grabbed my backpack, and tried not to run to check in. The dirt parking lot felt like a red carpet under my sneakers. I was a *CIT* this year!!

"Vanessa!" Bee checked me in with a big hug. Her hair was up in this braided faux-hawk do. She looked so cute. No wonder my brother secretly loved her.

"Bee!!" I grinned. "Where's Ben?"

"In Dam, stuffing his face." She smiled.

"Sounds like Ben." Mom came up behind us, carrying my bigger bag. "Hey, Bee"—she kissed her cheek—"is your mom around?"

"In the office." Bee nodded. "She said to tell her when you got here."

"I'll go find her myself, thanks!" Mom said. She kissed my forehead. "I'll see you next week, okay?"

"Sure, sure!"

I hugged Mom, and she went off in search of Nik. Our good-byes at camp were never super sad or long, because she came to visit a lot. Or to drop off something Ben forgot. And she always wrote me letters and postcards, even though we were only a couple hours apart.

I was just about to ask Bee what my cabin was, when I got *slammed* by Sophia, right in the stomach.

"Your bangs are so cute I'm going to die!!"

"Sophia!" I laughed. "You're going to kill me!"

"With love!!" she screamed, squeezing tighter.

When she finally released me, I took a moment to check out my best camp friend: dark tan skin, brown curly hair, wicked grin, shorter than me this year!! Wearing an all-pink ensemble, complete with pink handkerchief and pink sunglasses. Sophia took her color coordination seriously.

"I missed you so much!" she squealed.

"I couldn't tell!!" I smiled.

Somewhere behind her, my other best camp friend, Wallace, waved at me. I smiled—the same black, cowlick-y hair, ridiculously pale skin, and a *new* NASCAR T shirt. He was tall and gangly this year, which was weird. I waved back through Sophia's bubbling, and eventually made it over to say hi.

Before we could really catch up, though (I had to tell them both about the divorce and the big move), Bee ushered us into the dining hall with the rest of the CITs for our first meeting.

Walking into Dam was how I would imagine walking into the great hall in a castle. The big main room was made of beautiful, spiral-y wood. Slabs of enormous trees were loosely shaped into long tables. The walls were covered in fading charts and maps of Maine's animals and plants, and an abandoned wasp nest hung like a disco ball from rafters in the center of the room. The poles and cross-beams were wrapped in twinkle lights that were never turned off. At the back, there was a friendly window—the drive-thru window, we called it—where you could talk to the cook, Shane. And where you ordered eggs. Next to it, a narrow wooden door led back to the kitchen for dish duty.

Not even dish duty could make this place less magical.

"He-llo! Nessie?" Sophia's voice cut through my dreamy entry. "Come on!" Most people at camp called me by Ben's nicknames, which I always forgot at first. I jumped and went to go sit down with her and Wallace. At the table were the other CITs this year, Joe and Isabelle. This was their second year, which meant they got to be first-year counselors *next year*. I was so jealous.

"So," I said as I slid in next to Sophia and Wallace. "Did you guys know that Claudia chopped off *all her hair?*"

Wallace's eyes widened. Sophia's mouth dropped open. "*No. Way.* Why would she—"

"All right, kiddos! Welcome back!" We looked to the top of the room, near the fireplace, and there stood Nik and Andy, both in cargo shorts, green camp T-shirts, and baseball caps; both smiling; and both holding clipboards. If I'd taken a picture of them right now, that would be, like, the quintessential Nik and Andy shot.

First, they doled out cabin assignments. I got Moose with Margo!! I'd wanted Little Bat, but I guess it was covered, since it already had two counselors, and the Leonato sisters were the best counselors ever. But Moose was a cute cabin, with a cute purple bench out front. And I loved Margo, and now I'd get to hear her bedtime songs all summer.

Sophia got Connie in Puffin, and Wallace got Donald in Coyote. Wallace was really excited about it, and Sophia just shrugged. I knew she probably wanted Margo—she kind of worshipped her style. I felt a little bad.

"We're all so excited to have you here," Andy finished, after the last assignment. "And to get you guys trained so you can be the best Dogberry counselors ever someday."

"Much better than this year's," Nik added. "They're terrible."

"Hey!" called voices from the kitchen. Everyone laughed.

"We'll give you"—Bee looked at her watch—"fifteen minutes to stow your stuff, and then it's back here for the first hour of orientation. Now, we need three volunteers."

There were six of us total, and we all raised our hands.

"Excellent." Nik laughed. "You can *all* take out the compost buckets on the way to the cabins. Pairs are better anyway, since they're heavy. Let's get going!"

A couple other CITs, including Sophia, groaned loudly. I didn't say anything. Okay, so compost was gross—every piece of food scrap from the camp went in there—but *I* was determined to be the most hirable, helpful CIT there ever was. No way was I screwing up my chances of working here like Ben. Speaking of, guess who was waiting at the compost buckets?

"Hey, Nessie!"

I ran up and threw my arms around him. He gave me a squeeze, ruffled my hair, and turned and greeted the other CITs warmly.

"Now, who's ready to help the environment??"

The other CITs looked doubtful, but I raised my hand. After we lugged the gross glop to the garden, he grabbed my big bag and walked me to Moose.

"Everyone's really excited you're a CIT this year," he chatted happily. "All the girl counselors fought over you, gladiator-style."

"And Margo won?" I smiled.

"Naturally." Ben nodded. "She called on her vicious woodland creatures to help."

I laughed. I liked my brother even more at camp—he was more energetic and just . . . happier. He had that layer of magic camp dust on him now. Soon I'd have it too.

We paused outside my cabin. I wondered where Margo was. I wanted to make a new, profesh impression on her.

"So everything's good at home?" Ben asked. I knew what he wanted to know.

"Everything's good," I assured him. "He hasn't called more than he's supposed to. Layla and Ava are so excited to come next week once Jewish Community Center camp is over."

"Good old JCC."

"And Mom got an A on her first quiz in her summer courses," I offered.

He laughed and shook his head. "I don't even want to know how you found that out."

I smiled. "I have my ways."

Mom leaves her computer open sometimes. Or sometimes she leaves her phone out. Or not out, but easily accessible. I just like to make sure everything's okay.

"But yeah, everything's good," I finished, anxious to get into my new space. "Except Smooshie's definitely mad you left again. I feed him treats, but I don't have those magic Ben chin-scritching skills."

Our cat inexplicably loved Ben with every long, floofy gray tuft of fur on his body.

"I miss him," he said wistfully. "I hope he writes."

I laughed and gave him one more hug. "Okay, I need to go in."

"See you later, on Monarch!"

Oooooh right, evening games tonight, special for just CITs and counselors. I loved evening games. I guessed I would love them even more with Ben running them now.

The cabin was empty, but there was a colorful note from Margo on my bed—the one on the opposite side of the room from hers.

Nessie!

You're my CIT now. I promise to rule over you with fairness and as little gloating as possible. Here is a tiara I made Donald make for you. Also, I saved one of the baby goats for you to name.

Love love love,

Can't wait to see you,

Margo

I sighed happily, put on the daisy crown, and held the note to my heart for a brief second. And then I ran to orientation, because I realized I was already five minutes late!!

CHAPTER 21

Bee

THE ACTIVITY LEADERS WERE set to come that afternoon for a few hours to organize and set up their spaces, which meant Ben and I would be on opposite ends of camp, thank goodness, since I was Raph's improv assistant this year. Margo would be with Doc in nature, Donald with Nell in art, and Claudia, lucky her, with *Ben* in sports. Seriously, I couldn't believe he was leading an activity. Mom would neither confirm nor deny, but I suspected that he'd planned *nothing* this week. What a Ben-shaped train wreck.

"Raphael's here!" Mom called when I walked into Dam. She was sitting at the paperwork table. Dad was in the corner with the CITs, happily supervising their camp nametag creation.

I looked around wildly. No beautiful man. "Wait, *here* here?"

"Luna!"

"Thanks!" I grabbed a camp calendar and dashed back out the door, hearing the group chuckle on my way out.

Luna Moth was our all-purpose building, in between Painted Turtle (art) and the boat shed. It was newer than the other buildings and had bright green trim instead of red. The first floor of Luna's kind of a catchall for stuff we have at camp that doesn't have any other place. Part library, part counselor hangout, part trial room for Kangaroo Court. It was big and sunny, with enormous windows on all sides, and since there were squishy purple-and-pink rugs piled on the floor, it was the only building where you were allowed to take off your shoes. It was also where all improv classes took place, which made it the *best* building.

But it was only the *best* building when the *best activity leader ever* was inside it. And, actually, the only person in the world who knew my last-summer secrets.

I burst through the door and saw him at the back of the room, hanging up posters. "Raph!"

"Bee!"

I slid off my shoes and toppled into him. I was a lot bigger than he was. I barely had time to take in his slick new haircut—short on the sides and long, styled, and suave on top. I wondered if he partially did it to smooth out his receding hairline. Well, it totally worked. He wore his usual brightly colored shorts, salmon this time, and a striped tank top.

"It has been *forever*." He smiled. Raph had a perfect small mouth, with perfect small teeth.

"I can't believe you're finally here!!" I squeezed his hands. Now it really felt like summer had arrived.

"Neither can I, let me tell you." He sighed. "I had such a bad health year in New York. I got terrible asthma. Thank God for camp! I can actually breathe out here." He closed his eyes and took a big breath.

Raphael was in his late twenties, doing a masters program in directing in New York City.

"That's awful!" I shook my head. "I know you love it, but I get so claustrophobic when I'm in a city."

We'd done family trips to Portland and Boston, and one to New York City to see some shows. Amazing theatre, way too many people for me, and not enough trees or stars.

"So this means you're going to New Hampshire?" he asked.

"Oh." I'd forgotten that I'd told him about my acceptances but not my final choice. He'd written one of my recommendation letters. "No, I mean, I guess I'll get used to city life, because I'm going to EBU." East Boston University.

"Bee, I am so proud of you!" He pulled me in for another hug. How did he smell like a Macy's, even at camp? "You're going to love it!" He pulled back and handed me a poster to hang. *In the Heights.* "You're majoring in . . . ?"

"Education with a minor in theatre."

"That's my girl! Oh, I am just so thrilled for you."

When I said my major aloud to Raph, it sounded cool and confident. Like I knew what I was doing. Wouldn't it be nice if that were real?

We started moving around chairs and organizing Luna into our usual setup. We chatted about the shows we'd worked on this year—Raph had assistant directed *Sunday in the Park with George*, and my school had tried to do a production of *The King and I*, but I'd gathered a petition against it, seeing as we had *all white students*. Except me, and I'm not Thai. I'd won.

Raph shook his head. "I can't believe they even tried. That drama director is—"

"Out of touch as fuck?"

He laughed. "Putting it mildly, yes. What'd you do instead?"

"*Bye Bye Birdie.*"

"And you were Kim?"

"Naturally."

"Could've been worse."

"Could've been the most racist *The King and I* ever."

"Dear *God*."

I'd missed him so much. After thoroughly Broadway-ing the space, we spread out on the rugs to plan the games for the first session. Starting off with Statues, Machine, What Are You Doing?, Park Bench, and then more complicated games as the week went on. I was trying to figure out how to bring up Ben stuff with him, without sounding like I wanted to talk all about me. So far, no balanced phrasing had presented itself in my head.

"Well, I'm sure your new theatre department will be much more informed," Raph assured me, while he color-coded the lesson plan by age group. He'd given me the calendar to mark up for special events and theme days. His organization skills were on point.

"Oh yeah, I'm sure." My new theatre department. I didn't want to think about it.

"You'll get into the city, and it'll be such a relief, Bee," he continued.

"Right."

"That's totally how it was for me," he explained. "In New York, I could finally be myself. And then it was easier to be me here in Maine too."

"Great." I tried not to grit my teeth. Even if I was the only black girl in my class, Messina was still my home. Raph and I weren't coming from the same place on this. Maybe I'd made a mistake and I should stay here—

"Have you told Ben yet?"

I froze.

"Umm, told him . . . ?"

"That you're going to EBU?"

"Oh right, that. No. Nope. Definitely not." I'd managed to only answer college questions when Ben was conveniently out at Monarch. Or out on the trails. Or peeing.

"Iiiinteresting," he replied, drawing out his green highlighter with the word. "So, is there anything new to tell there? He's here, right? That wasn't the plan, if I remember correctly."

I bit my lip. Though I'd wanted to bring him up, now that the opportunity was there, I wanted to scream and duck into the pile of pillows, or make an emergency exit. Where was the closest fire alarm?

I took a breath. I was so used to hiding the Ben stuff from everyone, it felt weird to finally talk about it. But I really, really wanted to. I passed Raph the finished calendar.

"Yeah, he's here," I said, finally.

"And how's that going?"

I thought back over the week. "I'm, uh . . . not handling it well." By the end of the sentence, my eyes had filled with syrupy tears. I grabbed my lips to try and stop them from quivering.

"Aw, Bee." Raph put a hand on my shoulder. "I'm sure it's not as bad as you think."

I swallowed, forcing some crying down. "No, it totally is." I hated my choked voice. "And he's totally given up. I really think the whole thing is just dead now. Like, in the water. Like a dead seagull carcass floating in the water."

Raph nodded, his big blue eyes widening with sympathy. "I know, sweetie. It's the worst when you've thought about it for so long, and then it's over, like it never mattered."

I nodded back. I didn't want to speak again until I could sound like a grown-up human, not a homesick baby camper.

"I promise, it'll heal," he continued. "It'll always hurt, but it won't be everything, all-consuming, and you'll feel like yourself again."

I took a shuddery breath and sighed. Did I want to be myself without my feelings for Ben?

"Thanks. Sorry." I stood up. "I know you're right, I just wish he hadn't come back. It would be so much easier if I didn't have to *see* him."

"I hear you." Raph stood up too. "Here's some advice from the great beyond: *do not* hook up with your roommate just because he says he's moving out." He rolled his eyes at himself. "Because the housing hunt is brutal and he's probably actually not moving out."

I laughed. That's why Raph was awesome. He was older; he'd been through this stuff before. He made it all sound normal.

Of course, this was why love and sex and whatever was so unappealing to me. Because who the hell wanted this to be their normal?

We finished, and I walked Raph out to his car. Another hug, because tomorrow morning was a long way away, and he and his white SUV pulled out of the lot. I trudged back to Dam, his words sitting heavily on my shoulders: *it'll always hurt*. I pushed away the Ben stuff, but there was a lot left over.

The city, a new theatre department, a new life. The MHS theatre department was a nightmare, but I knew everything about it. It was mine. When there were problems, I felt like I could fix them. I didn't even know what the EBU theatre problems were yet.

I went to bed that night and woke up clammy from a dream that my new theatre was putting on an all-white production of *Hamilton*. With some water and the soundtrack, I coaxed myself back to sleep.

The next dream was one more familiar.

WHAT HAPPENED: PART 5

Bee

WE'D TOLD EACH OTHER secrets and promised to keep them. Our hands were touching, mine on top of his, skin-to-skin, and we were looking at each other like, like, like—it was too much. I broke it off.

"Wanna go for a walk?" I asked, standing up quickly

He paused for a beat, then jumped up too. "Sure."

We folded the blankets and stacked everything in a corner of the clearing. Donald and Margo and the rest could carry it down in the morning. Well, later in the morning. The stars had already begun to fade. I tried to ignore that.

Wordlessly, we wandered toward the opposite edge of Nest, toward the path that led down around the cabins. Getting down off Nest was steep and tricky, the path dirt was loose, and I had to carefully place each step. I felt Ben next to me, concentrating on his steps, too.

We're not drunk anymore, are we? But I pushed that thought backward. Because if we weren't drunk, what were we doing?

The trail leveled out. The water grew louder, waves hitting the shore nearby. We followed the sound down a small side trail that led by the off-season boat shed, Stickleback. We stored the kayaks and paddleboats there during the winter.

Past the barn, the trail came to a small point—rocks with a view of the water. We pulled up short at the edge. You couldn't swim here or anything, too many sharp edges below. But you got the nice view of Messina's cove, with the harbor, houses on the other side, and sailboats in the middle, rocking gently.

"The fog . . ." Ben trailed off.

The paling sky and still-bright moon illuminated levels of mist, a bridge over the water. It was pretty, but cooler down here. I pulled my hair out of the topknot and shook it all out so it would cover my ears.

I glanced over at Ben. His eyes squinted at the ocean. Neither of us said anything.

What now? I panicked. *I've ruined everything by taking us down here. We never should've left Nest.*

"We should probably go—" I turned around, but I must've been distracted, or tipsier than I thought, and misjudged the edge of the point.

As scary as it was, it only took about two seconds. I tripped, I started to fall to the side, saw my life flash before my eyes, my body splayed across the rocks below, and then I was scooped up into Ben's arms immediately. He held me close, and we breathed hard into each other.

"Hey, you okay?"

It wasn't even that far a fall; I probably wouldn't have died. I was fine. But automatic reactions took over: my heart pounded, my eyes watered, my cheeks grew hot.

"Ahhh! I'm sorry," I said, wiping my eyes. "I'm so tired, I must've—"

"I know," Ben said gently. "It's okay though, you're okay. You're fine."

I'd heard him use that soothing voice with campers, with his little sisters. It was kind of humiliating he was using it on me, even more that it worked. My breathing softened, *You're okay*, my heart slowed, *You're fine*. After a few deep breaths I looked up at him.

"Fudge," I whispered, laughing a little. "That was so. . . but thanks."

"What are friends for?" He smiled.

I smiled back.

And then we didn't kiss.

CHAPTER 22

Bee

MY DAD WOULD'VE SAID that the parking lot on the first day of camp was "abuzz," but that was too light a word for it. It was more ablaze, and it was our job to be constantly at the ready with a massive hose.

I stood under the tent with the group signs—the kids dropped their stuff off by age and cabin. Donald, Margo, Bobby, and Ellie were on lice check duty, supervised by Dad in the chairs set up outside the office. Hana was down at the waterfront, conducting swim tests with the Dogberry swim team. The CITs and John and Connie took care of lugging the gear, while Doug, Dave, and Jen were at the mini trading post we'd set up in Dam, selling mosquito netting and Dogberry T-shirts to the new campers and families. Ben, of course, was nowhere to be found, because that would've meant he'd been on time.

I tapped the top of my clipboard. This was my first year running check-in out here—usually we had another, older counselor. Somehow, now I was that older counselor, and as much as I hated to admit it, I was really nervous. What if I said someone's name wrong? Or put off an unprofessional air? What kind of air *was* I putting off? How did I change it? From where did that kind of air originate?

A yawn interrupted my worries—Ben, ten minutes late, the skin under his eyes still swollen from sleep. Like a troll. I'd somehow avoided him since the island party, but now there was no escape. Had he known Donald was going to ask me out? Was he just totally okay with that?

"Morning!" He gave me a tight smile. "We're under the big top, huh?"

"I am." I stiffened. "*You're* just getting here."

"I know, I'm sorry, I got stuck in my sleeping bag."

"Only Peter gets to use that as a valid excuse." Peter was our camper who got stuck in things. The bathroom, his sleeping bag, his luggage . . .

"Hey, look! It's Jay and Maddie!" Ben pointed to the entrance, where a big tan van had parked, and two kids were jumping out. Suddenly, all my nerves and Ben-related annoyance evaporated. Right, I reminded myself. This is about these awesome kids, not my checklist, and not my *coworker*.

Jay and Maddie tore toward us, their mom following at a normal human pace.

"Slow down!" I shouted. They almost tripped, taming their sprints into Olympic speed walking. When they were finally close enough, they flung themselves into our arms. Sometimes being a camp counselor was kind of like being a celebrity.

"Bee!" cried Maddie. "And *Bunny!*"

"*Bunny!*" Jay cackled, jumping up and down with evil glee in the middle of hugging Ben.

I watched Ben's expression flip from elated to a fake smile. "Okay, guys. LOL. But I'm not Bunny this year, just Ben."

"Oh, but you'll always be Bunny to us." I smiled.

"Not. This. Year. *Bee*." Ben grabbed Maddie and Jay's bags, and huffed over to their group's drop-off zone.

Whoops.

Last summer, for the first session, before the Fourth of July, Ben and I had led a group hike together to Blueberry Mountain. The trip was a *disaster*. It started pouring on the way, but we had half a dozen strangely determined kids, so we'd handed out extra ponchos and hiked anyway.

About halfway up the mountain, when we were basically climbing through mud and the kids were miserable, I got stung by a wasp. I'm really allergic to wasps, so I had to take a bunch of Benadryl, and we had to turn the group around.

Benadryl makes me *really* loopy.

So there we were, in the pouring rain, Ben trying to get these kids back down a mudslide safely, and me yammering on, high as a kite.

"Come on, kids!" Ben had yelled, as encouragement. "This trip wasn't a mistake if nobody dies!"

That got a laugh out of them, but they were still exhausted, soaked, and hungry. So my loopy self was keeping them preoccupied by asking them icebreaker questions. Like their favorite movies and colors and animals.

At the time, the older campers had it in their heads that Ben and I were dating. So when I asked their favorite animals, they asked me the same question, and I said:

"I *love* bunnies."

They'd figured out by then that I was out of it, so they egged me on.

Sophia, a camper at the time, giggled and said, "As much as you love Ben?"

"More," I'd shouted. "I love bunnies more than Ben!"

"What if Ben *was* a bunny?" asked Rudy helpfully.

"Thanks, Rudy," Ben had grumbled.

"That would be *the best case scenario.*" I'd laughed. "Bunny Ben. Hey, let's call Ben *Bunny* from now on. Ben, your new name is Bunny!"

And it stuck. All summer. It caught like wildfire, and it super bugged him. Even Doc and Judy called him Bunny. And I swear, John, Connie, and Bobby told each new session of campers coming in. Probably Donald did too. Ben hated it.

And he blamed it all on me. Clearly. Fantastic. "Guys, if Ben doesn't want to be called Bunny, we shouldn't call him Bunny," I said to Maddie and Jay, diplomatically. "Respect, remember? It's an important thing at camp."

Ben shot me a grateful look. It was probably the most civil moment we'd had yet, and it almost made me blush. I shook him off with a smile and changed the subject with Maddie and Jay. "So, did you have a good school year?"

"Jay has a pet frog now," Maddie told me, pointing at him as if he was being accused of something terrible. "He named it *Maddie.*" Oh, he *was* being accused of something terrible.

Jay snickered, holding his hand up to his mouth to hide it.

"Frogs are cool," I explained to Maddie. "I'm sure it was a compliment."

"Was not."

"Hey, you two," Ben said, returning from stashing their duffel bags. "You need to go get a lice check and then change and do your swim test."

Maddie tugged on the hem of my T-shirt. "Are you doing polar bear swim tomorrow?"

Ben grinned as I stifled a groan. Polar bear swim was a hellish tradition at Camp Dogberry, and the only one I fantasized about axing once I took over the camp someday. The kids were given the opportunity to wake up at *six a.m.* and go dunk in the ocean. If you perform this satanic ritual four times during your session, you get a certificate when you go home. I did this once as a camper—it was freezing and terrible and my least favorite thing ever, but I was *determined* to earn my certificate.

After one bone-chilling round of this, I realized the certificate was a sheet of blue paper with a polar bear on it. I could totally print that myself. I haven't participated since.

"If *you* want to go, just tell your counselors," I said.

"We will." Jay nodded. "But *you're* going to come, right?"

"Never." I laughed. "Not in a million years."

"But, Bee, you always say that!"

"Correct!" I smiled. "Because I'm never going to do it again."

"But you always tell us to try new things!" Maddie pointed out. These kids must've joined debate club this year.

"And she's already *tried* polar bear swim," Ben chimed in, taking Jay gently by the shoulders and turning him toward the lice-check area. "Now go get checked for bugs."

"But—"

"Go!" Ben prodded them.

Wow. Was Ben actually taking my side? "Don't worry. You can berate me more at lunch, if you want," I told the kids.

"Fine," Maddie said. "We'll berate you then." As they walked off, I heard Jay whisper to her, "What's *berate* mean?"

Next I checked in Meredith, the tiniest, gangliest, freckliest eleven-year-old in the world. She was a longtime camper and was notorious for losing her toiletries every year. This year we'd given her counselors an extra set already, so they'd be prepared.

"Hey, Bunny." She grinned a toothy grin at Ben, handing over her bag. "Long time no see."

"I'm not even going to dignify that with an answer," Ben groaned, tossing me a look. But his eyes were twinkling, just a little, and I let myself smile back.

CHAPTER 23

Hana

"OKAY! ERIC, BACK UP the ladder. Toyah, how would you like it if a giant fish tried to catch you? Leave that little swimmer alone, please."

First day of camp as a swim instructor was different. The youngest swimmers were the hardest. They *really* tried, but most of them needed to stay in the shallow end, no question. After Judy, the head swim instructor, announced the verdicts, they all sighed and slid back into their flip-flops dejectedly.

I *loved* being in the water the entire morning. Bee always said I was a mermaid because I floated like a balloon and my skin never pruned. Maybe that was true, because being in the water felt like my other world, and I forgot about everything else. On swim team, I wasn't particularly good at keeping track of laps, though. It never mattered to me how many I'd done—once I started swimming, I never wanted to stop.

When we finished our last swim test before lunch, I pulled myself up onto the dock and wrapped a towel around my waist. Technically, I was supposed to change out of my suit for the dining hall, but if I didn't, then Claudia might see me in it. My rash guard top, lifeguard official, hugged my chest, and though I wasn't Margo-epic, I knew I looked good.

I slipped on my flip-flops and thanked George, our day lifeguard, on my way out. I found Margo outside of Dam, by the flagpole, lying out on a towel in the sun.

"Hey, darlin'," she said, sitting up. "Nessa and Rachel are getting my group changed for lunch. How cool is that?" Margo had the littles, our youngest group of campers.

I smiled. "Pretty cool. Don't let my mom catch you tanning, though."

"Not tanning." She sighed, standing up and shaking out her towel. "Just freckling more."

"Beautiful freckling," I said. "We should head in and help set up."

"Oh wait!" Margo caught my hand and pulled me away from the veranda steps. "I forgot: I have a *plan*."

"You're starting to sound like Donald," I pointed out.

She steered us around the side of Dam, through the gate and into the garden near the carrot tops, where she shot the fluffy greens a brief glare, like she was threatening them not to repeat anything.

"Okay, so this morning, I got Jay and Maddie for lice check," she whispered.

"Oh, I got them too for swim test!" I said, normal volume. "They both passed into the deep end this year."

"Cuties!" Margo whispered, face lighting up for a moment as she temporarily forgot her mission. "Right," she said, becoming serious once more. "So, they were talking about how Bee never goes to polar bear swim."

"Oh, never." I shook my head. "She hates waking up that early and hates cold water." Two of my favorite things.

"That's a lot of hate," Margo admitted. "*But* what if we got Raph to take her to Kangaroo Court tomorrow and sentence her to a morning of polar bear swim?"

It was kind of evil, but I did love getting everyone to go to polar bear swim, and a public Kangaroo Court sentencing would be such good press.

"I'm in," I agreed, and Margo clapped in excitement. "But what does polar bear swim have to do with Donald's plan?"

"That's the *brilliance* of it," Margo said. "*Bee* is groggy in the morning."

"Yes." Bee was really out of it early in the morning. Sometimes she left for school without her books or tried to get in the car wearing pj bottoms. She was never late, but she was never with it, either.

"So it's the perfect time to *stage our trick*."

"You mean—"

"We plan it so she's coming down to the bathroom to change, and we're already there waiting outside, hidden, right?" Margo's voice got faster as she talked. "So we wait until she goes in, and then *we* go in, and talk about how Ben is *in love with her*!"

"Oh." This just got real, real fast.

"And she's so out of it that she actually believes us. What do you think?" Margo bit her lip.

I considered Bee's grogginess. I considered our acting skills. "I think it's our best shot?"

"Yes!" Margo squealed. "I'll go catch Raph." With one more silencing frown at the carrot tops, she hopped around the corner. Then reappeared a second later, and made funny eyebrows at me, whispering, "By the way, you look real cute in your swim top." She winked, and disappeared again.

Okay. That was sort of random. But a second later, it made sense: Claudia tentatively peeked out from around the corner. I smiled, and she closed the distance between us.

Back here in the garden, we were shielded from the world for a moment, and I could see her eyes take me, and my swimsuit, in. I took her in too, in her athletic shirt and cargo shorts. I imagined we felt the same way about each other's clothes. Like we'd rather we weren't wearing them?

"Hey," she said, voice low, wrapping her arms around my waist. She didn't seem to mind I was soaked.

"Hi," I whispered. "How was your morning?"

"No lice," she said. "How about you?"

I smiled. "No one drowned."

"You'll never believe what Donald's planned for Ben." Her eyes sparkled with laughter.

"Oh, I can probably believe it." Before I realized what I was doing, I'd gently grabbed her shirt. One small movement, and we crashed together. Our lips pushed against each other urgently. Her fingers entwined through my damp hair. My hands found their way onto her back, grasping her closer.

Was kissing Claudia ever not going to make the world spin double time? If it kept going like this, we were going to disrupt the solar system.

All at once, we broke apart, breathing heavily. Whatever was happening, it was super not camp appropriate. Breathing like that, looking into each other's eyes, I realized this was moving fast.

"To be continued?" I whispered.

"Mmm," she hummed back.

CHAPTER 24

Vanessa

OH MY GOD. My first day of camp was *exhausting.* I fell asleep as soon as the kids finally did. And then I had to get up and go to breakfast and start all over again.

I didn't even *think* about the fact that being a counselor would be like babysitting twenty of my sisters at once. Margo and I had seven-year-olds, who were a year younger and cuter than the twins, but maybe even more of a handful. One of them peed themselves the first afternoon, and another one turned into a dinosaur, which Raph and Bee *did* work into improv class flawlessly. Still, it wasn't as useful for our nature hike, because he scared away most of the birds and chipmunks.

"*RRRRGH!*"

Margo salvaged the hike with icky-looking plants. "Look at these gross *mushrooms*, though!"

"Ooooooh!" "Nice. That's disgusting." "Can we eat them??"

We spent all day ordering our littles in and out of places: in and out of the water, in and out of the bathroom, on and off the field, in and out of Dam. And half of them couldn't sleep that first night because they were homesick. Luckily, Margo had a bunch of stories up her sleeve.

"The trick is," she whispered, once the last one had drifted off, "to *start* the story really exciting, and then make it more and more boring. And voilà!" She gestured to our snoring cabin. "I'm going to go get a snack!" How she had the energy to move after all of that, I had no idea. I fell asleep ten seconds later.

The next morning, we were up at eight, changing, bathroom, breakfast. I barely said a word except "No, Howard. No." I never wanted to admit it, but Ben and I were both bad before ten a.m.

Standing in the breakfast line, the comfy smell of pancakes started easing me back to sleep. I felt my lids start to flutter. Could I sleep standing up? And then Sophia leaped in next to me, in a blinding shade of lime green. What a scary alarm clock.

"Nessa, you'll never believe what I heard."

"How did you hear anything?" I yawned. "Over all the kids?"

"Mine are eleven." Sophia pointed to a group of older kids in line at the eggs counter. Tall kids. Almost-our-age kids. Kids who looked like they could express when they had to pee, before the fact. I felt a little pang of envy.

"They're kind of mopey." She tilted her head at them.

"Lucky," I sighed. But then I saw my dinosaur camper, sneaking around the muffin basket, hunched over like a velociraptor. At least my group kept things interesting.

She poked my side. "Yeah, but ask me what I heard."

Gossip, Vanessa. Wake up. Get in the zone. "Okay, what did you hear?!"

"I *heard* that Claudia and Hana are *dating*."

That woke me up. There was nothing better than counselor

relationship gossip. Although it was weird when, like last summer, your brother was in the middle of it.

"Seriously?" I whispered. "Who told you?"

"Isabelle, who heard it from Rachel and Doug."

"Whoa." This was big. Actual counselor information. I guess being pre-counselors now, we got more reliable gossip. We grabbed plates of pancakes and fresh-cut strawberries. I eyed Hana at one end of the dining hall, pouring herself coffee, smiling at her mom. Dark hair in a curly knot, already damp, wearing board shorts and a short-sleeved lifeguard swim top. So pretty, no matter what. I looked and found Claudia sitting with her group, the nine-year-olds, playing table hockey with a melon rind.

Hmmm. They weren't looking at each other longingly or anything. But they weren't supposed to either. We'd found that out at orientation. *NO PDA. Boundaries, boundaries, boundaries.* Boundaries sure made it hard to snoop.

"But can you believe it?" Sophia continued seamlessly, as we got our tea.

"Believe what?" Wallace asked.

"Hana and Claudia," I whispered. "There's a rumor—"

"Oh man, yeah." Wallace smacked his forehead. "So embarrassing. I accidentally saw them kissing yesterday before lunch."

Sophia let out a little shriek, and I spilled hot water all over the table. We quickly mopped it up.

"You *did?*"

Wallace scratched his head. "Yeah. I mean, I didn't *watch*, but I went to cut through the garden, and they were . . . you know . . . *in the garden.*"

I had so many questions: Was it like a peck? Or were they in a *romantic embrace*?? But Wallace looked embarrassed enough already.

"Amazing," Sophia breathed.

"Well, I think they'd look pretty cute together," I said, picturing it in my head. Automatically, my brain put them in front of a wedding altar with Hana in a flowy white dress and Claudia in a sharp black suit. "I can see it."

"Yeah . . . but they're both girls?" The way Sophia said the last part, I wasn't sure whether she thought one of them was a dude, or whether she wanted to know if I didn't like gay people.

"Weren't you at orientation?" I fired back, suddenly terrified my friend was homophobic. "We had a talk about diversity, you know."

"Oh, I know," Sophia whispered. "I've just never *known* any girls who date, you know, each other."

"Well, now you do," I said firmly. They were the first girl couple I knew, too, but Ben had told me about that stuff. And now that we didn't live with my dad anymore, I didn't have to hide that I supported everyone.

"Hey, you're right!" Sophia brightened. "This is going to totally *shock* my school friends."

"I don't think that's—"

"Let's go discuss with Isabelle."

She jumped up, Wallace followed, but then three of my campers asked if I would come sit at their table. Who could say no to those little faces? As we crossed the dining hall to their perfectly selected spot, I scouted the rest of the room.

Rachel and Doug? Rachel and Jen? Doug and Dave? Who else was dating?

I could not *wait* to find out.

CHAPTER 25
John

IF I'M BEING HONEST, Hana and Claudia making out at the island party, after I'd asked her out, wasn't my ideal. My ideal was me making out with Claudia. So yeah, a small setback in the plan, but hey, everyone's gotta do their thing, and I didn't hold it against Claudia for liking girls too. That just made her hotter, as Bobby pointed out. And I couldn't deny Hana was cute, even though she was super boring. All that girl did was swim and smile. But she was fine for a hookup buddy.

I barely saw Claudia over the first two days of camp. I had the ten-year-olds, and damn did they have energy. And concerns. So many concerns. I missed working with younger kids (they were usually just cute as all hell), but Margo and Rachel got them this time. I did get to see Claudia, briefly, during sports, and she smiled and joked with me like usual. I figured I was in a good position to ask her to hang out on the weekend. Maybe for Saturday. The sparkler party was Friday, but my real aim was to get Claudia alone.

I snuck glances at her in the dinner line. The piercings all along the back of her right ear. The gentle smirk she threw at campers. She seemed to operate in the world so easily, so herself.

If I asked her out tonight, after Counselor Hunt, was that too desperate? Maybe I should wait till tomorrow?

"John, Lis says she *doesn't like* our president," one of my boy campers complained, jerking his thumb at one of the girls. "Isn't that unpatriotic?"

Out of the corner of my eye, I saw Connie by the piano, motioning at me to come over.

"What's to like?" I replied, nodded at Lis, and ducked out of line. I heard the boy huff as I dodged into the bathrooms hallway. Connie poked her head out of one of the single occupancies, and I followed her in. She shut the door hard, behind her.

"Pretty sure we're not supposed to be in the bathroom together," I pointed out. Suddenly, I was paranoid: if Claudia saw us come in here, would she think I liked Connie?

There was a knock at the door, and Bobby slipped in too. Would Claudia think I was having threesomes with these knuckleheads?

"What's up?" Bobby asked.

"I have bad news," Connie announced.

For bad news, she didn't look real upset. "All right," I said. "Make it quick. I have kids out there, and some of them have *dietary restrictions.*"

"You know how Claudia and Hana . . . ?"

"Only wish I'd seen it." Bobby sighed. I hit him in the gut.

"Yeah, so?" I prompted. I was pretty sure Connie was into me. She'd seemed overly excited that Claudia had made out with someone else.

"So they're a thing."

"A thing?"

"Like a dating thing."

My stomach dropped. They weren't supposed to be a thing, of any kind. A sexy thing, at the very most. "How do you know?"

"A bunch of people saw them in the garden yesterday, kissing."

"Where am I when all of this is happening?" Bobby demanded. I hit him in the gut again.

"Ow."

More kissing? In the fucking garden? That sounded sickeningly romantic. "So they're kissing." I tried to blow it off. "That doesn't mean anything."

"Well." Bobby held up a finger. "Combined with the fact that all the CITs know they're dating—"

"What?"

"Yeah, that was my second piece of bad news." Connie nodded. "Ellie told me, and apparently everyone else, that Hana and Claudia are a legit couple."

Fuck. Fuck, fuck, fuck. These girls always knew each other's business. And Ellie was friends with Hana, and she might've talked to her.

I kicked the door. Now I was back at this goddamn camp, because of my goddamn brother, and my goddamn pseudo-*father*, and my one chance . . .

No. That's not how this worked. People dated all the time. Hooked up all the time. They hooked up with people they liked, and people they didn't like. . . . All we had were rumors. And some kissing.

"This doesn't mean anything," I decided. "Until there's actual proof."

"But what more proof—" Connie started.

Bobby cut her off. "John's right," he said. "It's just two girls doing that experimenting thing. You know." Connie glared at him. But I'd seen plenty of girls go through that phase.

"But keep an ear out, yeah?" I said. "For actual proof. Like, online or something."

Connie rolled her eyes, clearly frustrated—she so wanted me—and shoved her way out of the bathroom.

"Dude, I'm totally hooking up with Margo later," Bobby whispered. "She gave me the nod."

"Good for you, man."

I slapped him on the back affectionately. Dude was in to get his heart mashed into papier-mâché pulp, third summer running, but who was I to stop him?

We split up. I went and found Marigold, who needed gluten-free pasta, and Caleb, who needed soy-free sauce. I had to stop myself from talking to them like my grandma: *"When I was your age, if someone was allergic to peanuts, they ate a peanut, died, and got it over with."*

CHAPTER 26

Ben

DAY TWO OF SPORTS went smoothly; I didn't have to send any-body to Andy/Black Bear for any kind of medical attention, which might've been a first for the sports program. I dug being in charge of the games we played, the sportsmanship lectures. When I'd been Pete's assistant, I had helped out, but *my* assistant, Claudia, was so disgustingly in love, I got to do everything myself!

Lucky me!

But whatever, I still liked it a lot, in spite of space cadet Claudia. I'd made her the permanent catcher that morning during tee ball so that she didn't have to hold a bat. That seemed wisest.

The routine of camp had wrapped itself around me like my cozy sleeping bag. I loved having every inch of the day planned for me. I loved being busy. I didn't love when I had time to think—like this weekend, and Fourth of July. We had the rare Friday Fourth, which meant the kids would go home after lunch. Which meant maximum sparkler partying.

Fireworks.

Picnic blankets.

Warm beer.

Bee . . .

I tried to shake it out of my head, like an Etch A Sketch.

Donald, however, could not shut up about it. He whispered to me in hushed tones when I sat in on the afternoon art class. Hana had volunteered to help out with an origami unit on her break, so everyone who was free came to hang out. Luckily, Bee wasn't free. Some kind of ropes course disaster.

"I'm making a booze and fireworks run on Thursday," Donald murmured, creasing a blue paper creation. "You want to come?" He handed me the finished product.

I ignored him for three reasons. One, seriously, a bunny? Fuck off. Two, I didn't really want to think about this party and all the memories that went along with it. And three, folding tiny origami stars takes a lot of concentration.

"Donald, I can't make a crane," Reading whined. "Can you do it for me?"

"Did you *try*?"

"No . . ."

☙

After dinner, en masse the kids poured onto Monarch for evening games. Tonight, a classic and a favorite, Counselor Hunt. The rules were simple: counselors hid, campers sought.

Each counselor was worth a different amount of points. The more points the counselor was worth, the harder they were to find. We used to ask the kids to assign the points, but now we did it randomly, because it became a terrible popularity contest, and Donald always won.

One setting sun, sixty or so campers, a dozen counselors, half a dozen CITs. *Mayhem.*

"All right!" I called out over the field. The murmuring and excitement began to die away, but Bee's voice cut it down like a machete:

"Listen *up*, Camp Dogberry!"

Sixty silent, attentive faces. You could hear the peepers.

Skills.

"Thank you." I nodded at her. She winked in response and my heart backflipped. It was almost like old times. "So tonight, we're playing Counselor Hunt!" Applause erupted from the field, but they quieted down quickly for the rules. I ran through the basics for the new kids and then looked behind me on the grass, where I'd set down the points cards—colorful poster board with lanyard ties. The counselors wore them around their necks, like nametags.

"Where—"

"Bee is worth *one thousand* points!"

I turned. Donald was already assigning Bee her points card, dramatically placing it over her head. The campers clapped, giddy. Great.

"Donald . . ." I tried. He dodged around me and continued.

"Hana is worth *an entire birthday cake!*" Everyone cracked up. "Which is equivalent to three hundred points." Hana dipped her head through the loop and gave a little wave. "Claudia is worth *five hundred* points, *and* half an ice cream cake."

All right, well, he'd taken my job, but the entire field was rolling in laughter. Except John and Bobby, who were, predictably, worth ten points each.

Finally, he got to the end of the line, awarded himself a thousand points plus the best sunglasses award. That was not a thing at all. Then he got to me—

"Finally," he said, holding up a points card. "Our young Benjamin is worth *three thousand points.*"

We didn't even have that card. I looked at what he put over my head: he'd added two zeros to the thirty points card.

"You, my friend, are the Golden Snitch!" he announced proudly. That reference was lost on the majority of our campers, but they clapped anyway.

After the fancy part was over, Donald handed it back to me for the actual game work. We divided the kids into teams and assigned them each a CIT or first-year counselor. They had to give us ten minutes to start hiding, and then BLAM. The older counselors had a quick huddle before we set off.

"No hiding inside, under, or on buildings," I reminded them. "And nobody take the waterfront." I put my hand in the middle, we all did: one, two, three, *Camp Dogberry!* And we broke off.

"Better hide somewhere good, Rosenthal," Bee whispered, as we headed out. "Gotta live up to those points."

There wasn't even any sarcasm in her voice. I grabbed the olive branch and tried not to do a maypole dance around it.

"Back at you, Leonato." That sounded normal.

"Pshh," she scoffed. "I'm apparently only worth a third of you."

"It's hard being the best," I admitted. "But someone's gotta make the game interesting."

Pink sunrays hit her brilliant smirky smile; I tripped over a tree root. By the time I got up, her snickers were echoing down the trail. Donald, Claudia, Hana, and Margo had already disappeared.

Hide, Ben.

Right.

Three thousand points. We'd never assigned that many. I ran

through my options: goat shed, haystack, tire swing pine trees, under the outdoor clay sink? Could I burrow into the sand at the volleyball court? Impersonate a log at the sing-along fire pit?

Suddenly, a thought occurred to me. I didn't *like* the thought, but my feet started moving without my consent, as my stomach twisted.

Quickly, I jogged past the waterfront, behind Dam, up the trail, out into Nest, where I found the fuzziest dogberry bush of the bunch, crouched down, and inserted myself into the branches. The raw, sticky wood rubbed at my skin, but eventually I found a position I could tolerate. It *was* the perfect spot: Nest was an easily forgettable location. The campers didn't come up here often, maybe only for stargazing once in a while. And three thousand points was a lot of hiding responsibility.

Still, I thought. I had other options. Why had I returned to the scene of the crime?

A few minutes later, I heard distant hoots and hollers: the race was on!

Over the next hour, voices floated up from Dam and the garden. There were screams of victory, and cries of defeat carried up to me on the wind as counselors got away.

Finally, I heard footsteps coming up the trail. At this point, I was ready to be found. Usually I was a patient hider, but this spot I'd picked . . . I'd just been staring out into the middle of the clearing, watching the sun set, the stars come out, the scene in my head projected onto the space before me. There was Bee, there was me, there was my arm around her, there was the briefest hint of possibility. I couldn't decide whether I wanted our former selves to scrap the whole thing and go to bed, or whether I wanted them to try harder. To be more honest with each other. What if she had just told me that she only wanted to hook up—nothing more? Would I have said fine and done it and been hurt anyway?

So yeah, after an hour of that circle of hellish thinking, I was A-OK with being found.

But it wasn't campers.

"Is he here?" Donald's voice at the top of the trail.

"I don't see him, but where else could he be?" Claudia.

They must've been found already. Suddenly, I saw this for what it was: an excellent opportunity to scare the crap out of my friends. I could see their outlines in the dark—they turned and started seeking on the other end, making their way around Nest's edges. Soon they'd be close enough that I could reach out and grab their ankles.

Their voices were lower on the other end of the clearing, so I couldn't hear them. I was mostly focused on the space in front of me, holding my breath till I could see their shoes.

Footsteps and voices sounding closer, closer, closer. Shoes. Yes. I could grab one of each foot. I slowly, silently wove my hands through the bush's branches. I was just about to reach out—

"I told you: we definitely can't tell Ben," Claudia said.

Wait, what?

"Bee is *in love with him*, and we're not going to tell him?" Donald asked.

CHAPTER 27

Claudia

"NO WAY," I REPLIED. "We're not telling him. What good would that do?"

Donald eyed the bush, trying not to laugh. We'd both just heard Ben *squeak*.

"I don't know . . ." Donald managed, grinning like a madman. "I feel like he deserves to know."

He looked at me expectantly. Crap. I'd completely lost my lines. Everything we'd rehearsed had gone right out of my head. And I hated improv.

Donald mimed smacking his forehead but picked it up: "I know Hana told you *not to say anything*."

"Right!" I said. "She *did* say that! She told me not to tell anyone!" This didn't sound super realistic coming out of my mouth. What were words, what was saying things? Did I ever sound realistic?

"I get that, but how can she drop this news on you and not expect us to tell our friend?" Donald continued. *Okay, okay, Claudia. Focus.* What came next?

"Yeah." I snapped my fingers. "She said that Bee was *going crazy* with Ben being back this summer."

"Like how?" Donald prompted.

"She's so obsessed with him she can't think about anything else!" I said. That sounded good. And currently what I was experiencing with Hana. "And she can't sleep! Or . . . eat dairy!"

"Dairy?" Donald said, genuinely surprised. I was on a roll.

"Yeah, her stomach gets upset," I explained. "Bad poops. She's so stressed. She can't even shower!"

"Shower?" Donald repeated, raising his eyebrows.

"Yeah, she keeps forgetting to shower," I said. "Because she's so in love with him?" This was starting to sound fake. I quickly added: "That's what Hana said, anyway."

Donald held a hand over his mouth, literally holding in laughter. Jerk. After heaving a few deep breaths he finally spoke in a rush of air: "Well, you know, love is a powerful thing, man. So is stank, though. I hope she's swimming . . . and avoiding dairy."

"Me too," I said. Was this over yet?

"So anyway, I guess what you're saying is, we can't tell Ben because he would never, ever admit to liking her back."

"What do you mean?" I asked. *Stick to questions, Claudia, not statements.*

Donald glanced in the direction of the dogberry bush, then winked at me. "Well, you know Ben. He's got the emotional depth of a dinner plate."

"Maybe a canoe?" I offered.

BEN

Seriously? Fuck these guys!

Claudia

We heard another small, indignant noise from the branches, and out of the corner of my eye, I thought I saw the shadow of a middle finger.

"Did you hear a mouse?" Donald asked innocently. We both cracked up, silently, but I pulled out of it fast: I didn't know how much longer Ben could hold it together. "So yeah. I don't think he's, um"—there were a few stray tears of laughter running down Donald's face—"I don't think he can deal with . . . *feelings.*"

"Tell me about it." I rolled my eyes. He'd been such a jerk when I'd told him about my feelings for Hana.

"And he's never even *had* a girlfriend."

"So true," I said, feeling the smug slip out. I mean, *I* had a girlfriend.

"Now that I'm thinking about it," Donald pondered. "Even if he liked Bee, he would totally shoot her down or fuck it up somehow." I couldn't tell if that was acting or not.

"You're right," I said. Because that seemed to be what Donald wanted.

"And Hana's right," he said firmly. "We wouldn't want Bee to have to deal with that. It's probably better this way. Her feelings'll fade eventually."

"Yeah. I wouldn't want that to happen to her. *Rejection* from *Ben.* Double ouch." We both laughed.

"Me neither." Donald sighed. "Bee's kind of the greatest."

"Well . . ."

"Yeah, yeah." Donald shoved me lightly. "Something about how 'her sister's cool, too.'"

"She *is*."

"Speaking of which, shouldn't we go? The game's almost over, and I feel like you're gonna want to gaze adoringly at Hana across the fire."

I frowned at him. But then I realized that's totally what I wanted to do.

"Yeah, let's go."

He put an arm around my shoulder and started steering me toward the trail again. As we left, I tried not to look back at Ben, who I'm sure was throwing the most dramatic fit of all time.

CHAPTER 28

Ben

THEY WALKED BACK TO the trail, trampling through my dreamscape of Bee and me on the picnic blanket. I waited for an extra thirty seconds, just to make sure they were really and truly gone, then I stepped out into the clearing and sat down. Hard.

Dam's generator whirred from down below. The moon and starlight hummed. A beetle landed on my forearm and stared up at me judgmentally.

Bee *liked* me?

The back of my neck burned. Was I sunburnt or blushing or both?

I closed my eyes, pictured Bee. Her high forehead and cheek bones, her round, dark eyes flanked by darker lashes. That smirk on her lips—*her lips*—that so easily broke into a grin. Crossing her arms. Bursting into laughter. Pointing one finger with such command that an entire room of children pretending to be jungle animals instantly became taxidermy.

The greatest. Donald was right. She was.

And she liked me—*loved* me?

My heart beat into my stomach, into the grass and ground beneath me.

I loved her.

If a nearby pine tree had fallen on top of me, that would've been a lighter blow than this.

"Ha-ha, *what?*" I said out loud. To no one. Maybe the judgmental beetle.

I launched off the ground, almost blacked out from dizziness, steadied myself, and started pacing around in circles.

I loved Beatrice Leonato. *Really, her full name?* a part of me protested.

My pacing picked up—I jogged in wider and wider circles. It helped me think, break this down.

Claudia had *said* that Bee was afraid that I'd reject her if she'd said anything. But I had told her last year that I liked her, and she'd rejected me: *just friends. She'd* rejected *me!* But maybe she regretted it now? And thought I wouldn't forgive her?

Or had something else happened that night? Something I hadn't understood?

Donald and Claudia clearly thought I would fuck things up if the opportunity presented itself. Maybe they weren't wrong.

Sidenote: Why had I spent so much time in bushes listening to people making fun of me this summer?

WHAT HAPPENED: PART 6

BEN

THE MUSIC SWELLED, THE stars danced, and fireworks went off—prematurely. Because we were standing on that rock, holding each other, our pulses racing, lips moving closer. And then we were distinctly doing none of those things.

Okay, so she didn't want to kiss me. Or . . . well, we'd both jumped back before it could happen. And then I'd tromped behind her on the trail, trying to wrack my brain for a memory made a moment ago. Did one of us jump back first? Which one?

The brown boat shed, Stickleback, came into view. If we took a hard right, it was a fifteen-minute walk back to camp. A rough fifteen minutes. I wasn't looking forward to it. I felt all of this, whatever it was, slipping away as the sky grew ever so slightly brighter.

"Do you think the Bandytails are in there?"

I almost bumped into Bee. We'd stopped. She walked up to one of the murky windows and was peering in.

"We could check?" I offered. My heartbeats grew more deliberate.

"Why not?" She opened the door. I followed her inside.

Stickleback was dark and dusty, but my eyes adjusted. The air smelled stale and musty, but my nose adjusted. Odd wooden chairs and heaps of sunfish sails, looming empty boat racks.

A pair of raccoons, called the Bandytails, often camped out in Stickleback. They left behind plenty of poop, footprints under the windowsills, and sometimes tufts of fur caught on the metal racks. Staff and campers had logged only a few actual sightings because they seemed to invade at night exclusively.

Bee and I checked the couple old paddleboats in the back—no cute faces staring up at us. We checked in the tackle cubbies. We checked the closet with rigging, too. Nothing. We gave up.

So much for those deliberate heartbeats. This was so over.

Except on our way out, I tripped on a rope. I swear I didn't mean to. I don't think.

I grabbed Bee on my way down, and laughing tiredly, we both fell onto a pile of tarps. We landed with Bee on top of me, face-to-face, chests pressed against each other. She stayed there.

"This is actually pretty comfortable," she whispered. I nodded. "Is there any poop?"

"I don't think so."

With those magical words, her lips were on mine.

CHAPTER 29

Ben

MAYBE SOMETHING HAD TANGLED that night. A misunderstanding. This whole time, I'd thought that I was the one confused and Bee had known what had happened. But it sounded like we were both in the dark. So maybe this wasn't over.

Holy crap, this isn't over.

A shadowy figure appeared at the top of the trail.

"Ahhhh!" I screamed.

"Ben? What are you doing?"

Oh, it was her. Her voice demanded, sparkling with irritation. Like a powerful, angry bell, sounding through the windy silence, vibrating my entire heart and soul.

She was standing with her hands on her hips in the middle of the clearing.

"Bee! Hey!" I ran over and nearly slammed into her, stopping just short. She jumped, with sharp intake of breath, then relaxed and rolled her eyes. I quickly looked her over. She did seem a little grungy. . . . *She wasn't showering.*

"What are you—" She narrowed her eyes at me. "Whatever.

Never mind." She waved a hand. "They sent me up here to find you. Were you even hiding?"

I stared at her for a minute. I didn't know if I could talk.

Hiding? Why would I be hiding?

"Oh, yes!" I shouted, suddenly remembering, startling her again. "For the *game*. In that bush, for most of the night."

"Well, the game's over, Houdini." She sighed. "Nobody found the snitch. Hiding that well is kind of poor sportsmanship."

The game was over. I had no idea what else she said. "Thank you so much for coming to tell me." Why did my voice sound so formal?

She scrunched her brow. "You're welcome? I got *sent* to find you. You're, like, an hour late for s'mores."

"Oh, I see," I said. "Sorry about that—didn't mean to make you worry." I smiled at her and strode toward the trail.

She didn't follow. I looked back, and she was staring at me as if I had horns. Would she still like me if I had horns? From what Claudia said, probably. Cool.

"I wasn't *worried*," she said, and then stomped over. "It's not like I *care*. You're in trouble with everyone else."

Aha! "So you wanted to give me a heads-up?" I asked. "Thank you!" We came out at the bottom of the trail.

"What?" she snapped. "No. Why are you being so weird?"

"I'll grab extra supplies, to make up for it." Before she could protest, I jumped into Dam's kitchen to grab an exorbitant amount of marshmallows and chocolate. And some extra bug juice mix, just in case. I threw all of it into a cooler while Bee watched.

On our way out, I had a sudden thought and pointed to the bathroom. "Do you need to go before we head over?"

She looked at the door, then me, then the door, then me. Maybe

I shouldn't have suggested it—but I didn't want her to be in any sort of discomfort, and I *had* seen her eat a cheeseburger at lunch.

"Ben, if you're stoned," she said slowly, "I won't tell anyone, but you need to go lie down until you're sober."

"I am not stoned!" I laughed. "Just being considerate!"

She shook her head. "Fine. But I'm not a camper, and I don't need a bathroom reminder. Let's go."

We walked up toward Dam's front doors in perfect silence. I'd read somewhere that the best relationships are ones where you can be silent together. That was important. At the threshold, she paused to look at me.

"Fudge nuggets, Ben!" she hissed. "Stop smiling at me like that!"

"Like what?"

"You know what?" She lifted the cooler from my hands. "You're obviously high, and I don't know on what, but you should go to bed. I'll tell everyone you're puking or something."

"I'm fine," I assured her. "But okay."

"If you're fine," she said, rolling her eyes, "you're more of a weirdo than even I realized. Go to bed."

It was just as well. Though being around her was incredible, I knew I probably needed time to cool down before I did or said something stupid.

I lingered for a moment in the doorway, watching Bee trudge down the slope. I thought about how we'd been apart for a whole year. And now we'd finally be together again.

Just as long as I didn't screw this up.

CHAPTER 30

Bee

I FELL BACK ONTO the poofy brown love seat in Luna. "I thought that last round was never going to end."

"We can't pair those two up again." Raph gathered up the few slips of paper left on the floor. "Reading loves the spotlight too much, and Meredith doesn't know what to do when she starts screaming like that."

"Do we even know?" I asked. Raph had "turned down the volume" on the game, but Reading had a knack for whisper-screaming.

"And just once, I want Meredith to play something other than an inanimate object."

"I thought her salt shaker was very convincing."

"That's the problem."

I laughed. I'd spent day three of camp so blissfully busy I'd barely had time to think. Wake up, set up, CIT assignments, lunch, improv all afternoon, dinner, campfire, games, crash. The routine made me so happy I could burst. No way college was going to be this much fun.

Raph stayed for dinner, and I quietly filled him in on Ben's antics the night before. I was hoping he'd have ideas about what was going on, but neither one of us could explain it, so we chalked it up to boy PMS.

"See you tomorrow!" I smiled at him on our way out.

"Oh, hold up!" He grabbed my shoulders and steered me back toward Luna. "Kangaroo Court tonight."

"Oh shit!" I said, too loudly. I quickly looked around—no close-range campers. "I mean, oh shiitake mushrooms. I completely forgot!"

"No, you didn't," Raph assured me. "I didn't put it on the schedule in Luna."

"You didn't?"

Raph got a scary gleam in his eye. "No."

"Why?"

"Because then you'd've asked me who was on trial. . . ."

I stopped dead in my tracks in the grass. Are. You. Kidding me?

"Raph," I said, slowly. "This better not be about polar bear swim."

"Oh dear." Raph patted my shoulder. A swarm of kids poured out of the dining hall toward us, thrumming with excitement.

Kangaroo Court was one of the best traditions we had at Camp Dogberry, started by Raph when he worked here in college and had joined the mock trial club. We would squish the whole camp into Luna, which became the Dogberry courthouse. Raph was the judge, the campers sat as jury members, and the CITs served as lawyers. Every session a couple counselors were put on "trial" for various "crimes." Singing in the shower (Donald), irresponsible sunburning (Margo), sleeping late (Ben), and one year, flirting with the day lifeguard (Francis, the art assistant from last year).

The system was a little twisted, because anyone could suggest a case to Raph, and he usually picked whatever sounded the most hilarious.

He married people, too. Mom and Dad, Francis and Sam, and he'd *tried* to marry Ben and me when we'd "dated" in seventh grade, but I wouldn't let him. It occurred to me, sitting in my defendant chair that evening, trying not to pout, that maybe Claudia and Hana could get married this year.

I was practicing my pitch in my head, when I realized we were starting. Over dinner, the CITs had set up the courtroom. Campers were crowded in, doubling up on chairs or snuggled against pillows on the floor, and a special group of them were positioned to my right, at a long, narrow card table. These were the jury. I smiled at them. A little waved back at me. Then Maddie whispered to the kid urgently, and his expression went neutral.

How did *Maddie* get on this jury? She was so clearly biased.

"Order in the court!" Raph banged his gavel on his tiny folding table. The gavel's name was George, and it had a bowtie and googly eyes. The crowd hushed, except the rest of the counselors, who smirked at me from the back of the room. Ben waved, with this bizarre smile, and then winked. What the actual frick?

"This court is now in *session!*" Raph declared. We didn't have a judge's wig, so he wore our family's Santa beard. "We bring to trial the case of the People—"

He gestured to Wallace, the prosecutor, who waved at me cheerfully. Cheeky.

"Versus Beatrice Leonato."

I did a queen wave. Nessa, my lawyer, shifted in the chair next to mine.

Raph turned to Wallace. "What are the charges?"

Wallace stood confidently. He'd done this last year, too. "Your Honor, the defendant is charged with cowardice and hypocrisy."

"*Hypocrisy?* How dare you!" I cried out, slamming my fist on the table. The room shook with laughter.

Raph looked at Nessa. "Counsel, get your client under control."

My lawyer turned red but then looked at me, held a finger to her lips, and deliberately patted my knee. The room giggled again. She was good.

"Prosecution, please be more specific," Raph entreated.

"Specifically," Wallace declared dramatically, "she is charged with skipping out on polar bear swim *while* encouraging everyone to be a team player. *Constantly.*"

Laughs again, especially from the returning campers. Margo and Donald whistled in agreement at the back of the room. I mentally gave them the finger.

But okay, so I did use the term "team player" a lot—especially in improv class. Even if we explained the rules, there were always actions during games that Raph and I had to gently stop: campers would whip out guns and "shoot" the other campers in a scene, or one camper would be a dinosaur—"I'm a dinosaur"—and the other would say, "All the dinosaurs are dead." The best way to not shame the kids, but also let them know that wasn't okay, was to frame it under teamwork. *"Pause! Okay, let's start rewind a little, and everyone try to be a team player!"* Once I'd figured this out, it kind of became my catchphrase in class.

"So you see, by skipping out on a Camp Dogberry team-building activity, i.e., polar bear swim"—Wallace circled a hand thoughtfully—"Bee is being *cowardly* as well as *hypocritical*. The prosecution rests."

He sat to thundering applause.

Well, I was doomed.

CHAPTER 31

Hana

FIREFLY TAG. LIGHTS FLASHING, screams of joy, and definitely some actual crying. Somebody'd tripped on the other side of the field.

"Everyone okay?" I called out breathlessly.

"We got it!" I heard back from Ben.

I dropped back down to the ground. I'd been tagged for a while—I'd let a little catch me—and I was waiting for my opening to get back in the game. I heard footsteps approaching from behind, I turned in my awkward squat—

"Quick." She caught my hand and dragged me backward, into the trees. We stumbled through the brush and came out on the dirt road behind camp, the streetlamp illuminating our faces.

Claudia reached forward, grabbed my cheeks, pulled me in. Lips and tongues and breath. I felt light everywhere on my body.

"Sorry, I just couldn't—"

"I know." I smiled. "But we should go back."

She stared into my eyes, her forehead pinched in thought. There was something she wanted to say. My legs shook, just a little, from the anticipation. Or maybe from other things too.

"I don't want this to end," she said finally.

"Me neither," I agreed. Who would ever, ever want that?

"I mean," she breathed, "when we're together, I don't want *this* to end."

My turn to stare at her. I knew what she meant, but did I have the courage to say it back?

Instead, I ran my fingertips across her forehead, brushing her temple, down her face and neck. I pulled her T-shirt's neck down, kissed her collarbone, in a way I hoped—in a way I *knew*—was sexy. She shuddered. I pulled back.

"Me neither."

"So, then." She shuddered again when she spoke. Kind of a spasm. It was so hot. "Fourth of July is Friday."

I barely followed. My mind was so many places. "Yes."

"There's going to be a party."

"Yes."

"So let's get a tent, for after the party."

Suddenly, my mind was just one place: in a tent. With Claudia. And our clothes were off.

"Mmm . . ." I let out the tiniest moan. Maybe I should've been embarrassed, but she'd just shudder-spasmed, so I think I was okay? She smiled and pushed a loose curl behind my ear. I was okay.

"Sounds good?" she confirmed.

"Sounds perfect."

One more kiss that I felt down to my curling toes. She went back up to the game first so we wouldn't seem suspicious.

As I stood there in the dark, tingling all over, I realized:

A tent. Was I really going to have sex for the first time in a *tent*?

CHAPTER 32

John

DURING THE THIRD ROUND of Firefly Tag, I got my proof. Did I ever.

I'd tried to keep an eye on Hana and Claudia, where they were on the field. This game seemed like the perfect opportunity to slip off and hook up somewhere. That's what Margo and Bobby did.

My plan only faltered once, when I got too into the game and tagged, like, twenty campers in a row. I finally let Jay catch me because, you know, that kid was cool.

Crouched down in frozen mode was when I saw it: Hana hunched over in front of me, maybe twenty yards away. In one motion, Claudia approached, grabbed her, and they disappeared into the woods. I quickly switched off my light and followed them.

They retreated down the little hill, to the road that runs behind Camp Dogberry. The girls paused under a streetlamp. I followed and positioned myself behind a tree, far enough away that I couldn't quite hear their whispers. Then they kissed, and I could see this *thing* between them. My breathing felt sharp. Then, at the end of the conversation, before they made their way back toward the field, I actually heard Claudia say—

"So let's get a tent, for after the party."

And I realized: Claudia had completely forgotten about our conversation. The hangout that I was agonizing over wasn't even on her radar anymore.

Asshole.

I watched Claudia romp off into the game again. Just like that. Like I didn't matter in the slightest. I felt that familiar heat rising in my stomach.

"Where's John?" I heard a camper's voice call.

Firefly, I thought to myself. You're a *firefly*. Bzz. I switched on my flashlight, switched off my brain.

But I couldn't get back into it. After another round, I handed my flashlight off to a CIT who'd forgotten his and stalked back to my cabin, knowing Bobby and Connie would eventually turn up. They did. Good old lackies.

"Dude, sing-along?" Bobby poked his head in. Connie's appeared too, but the minute she saw me, she stopped smiling and looked concerned.

"You know, singing," Bobby reminded me. "It's like words that you say with your mouth, but you say them longer?" I didn't respond. "We say them around a campfire, because we get paid to. . . . Yeah, it's making less sense as I say it out loud." He sat down on a camper's bed.

"What's going on?" Connie asked.

"You guys were right. About Claudia and Hana," I said. I swung my legs around and leaned forward on my bunk. "I need to come up with a plan."

CHAPTER 33

Bee

I DIDN'T BREAK RULES, and this was a super obvious one: the sun was supposed to wake you up. Anything else was against nature.

Unless you were a nocturnal animal, like a bat. Most humans are *not* nocturnal, though, I thought to myself blearily. There's absolutely no reason for me to be awake for this activity invented by Satan. Or whoever came up with polar bear swim. The name made it sound cute. But we were *not* polar bears, and I bet polar bears would think we were insane for doing this.

Team player, Bee, you're a team player.

But my teammates were so evil! I vowed to get back at Raphael—maybe I'd take *him* to court for . . . being a jerk. Loving Lin-Manuel Miranda inordinately. Wait, that was impossible. My brain was too tired to think.

Stop. Just get up, Bee.

I took a deep breath and opened my eyes, which actually *hurt*—every blink felt heavier. I rubbed at them, flattening the puffy lids. I gritted my teeth and pushed back the sleeping bag and almost screamed from the cold. As I pulled on sweats and a sweatshirt, I checked Hana's bed: she was already gone. Probably down at the docks warming up. How did that girl wake up freezing every morning? I'm sure she thought it was invigorating or something ridiculous like that.

Only one other camper from our bunk had gone down with her. Though it pained me, I wrote on our little whiteboard that Hana and I were at polar bear swim, in case of an emergency. Little Bat was, blessedly, only a couple minutes from the waterfront, and we had the oldest girls, twelve-year-olds, so they'd be fine for an hour. I shoved my bathing suit and towel under my arm and headed to the bathrooms.

Gulls barked obnoxiously over the harbor. A breeze took a swipe at the back of my neck. The sky had just started to go from gray to a pink; the transition looked disgusting. Worm colored, as far as the eye could see.

That was mean. Margo loved worms.

The fluorescent lights of the bathroom hurt too. I punched open a stall door and sat down on the toilet lid. Where was *my* camp counselor to tell me not to sulk? I sulked a bunch.

Finally, I stood and stripped in the stall. My body immediately began shaking. My teeth started chattering, for real. As I pulled my *damp bathing suit* over my *shivering body*, I heard the swinging squeak of the door, and then Hana and Margo coming into the building. Laughing. Like the demon polar bears they were.

"Is she even up?" Margo asked. Margo didn't come to polar bear swim that often, so clearly she was just here to watch me die.

"I don't know," Hana replied. "Maybe we should go get her?"

I couldn't decide what to do. Should I scream and terrify them? Burst out of the stall and terrify them? Anything that ended in terrifying them.

"Are you going to tell her today?"

What?

Hana paused, then shook her head, I could hear it. "No, I don't think I'm going to tell her at all."

Tell me what? I leaned forward.

"Seriously? You're not going to tell Bee that Ben's in love with her?"

What?

My legs gave out. I wrapped my towel around me and sank back down onto the toilet seat, as softly as I could.

CHAPTER 34

Hana

I FELT BAD, THINKING about Bee, still mostly asleep, trying to understand all of this. We'd been waiting in the bushes outside and watched her fumble into the bathrooms, then followed her in after a minute or so. I knew Bee would take forever to change. We'd timed it right, at least.

Margo nodded at me. She had bags under her eyes that almost matched her purple hair. How late had she been up? Well, she had the littles this session.

"Yes, I'm sure." I nodded back. "I'm *not* going to tell her that Claudia told *me* that Ben told her and Donald that he's *in love* with Bee."

Keeping all of that straight felt like being a CIT again.

"Right, right." Margo eyed Bee's feet under the stall door. "And Claudia told *you* to *tell* Bee?" She'd decided beforehand that I should be the one with the info that Ben liked Bee. Because if this were actually *real*, Claudia might've told me. I got the reasoning, but I was afraid Bee would hear all the lies in my voice.

"Yeah," I confirmed. "*And* Claudia said Donald thought I should tell Bee, too. But I realized I couldn't."

"Really? Why?" Margo prompted, with a goofy grin that didn't match the fake sincerity in her voice. I had to look away and collect myself.

"Because," I said finally, "Bee doesn't *like* Ben." Well, she hadn't told me otherwise, had she?

"Are you *serious*?" Margo pealed laughter. "She totally likes him. She just won't admit it!" I swear I could hear Bee's breathing.

"Maybe you're right," I said, pretending to think about it. "It feels like something happened between them last year, but she won't tell me about it."

"Well, they can't have hooked up." Margo shook her head. "Because lord knows Bee doesn't think *anyone* should ever just hook up."

I froze. Had this just become about Margo and Bobby? And was it suddenly real? I glanced at the stall, and then back to Margo, indicating that she should keep going.

"But anyway, Ben!" She snapped back into the script, thank goodness. "He's not a hookup person, either. They could be dating snobs together, in snobby, snobby romance land."

"Totally." I laughed. "And he's definitely the kind of guy I could see Bee with."

We *almost* heard a snort. It was like a stifled snort. We paused. I didn't know what to say next.

Luckily, Margo had it covered. "Maybe you're right, though." She sighed. "I wouldn't want him throwing himself at someone who wasn't interested. He's, like, the sweetest guy."

This I could speak to. I really did think Ben was the best. "Totally. He's hard-working and *goal-oriented*, and he's so good with his little sisters. And he might be the nicest person at camp." When I said it out loud like this, I really did believe that Bee and Ben would be perfect for each other. I almost couldn't believe it hadn't happened already.

Margo nodded along, and then, as I finished, got that wicked grin on her face. "Wait, what about Claaaaudia?"

"Claudia's not nice like Ben's nice," I explained. But that sounded bad. Whoops. "I mean, she's nice, but she's also . . ."

"Dark? Brooding? Sexy?" Margo wiggled her eyebrows at me.

"Maaaybe." I giggled back. Sexy. Tents. Sexy tents.

"But, wait—why don't you just tell Bee all that about Ben?" Margo leveled suddenly. "I mean, you're her sister—wouldn't she listen to you?"

"To me?" I laughed. "No way. Ben's kind of an off-limits subject. She's never . . . She wouldn't let me, even if I tried to. She'd just change the topic or distract me." It was true. It usually worked on me, too, embarrassingly.

Margo nodded. "She hides those feels so well. . . ."

Did she?

". . . She can be tough."

"Very tough," I said, hoping Bee would like that. *Tough* was a Bee word.

"And besides, if she knew he liked her, she'd have so much more ammo to make fun of him," Margo pointed out.

"Oh yeah," I said, before I could stop myself. "I wouldn't want him to get hurt." That was true. I was terrified that Bee was going to hurt Ben—or vice versa—more than they already had. I knew what heartbreak was like. Suddenly, I super wanted this conversation to be over.

"That's real," Margo said. "I guess Ben'll just spend the summer hiding sad erections in his sleeping bag."

I choked on my own laughter.

Suddenly, the toilet in Bee's stall flushed.

"Ghost toilet!" Margo screamed, and we both burst out laughing and tore out of the bathroom, down to the waterfront, leaving my sister emotionally reeling in a toilet stall.

CHAPTER 35

Bee

I CAN'T MOVE. *I can't breathe.*

I'd climbed up onto the toilet back and accidentally stepped on the flush handle on the way down.

After Margo screamed and they ran out of the bathroom, the familiar whirring started in my ears. They pulsed hot. I stumbled out of the stall, yanked on a faucet—cold water—and splashed it on my face and ears.

Ben, telling Claudia and Donald that he's in love with me?

In *love* with me?

I heaved a breath, looked up at myself in the mirror. Early morning puffiness, braids flopping to one side, boobs kind of lopsided in my one-piece.

Me?

Seriously?

After all of that?

WHAT HAPPENED: PART 7

Bee

IT SHOULD'VE BEEN UNCOMFORTABLE to make out on a stack of tarps, but I barely noticed. Every once in a while I could feel them crinkling under us.

First I kissed him, and after a moment, he kissed me. And then I lost count, but it just seemed like we were kissing each other. Press, push, tongues, release, repeat. Passing breaths back and forth. Why did it feel so good?

Ben's arms held me close, and almost every part of me was touching every part of him. Maddening. I wondered which move, which kiss, brush, or graze, would strike and burst us both into flames?

Now his hands were on my neck, his lips on my ear. I shuddered. If I did the same thing back to his ear, was that copying? I tried it. He didn't seem to care if it was original.

His hand moved down; his fingers paused at the edge of my T-shirt hem.

"Yes," I whispered.

Then my shirt was off. Then his shirt was off. Skin against skin, I felt dizzy. It felt like I'd always wanted to touch him like this. Be touched like this.

But even with all the contact, it still didn't feel like enough. Because we needed to be closer than this. This was nowhere near close enough. Whatever that feeling was, it kept us going. . . .

Finally, after what felt like hours, we drifted off in each other's arms, shirtless with bruised lips.

And when we woke up, everything had changed.

CHAPTER 36

Bee

I DRIED THE COLD water off my face. Had Ben been feeling this way this whole year, just like me? Did he really want me? *Me?*

Of course you.

Because Ben's yours, too.

The thought popped into my head without warning, and I gasped. Actually gasped, by myself alone in the bathroom. But I'd been so harsh to him since he'd arrived. How could this be real?

But how could it not? Why would they all know otherwise? Did Hana and Margo really think I was too proud to admit I was in love with Ben?

Wasn't I?

I took deep breaths, but that just let in a suffocating rush of bathroom mildew and bubbly antibacterial soap.

I needed air.

I pushed open the bathroom door. Outside had changed. The sun was finally beginning to rise, now pink-and-gold. The grass, dew, cabins awash with yellow glow. My feet automatically steered me down to the waterfront.

"Hey, sleepyhead!" Margo called as I approached.

Margo. She clearly thought I'd judged her for hooking up with Bobby. Well, I had. And for the first time, I actually felt bad about it.

"Morning!" I replied, my voice somehow working without me.

A dozen campers swarmed me, and I gently led them back down to the water, patting heads and asking questions, not quite sure what I was saying. Maddie and Jay bragged to the group that they'd gotten me sent to Kangaroo Court. I managed to act put out.

"You missed the warm-up," Hana said, concerned. "Why don't you do some jumping jacks, and we'll wait?"

"Okay," I said. Because what else would I do. "Will you all count for me?"

My trusty, disloyal campers cheered me on, and once I was through, we went out to the dock and lined up all along it.

"Polar bears at the ready?" Hana called.

"Ready!!" The kids screeched, giggling.

"One . . . two . . . three . . . jump!"

I didn't jump immediately. The spray hit me, fiercely cold, and I balked. But there was no turning back now, particularly because I knew if I didn't jump, the campers would pull me in, waterfront safety be damned.

Instead, I sat on the edge of the dock and carefully lowered myself in. Torturous, but somehow more manageable than a plunge. When I was up to my waist, I let myself fall—icy liquid closed over my head, and I came up screaming, much to the delight of everyone around me.

That was the worst of it. I went under again and again. Partly because then no one could accuse me of half-assing polar bear swim and make a case for extending my sentence.

And one more reason.

When I dove under, I was alone, and if only for a few freezing seconds, I could think. The cold water cleared my head. Voices giggled and shouted above me, people who wanted my attention. But I wasn't really there. I was sinking, floating, feeling minuscule grains of salt pricking my skin in a million places.

And I knew I hadn't imagined or dreamed it.

Any of it.

Ben.

Every time before I submerged, I took a breath and held Ben with it, tightly suspended in my chest.

I loved him.

I loved him.

I loved him.

CHAPTER 37

Vanessa

I HAVE TO TELL you, I was totally relieved when we got to Pirate Day. Thursday Theme Days at Camp Dogberry were always fun—we dressed up, there were special activities—but as a camper, I never appreciated Pirate Day the way I did now.

Because the kids spend the second half of the day on boats, being all pirate-y. And those less waterfront-inclined counselors/CITs get the afternoon off. We made up for it by working on another theme. I'd signed up for Halloween Day in a few weeks. So today, Pirate Day, I got a whole afternoon. To myself. I dropped off the kids at the water and thought for a sec about going back to my cabin. I could spend the break catching up on sleep.

Well, as soon as I finished an extra dish shift. That was part of the price for my afternoon off. An extra chore during your break. Campy Dogberry's fairness felt a little annoying to me at this exact moment.

I dragged myself through Dam, into the back. Sophia and Wallace were already at work in the big sinks with the hoselike faucets. I grabbed a pair of dish gloves.

"Nessa!" Sophia shouted above the spray. "Did you hear about tomorrow?" She'd drawn on a blue beard to go with her outfit.

I flicked up my eye patch. "What's tomorrow?"

"The Fourth of July!" she reminded me. "It's a *party*, like, a real one."

"Reeeeeally?" A party sounded like heaven.

"Totally. With sparklers and beer and everything." Sophia smiled, despite the gross bean dip she was scrubbing out of a bowl. "I heard Donald talking about it at art today."

"Wow," I said. "We're going to a real party."

"I know—"

"Except that we're not invited."

Wallace, loading the industrial washing machine, in a skull and bones captain hat, looked at both of us like: duh.

"We're not?" Sophia shut off the water.

"No way." Wallace shook his head. "CITs don't get to go to those kinds of parties. Doug told me."

"How do you always know everything?" I wondered aloud.

Wallace shrugged.

"Well, that's the worst." I sighed, flipping a pot onto the drying rack. "But we can probably grab some sparklers and hang out together—"

"Is this the way the entire summer is going to be?" Sophia demanded. "We bust our butts, and we don't get any perks?"

Wallace shrugged again. "We get weekends and some time off."

"To do what?" she replied. "Make more friendship bracelets??"

"It sounds like a cool party," Wallace agreed sadly. "It's up in Nest."

"The view from up there is so beautiful," I said, remembering that year Doc had taken us on a stargazing trip, when I was a little camper. I hadn't been there since.

"Too bad we won't get to see it," Wallace said.

"What if we go on strike?" Sophia suggested.

"Isn't a strike kind of hard to pull off when your parents are paying for you to work?" I said. "Plus, I don't think Nik and Andy would care too much about CITs not getting invited to parties that are probably *inappropriate*. And then the counselors would hate us for bringing it up."

"Good points," Sophia sighed. "Wait . . . What if we talked to one of the counselors about it? Ben?"

"Nah." I shook my head. "I don't think he'd be super sympathetic . . . but *maybe*—"

Suddenly, Bee's head appeared in the drive-thru window. "Hey, all, great teamwork!"

We startled and looked at one another, then at the kitchen around us. None of the faucets were even running. We looked back at her dubiously.

"Hint, hint." She smiled, knocked once on the doorway, and then disappeared again. The side door slammed. We quickly got back to work. I had an idea now.

After dishes, I ran and found Margo—I knew she'd be sunning herself outside our cabin.

"Hey, chickadee!" She smiled as I walked up. She was lying out on her beach towel, wearing a swimsuit and her big star-shaped sunglasses. No shoes. Scandalous.

"Hey." I sat down in the grass next to her. "Can I ask you a question?"

She smiled into the sun. "I know everything about birds, fungi, *and* periods. Ask away."

I laughed. "It's about the party on Friday."

"Ooooh." She sat up and slid her sunglasses back onto her head, pushing back her purple curls. "What about it?"

"Do you think that—"

"Aww, sweetie." Margo shook her head. "Sorry, but CITs totally can't come."

"Oh, okay." Margo'd been so nice and welcoming, and she was a lot less scary than Bee, and cooler than my brother (sorry, Ben). So I figured maybe . . . Now my ears were burning. I felt so juvenile for even asking.

"Hey." Margo snapped me out of it. I looked at her—she looked kind of pained. "I'm *really* sorry." She ducked her chin emphatically. "It's just, it's an older person kind of thing."

"But what if it was just me and Sophia and Wallace?" I ventured. "We wouldn't tell the others, and we'd be really cool there, I promise."

She smiled her dimply smile. "You're the coolest, Nessie. But if we brought you, we'd for sure all get fired."

"Oh." I hadn't even thought of that. Of course they'd get in trouble.

"You'll be able to go when you're older!" Margo slung an arm around me and squeezed.

"Right."

"*And* I'll totally sneak you guys some sparklers, if you'll be careful. You can have your own hoppin' Fourth!"

I grinned, the disappointment starting to fade. "That would be great! Really?"

"You got it. I'll make Donald get you some outside snacks from town, too."

After another hug, I went and found Sophia and Wallace in Luna. Neither of them had had any luck, either.

"I ran into Hana at the bathroom, but she totally blew me off," Sophia complained. "She just said, 'You won't be a CIT forever!' and then left. Probably to go make out with Claudia."

I was glad I'd got Margo, at least she was super nice about it. We both looked at Wallace.

"Oh, I chickened out," he said quickly. "I didn't ask anyone."

Neither one of us said anything, because we'd figured he wouldn't.

"Look," I said. "Margo's getting us snacks and sparklers. It'll still be good."

"I guess." Sophia sighed. "But we won't get to be in the middle of all of that action!"

A thought occurred to me. "But, Sophia"—I nudged her shoulder—"we'll be *around* it. . . ."

Her eyes widened. "We'll totally have to do some surveillance."

"Yes!" I agreed. "It'll be like a scavenger hunt. For *gossip*."

"Totally!" she squealed. "And, Wallace—"

"Yeah?" he said excitedly.

"You keep doing whatever you're doing," she finished. "Because somehow you always wander into it."

"Got it!" He saluted, beaming. Sometimes I wondered what Wallace thought about all of this gossip stuff, but looking at his smile, I realized he probably didn't care what we were talking about as long as he was talking to Sophia.

Then I told them I had to go check in at the waterfront, because Rudie never reapplied his sunscreen unless I sang to him during the process.

CHAPTER 38

Claudia

THURSDAY AFTERNOON, DONALD GRABBED Bee and me for a run into town for party supplies. Apparently, Donald had set up a contact to sell us a few fireworks, too. Bee claimed she just needed time out of the woods. I wanted to get a present for Hana, for the party. We piled into Donald's green Mercedes—Bee and Donald in the front, me in the back.

I clicked in my seat belt, lost in thought. A present. I wasn't sure what kind of present you bought for this kind of occasion—the we've-made-out-a-lot-but-we've-got-a-tent-now-so-we-both-know-this-is-going-to-go-further occasion.

Maybe chocolate?

A knock on my window startled me.

"AHH!" I yelled at Ben's face.

"AHH! is right," Bee snorted.

I rolled it down.

"What's up, creeper?" Donald said.

"Can I come?" Ben asked. "I need Capture the Flag stuff."

"Capture the Flag isn't till next Wednesday," Bee pointed out.

"Just planning ahead." Ben grinned.

She shook her head and turned back around.

The car went silent for a full three seconds. I looked at my knees, just in case Donald was looking back at me. I knew we'd both crack up.

No complaining from Ben about the Capture the Flag change. No "Oh, planning ahead for once in your life" from Bee. That was the most pleasant exchange between Ben and Bee that we'd seen this year.

"Makes sense," I said, finally. I opened the door for Ben and slid over.

"Thank you!" Ben said brightly, and climbed in. Since Counselor Hunt, being around Ben felt like hanging out with a cardboard cutout version of him who showered more. As I scooted toward the middle, suddenly the other door opened. John.

"Hey, guys, heard you're making a run?"

Before Donald could flip out, Ben said, "Sure, you need something?"

"I just want non-camp coffee," John explained, sliding in next to me.

I nodded at him. I missed real coffee too.

"Well, we can bring you some," Donald offered lightly. "Or not. Either way, you need to get out of my car."

John froze. "It's my car too, for the summer."

"Cool, you can have it when I'm done," Donald shot back. He was being stubborn. Whenever there was a town run, we took whoever.

Bee touched Donald's hand on the gearshift. "Hey, we all need a break from camp. Let's just go."

Donald took a breath, paused, then shifted into drive. "Fine. Let's go."

He pulled out of the lot at a speed most of us would find dangerous, but Donald seemed completely comfortable with—in fact, he
kept it up the entire way to downtown Paris, the closest actual town
to Messina. When we finally found a parking spot and pulled over, I
think everyone felt on the brink of puking.

"I vote John drives back" was all Bee said as we got out.

"It's only fair," Ben agreed, then after Donald's scowl, added,
"Equal share of the car!"

"So, should we have a Maine Adventure?" Bee asked.

Reny's was this wild department store they had in Maine, and
their tagline was "A Maine Adventure" because they stocked *everything*. Clothes, toys, household stuff, pet supplies, hunting gear, not
to mention a wide variety of quality hiking socks. I knew I could
find something for Hana there. A person could probably find their
long-lost cousin there.

"Reny's!" Ben snapped his fingers in her direction. "That's a
good place to go! Yes!"

I inwardly, not outwardly, groaned at Ben's weirdness, which
took a lot of effort.

"Welcome to Reny's!" A woman in a green smock smiled at us
as we came in. After weeks in the woods, the bright fluorescent
lighting slapped my eyes in the face, and the AC felt like walking
onto frozen tundra.

None of us knew what to say. What were real humans, again?
It had been two weeks of nothing but camp. I felt the sense that
we were all suddenly, painfully aware that we wore dirty T-shirts,
athletic shorts, and sneakers. Oh wait, and pirate costumes. I don't
know how we forgot we were wearing pirate costumes.

We split up. Donald took off to look for sparklers, Bee toward food, and who knew where Ben was going. I found myself in the swimming stuff aisle, looking at inner tubes printed to look like sprinkle donuts. Didn't feel exactly right, though.

In the next aisle over, I saw Ben studying a bottle of mouthwash. He shoved it in his basket the second he noticed me.

"Capture the Flag supplies?" I asked innocently, peeking into the basket. There were half a dozen deodorants in there.

"For our older campers," he explained quickly. "Next week's supposed to be hot, and they always smell."

Well, that was true.

"And the mouthwash?" I asked.

It was a gallon-size container of acidic teal. He looked down at it; his face went completely blank for one second. Then—

"Too much bug juice," he explained. "I'm gonna get cavities."

I made a mental note to tell Donald about this hilarity later. Emergency mouthwash, right before the sparkler party? Dude had plans. He then kind of sprinted away from me down the aisle. Maybe to pay and bag before anyone else could call him out. That's what I'd do.

Which brought me back to my task: try to find anything that looked like something Hana would want me to give her. I'd just made it to outdoor living, the bird section, when John showed up.

"Hey, they accidentally gave me two," he said, holding up two white coffee cups. "You want one?"

"Hell yeah." I grabbed it from him and immediately took a scalding sip. Black, not burnt, not instant . . . I hadn't wanted to spend the money, but damn. This was almost as good as kissing Hana. Was coffee-flavored lip gloss a thing? Should I buy it for her?

"Thaaaank you," I sighed, bringing it away from my lips.

"Sure thing." John nodded. "That's one of the perks at Yale—excellent coffee."

"Cool," I said.

"Hey, listen," he said, moving in toward me and the birdseed. "Can I talk to you about something?"

Did anything good ever start with that sentence? Was he going to want to talk about what happened on the island? I thought he'd probably taken the hint, given that . . . well, whatever.

"Yeah, sure, go."

"Okay." He leaned up against the shelves, lowered his voice. "I've heard this rumor you're hooking up with Hana."

He paused. I didn't say anything back.

"Okay," he continued. "I just wanted to bring it up because before I heard that, I'd heard she was hooking up with some townie who's sneaking into camp at night, after quiet hours."

Did he just say words? I must've looked shocked, because he took something I did as an invitation to keep going.

"Yeah, Connie told me she saw them down by the volleyball net." He nodded. "Like, a couple nights this past week. Hey, are you okay?"

I sipped my coffee. Stay calm, stay calm, stay calm. Was this even possible? "I'm . . . fine," I said. "Why . . . Why are you telling me this?"

John's pretty face pinched into some expression between anger and embarrassment.

"Because I like you," he said. "I know you're friends with Donald but . . . And I would want to know, if I didn't know. Did you know?"

I stared at him.

"Guess not," he said.

I was really done with this conversation.

"Well, thanks." I held up the coffee.

"No problem, I hope . . ." He turned away, then back again. "I hope I didn't fuck up by telling you?"

My brain caught up with my emotions for a split second. "No, no." I rubbed my cheek with one hand. "I . . . Yeah. Thanks."

He nodded, then disappeared at the end of the aisle.

I looked at the miniature bird feeder on the shelf, the red one, the one I'd just decided to get for Hana. I thought she could hang it outside her window in Little Bat. It seemed like something she'd love.

Could this really be a thing? What townie? I'd known, like, last year, there'd been a guy who'd messed her up. Was it him? What was his name? Chris?

"Christopher?" Bee's voice from the aisle next to me.

A spastic chill shot down my neck. What the hell? I turned around and walked slowly, quietly to the end of the aisle.

"Yeah, hey, Bee," said a dude's voice. "How you been?"

"Fine." She sounded tense. "How about you?"

"I'm doing good, busy summer."

"Really."

"How's your sister?"

"Why?"

"I just thought—"

"She's doing *great,* and she doesn't want to talk to you."

"Really?" This guy sounded like a total dick.

"Really. Stay away from her," Bee's voice growled. If I were this guy, I'd be retreating.

"If she doesn't want to talk to me, then why does she keep texting me in the middle of the night?"

A brief moment, which felt like the pause before Bee punched his lights out. I waited for it, because if she didn't, I felt like I needed to.

"You're lying," Bee said.

His voice sounded amused as he replied, "I can show you the texts right now."

But instead, she marched out of the aisle and walked right into me.

"Fudge nuggets!" she exclaimed. Camp swearing. "Claudia, the fuck?" Regular swearing.

"Sorry," I said, then held up a red bird feeder. "Do you think Hana would like this?"

Her harsh expression immediately softened. "Oh, that's so sweet." Her voice went from razor to butter knife. "She can hang it on the roof edge outside her window."

I smiled. "Yeah, that's what I was thinking." Out of the corner of my eye, I saw a guy pass by at the other end of the aisle. I turned, but only caught the back of his blond head, in a UMaine sweatshirt. I wanted to run after him and get a better look, but of course I didn't.

Bee frowned, then handed the bird feeder back to me. She searched my eyes for a half second, then said, "You're cool, Claudia."

"Thanks." I nodded. "What did you get?" I pointed to her bag.

She froze. "Um, deodorant."

I headed toward the counter to pay. Don't act weird, don't act weird. I bought the bird feeder, I didn't know what else to do. As the smiling woman rang it up and bagged it, I wished so much that this whole trip had never happened.

On the ride home, John drove at a much more normal pace, Donald glowering with sparklers, fireworks, and mysteriously obtained alcohol in the front, Ben under his massive pile of toiletries on my right, Bee lost in thought to my left. I felt suffocated in the middle.

I closed my eyes and retreated to the corner in my head where I kept everything shitty.

The confused look in my mom's eyes. My "friends'" mocking laughter. My uncle's sneers. Long strands of black hair.

I added the bird feeder to the pile, scattered a handful of paper stars. I couldn't bring myself to leave her smile there yet, though.

At dinner, I watched Hana from across the room—she always sat with the emptiest table. I usually snuck glances at her, but this was different. I looked for signs of anything, suspicious behavior of any sort.

Her dark curly hair hung damp and tousled.

But there it was: I saw her look down at her pocket, take out her cell phone under the table. She stuck it back in, then got up and went to the bathroom.

I felt like I might throw up.

Maybe she was just texting a friend.

I had to know for sure.

I grabbed Donald and dragged him out to the flagpole.

"I need your help," I said. "I need you to come with me to the volleyball court tonight."

"I'm flattered." Donald smiled and raised an eyebrow. "But I don't think I'm your type."

"Ha-ha," I said. "Your brother told me that Hana's hooking up with some guy from town, and when they get together, it's at the volleyball court."

I expected him to be shocked, but he just nodded, slowly. "Is his name Christopher?"

"You know him?" I gulped down a scream. *Donald* knew about this guy, too.

"No. Just of him." He ran a hand over his face in thought. "I don't think . . . I mean, I don't think Bee would let Hana get back together with Christopher."

"Well," I said, "contrary to popular belief, Bee doesn't actually have control over what her sister does."

Donald stared at me, puffed out his cheeks, let out a sigh of air. "I mean, John's the worst . . ." He trailed off. "But he doesn't usually lie. I don't think."

I looked at him sharply.

"I'm a virgin, so."

I nodded. "Right, so."

"But this *is* Camp Dogberry," Donald continued. "So he might just be repeating a rumor."

"Right, but . . . I heard Bee run into this guy, Chris, at Reny's. They talked about Hana—it sounded like she's still talking to him."

That brought Donald up short. "Maybe we should talk to Bee?"

"No way." I shook my head. "If Hana was hooking up with someone else, it's not like Bee would tell us."

"Maybe she doesn't know," he mused. "So talk to Hana?"

"I don't want to accuse her of anything until I know this is real," I explained. "If John's wrong about this . . . I can't risk it." Truthfully, I couldn't imagine asking her.

"Should we tell Ben?" He jerked a thumb in the direction of Snowshoe.

"No way. He'd throw a fit. They're like family. So are you in?"

Donald paused, then nodded in agreement. Say a lot of things about Donald, but he's a loyal friend.

"Oh, and speaking of Ben," I said. "Did you see that he bought a crap ton of mouthwash?"

CHAPTER 39

Bee

OWLS HOOTED, STARS DANCED, I wrestled out of my sleeping bag. Luckily, our twelve-year-olds in Little Bat slept like logs, and salty Hana had crashed right after sing-along, done in by five hours of swimming and the ten verses of "Princess Pat."

Normally, I would've been crashing too. Ever since polar bear swim, my head had been spinning like a wheel of fortune, landing randomly on a hundred different tasks: Were the CITs okay? Were they in their right spots, doing their work? Did Raph have everything he needed? Were the campers bored of pretending to be stuck in Jell-O? Would they remember how to improv for the parents performance? Please remember how to improv. Are the goats good? Did everyone look adequately like a pirate?

This evening, in moments of brief camp pause, the wheel sometimes landed on: Was Hana getting in over her head with Claudia? Why was she texting Christopher again? Was Donald still hurt that I'd shot him down?

But tonight, the wheel had spun and stuck on what I'd been avoiding, and I had to get out of the cabin.

I threw on my sandals, grabbed my Reny's bag, and tiptoed down the porch steps. The salt cut through my big, emotional breaths. My legs shook.

"Calm down," I whispered to them. *"Calm down."*

I thought about going to the art building. Maybe do some origami, like Hana did when she was feeling the feels. I couldn't sit still, though. I hiked forward.

I stopped in Dam, flicked on the lights, went into the bathroom, changed my shirt. I stared at myself in the mirror:

Wow.

Gross.

Wow.

Gross.

I mean, I looked good, really good, but I was simultaneously utterly disgusted with myself. I wanted to fist-bump the girl in the mirror, and tell her how gorgeous she was. Alternatively, I wanted to shake my head and dismiss her for being so naive.

I changed back into my pajama shirt.

Outside again, I followed the moonlight past Dam, past the garden, past Luna. I stopped briefly to look out at the ocean. Something was still wrong. Why could I barely breathe?

The moonlight led me to Stickleback. I stepped inside—the Bandytails had been there. It reeked of raccoon poop. I walked through the maze of rope and metal clips on the floor, made it to the old dinghy in the corner, sat down in it, and immediately began to sob.

Now my whole body shook from crying. Long, low moans and shrieks escaped me, vibrating my lips. I couldn't keep up with wiping the tears away. I curled into a ball, to try and suppress it, but whatever was in me forced its way out: I must've cried for an hour straight.

And then all at once, it was over, and I was whimpering. My head felt clearer. I could hear what I was thinking—

College. I don't want to. I don't want to leave.

Hana. I don't want to leave her. She's messed up still. My parents can't handle it. They don't get it.

Donald. I don't want to lose him. He feels further away now.

Raph. Could he please shut up about how the world is better somewhere else?

Everything's changing, no matter what knots I tie.

Ben.

I'd avoided Ben as much as I could today. Both in person and in my head. But then it rushed at me all at once:

Ben, I like you, too. Wanna, like, do stuff?

Ben, I heard you're, like, in love with me. Is that true? 'Cause ha-ha-ha-ha, me too.

Ben, PLEASE ACTUALLY END SPORTS ON TIME FOR ONCE.

Memories pushed forward. I couldn't stop them. Smiles, hikes, hands, inside jokes, text messages, video chats. There was so much, so much I had shoved down and away.

Last summer.

I thought about it. I *really* thought about it. Not just thought about not thinking about it. I remembered the whole thing, all the way through.

And then I remembered it again.

And again.

I played the memories over and over, and they hurt more each time, like biting down on chapped lips.

I tried to add the new information to them—that though these were painful things that had happened, we had liked, maybe loved, each other this whole time.

It was baffling.

Ben, you totally baffle me.

I started to cry again, softly this time. I drifted off, crying in a boat in a raccoon-pooped shed. And then, just as I lost consciousness, I felt a little better.

CHAPTER 40

Claudia

ONCE QUIET HOURS STARTED, around nine, Donald and I ditched our cabins, jumped on the trail, and made our way up to Monarch. As soon as we got to the edge of the clearing, I wished I had never come at all.

Illuminated by the moon, two figures. One a girl, with dark curly hair, splayed out in the sand. The other a blond guy, in a bright white UMaine sweatshirt, pressed on top of her. I watched as they rolled over. Donald's sharp intake of breath next to me confirmed that it wasn't one of my paranoid nightmares. This was actually happening, right now, in front of me.

Donald's hand reached for mine. "Claud, I'm so sorry—"

I turned and sprinted back to the path, back to the crossroads at the waterfront. I stopped there, bent over, heaved up giant bursts of air. Black dots splattered my vision. Every bad emotion shimmied up my spine, into my head, pounded in my skull.

"Claudia!" Donald caught up with me. He kneeled down so we were face-to-face. "Are you okay?"

I didn't respond. It was a pointless question.

"I need to . . ." I started. But then I realized I didn't know what I needed. I needed to have never fallen in love with Hana Leonato.

"Look," Donald started. "Did you two . . . Ah, did you ever say you were exclusive?"

I dropped to sit, right in the middle of the trail. I racked my brain.

"No," I eventually whispered. We hadn't. I'd just felt it. I'd just thought.

"So maybe she didn't realize it was a big deal to you," Donald's voice floated in through the storm clouds.

My heart clung to that idea—that she didn't know how much it would hurt me. If she had, she couldn't have done it, right?

But my brain latched on to another thought—that she hadn't told me. We talked about her depression, her sister, her school . . . and she hadn't told me Chris was still in the picture?

"I can't deal with this right now," I said.

"Let's go back to the cabins," Donald suggested, and held out a hand. "Maybe you should sleep on it."

"Good idea."

He helped me up and looked me in the eye. "It's going to be okay."

"Okay," I replied, even though I couldn't see how.

He squeezed my shoulder before we split up, walking back to our separate cabins.

I got in my sleeping bag but did absolutely no sleeping.

CHAPTER 41

Bee

I WOKE UP AT five a.m., and at first I thought I just felt gross because I'd been sleeping on a tarp all night. But as I trudged back onto the trail, my nose started to run. Bee's Midnight Romance Worries had clearly been a walloping success.

I diverted to Big Bat, AKA my house, and crawled onto the couch in the living room. An hour or so later, Mom woke me up and shepherded me to the dining hall for early morning pancakes, which were almost worth the terrible sleep. It was nice to spend some alone time with her—although she kept asking me if something was wrong. I pleaded lack of REM.

"You're sick?"

"I think just tired." I blew my nose. "It'll probably clear up on the weekend, when I can sleep forever."

She laughed and ran her hand over my hair. "Well, try to get a nap in this afternoon after checkout, or you'll be drifting off during the fireworks. Have you checked your mail? You got more stuff from EBU."

I shook my head.

"Well, you can take care of that this weekend, too," she said, like it was no big deal. College paperwork. It took the fun out of paperwork.

"Mom, is Hana . . . Do you think she's okay?"

Mom rolled her eyes but smiled. "Apart from coming *dangerously close* to breaking every PDA rule in the book, she's fine."

"Okay." I bit my lip. "But I think she might be talking to *him* again."

Mom paused as she chewed a bite of her pancakes. "Why do you think that?"

"I saw something on her phone. . . ."

"You two need to get off your phones." She pointed her fork at me.

"I'm not on my phone! This was her phone!"

"So get off hers, sweetie." She laughed at my defensiveness. "If she's still talking to him, she'll stop soon. I think Claudia will prove a good distraction." She kissed my forehead, cleared our dishes, and got back to being the person in charge of, like, a hundred children.

◈

That night, after the fireworks, Margo, Hana, and I piled into the Dam bathroom again to get ready for the party. In my case, that meant blowing my nose a lot in the corner. I had my new shirt with me but didn't have the guts to change into it yet.

"Bee, you don't look so good," Margo said. "Maybe you should talk to Ben."

I froze, mid nose-blow. Which was gross. I finished the nose-blow.

"What? Why should I talk to *him*?!" I said it louder than I meant to. Margo raised her eyebrows at me. Hana glanced over from the mirror, without moving her head.

I quickly blew my nose again.

"Well, he's going to be a doctor, right?" Margo went back to touching up her eyeliner. "Maybe he's got a cold cure-all or something?"

"I've got the keys to the first aid office," I protested. "I think I'm good." I checked my watch. "We should get going soon. We're already ten minutes late."

Hana *eeped!*, and Margo quickly piled her own curls into an inspired messy bun. I looked at them both, so glam. It was now or never. I ducked into the bathroom, flipped off my top, pulled the new one on, adjusted my boobs a little, took a breath, unlocked the stall door.

"Bee!" Margo immediately screamed. You could count on her for the big reaction. Hana turned from doing her mascara, and her whole face lit up.

I looked at myself in the mirror again, this time bolstered by my friends. A stretchy white halter, with a delicate green vine pattern moving up the straps.

"Do you like it? I got it at Reny's. You really can find anything there." I put in my big silver hoop earrings with silver dangly bits, all nonchalant.

"You look *gorgeous*," Margo gushed. Hana's big eyes shone, almost watery. I'd expected the squealing, but why was everyone so emotional suddenly?

"So let's go?" I asked, before everyone started crying about my halter top.

"Let's go!" Margo pushed us out the door.

My stomach zigzagged as we made our way up the steep path. What was really going on here? Was I sick, or just nervous? What could I possibly be nervous about? I didn't have to do anything about the Ben thing, if I didn't want to.

It's my last summer. Just friends. He'd said those words exactly one year ago. What was I supposed to believe?

When we were nearly at the top, I got outside of myself enough to pull Hana briefly to the side of the trail.

"Oh, I forgot matches!" Margo exclaimed, and ran back down the hill. She was such a good sport about sister moments.

Once we were alone, I brushed Hana's arm. "Hey, so you and Claudia?"

My beautiful little sister blushed in the twilight, hiking the tent strap over her shoulder. With her hair done, and that glow around her cheeks, she'd never looked cuter. "Yes?"

"Ahh, you know . . ."

"Bee, what?"

"Sex?" The word popped out. I was trying, but the dizzy feels and the Ben stuff took up so much of my mind, it was hard to find tactful words. "You're going to have sex, right? Tonight?"

"I don't, uh . . ." She looked down at her feet. "I think so?" she finished, finally. "Maybe? That's what I think we planned, but with the swimming demos and checkout, we haven't talked today."

My lips pursed automatically. "Okay, well, as your big sister, it is my duty to remind you that you *should* talk about it first."

"Okay."

"And about STDs and stuff."

"Okay." She nodded.

"*And* about how you feel."

She stopped nodding. "How I feel?"

"Look." I sighed. "I've never done this before, but I do know people who have, and it's *really* important that you talk about how you feel about it first."

I glanced pointedly in Margo's direction up the trail. "I mean, I have friends who have done this before they're ready. Before they know how they feel, and how the other person feels. And it *messes things up.*"

"Right."

"Oh, and also," I said, rushing this part. "If you have feelings for someone else, it's probably not a good idea to sleep with another person without talking about it."

Hana's eyes got wide. "Bee—"

"And *consent!*" I finished. "Yes means yes. Got it? Great, let's go!"

I pushed my baffled sister up the trail. I might have been weird and out of it, but I needed to make sure she knew how I felt. My mind kept flashing back to yesterday—running into that douchebag at Reny's. He made me feel so powerless. Well, fuck that, Christopher, you have no power here.

At the top of the clearing, I felt the extreme urge to run into the trees and throw up. It was all too familiar. If I just avoided Ben the whole night, though, it couldn't possibly go the same way.

Maybe, I thought to myself, I should not have worn this shirt.

CHAPTER 42

Hana

THE EDGE OF THE clearing felt like the end of the high dive. I paused, the tips of my toes clinging to the familiar surface.

Talk first, I reminded myself. Bee was right, of course—although I didn't know if she was right about Christopher. What did she know about Christopher?

Bee gave me a squeeze as she walked by. I saw Ben's eyes widen to moon-size as she made her way across the lawn. Maybe tonight, Bee and Ben would finally begin. My chest warmed at the thought, and then burst into wildfire at the sight of her—

Claudia, sitting on a picnic blanket that she probably brought for us. She wore a blue flannel. The silver in her hair flashed in the moonlight. She picked at the grass around her. Did she feel as nervous as I did? That felt comforting.

I vowed then, there, that I would never talk to Christopher again. Over the edge, there was something so much better.

I stepped out and fell toward her.

CHAPTER 43

Claudia

HANA RADIATED IN THE darkness. She appeared like a star growing brighter on the navy sky. A small beam of light, bringing all good things.

It wasn't fair. I hadn't even told her I was in love with her yet.

Slowly, she made her way over to me, through the sparklers and the beer and the others.

"Hi!" She sat down on the blanket next to me and set the little green tent bag behind us.

"Hi," I managed. This was so much harder than I thought it would be.

"How was your day?" She ran her fingers over the back of my hand. I flinched.

"It was . . ." Distracted. Torturous. Fine!

I didn't want to talk like this wasn't happening. I tried to remember how I'd rehearsed with Donald.

"Look, we need to talk about something." That was the first part.

"Yeah." She settled in, leaning on her right hip and putting a hand on my leg. "I think that's a good idea."

Stars shot up my body. *Stop, stop, stop, stars.* I took her hand off my leg. She looked confused.

"I need to ask you something."

"Okay."

I brought my eyes to meet hers. I almost wanted to lean in to kiss her—that's always what happened after we looked into each other's eyes. I forced myself not to. "Are you . . . Are you and Christopher back together?"

Her mouth dropped open, but she regained composure quickly. "No! No, no, I'm not. That was . . . That was over in March, remember?"

"So you're not talking to him?"

She bit her lip. "No."

Not convincing.

"And you're not hooking up with him?"

"What?!" Her voice got strained and high-pitched. "No! No way. Why are you asking me about this?"

"Please don't lie to me," I begged.

"I'm not lying, Claudia."

"Can I look at your phone?" I held out my hand. It was shaking.

Hana reached down to her front pocket but paused. "Actually, no." She looked back up at me. "You can't look at my phone."

The fierceness in her eyes startled me. I felt like I'd been slapped across the cheek.

"I need to go." I stood up, pulled at the blanket. Hana scrambled up. The tent rolled away.

"Wait, Claudia—"

I had to get away from her. I jogged across the clearing toward the trail. Who knew why I'd brought the picnic blanket with me. As I reached the edge, her hand touched my shoulder, I knew it was hers, and I spun around automatically.

Big mistake. Hana's enormous eyes bored into mine. Her perfectly braided hair was wisping out on either side, like static electricity.

"Claudia, who told you all of this?" she demanded. Loudly.

Behind her, I saw Donald break away from the group and start coming toward us. Good. I needed backup.

"Stop," I said quietly. "Just stop. You're a liar, Hana."

Her face crumpled in reply. I could feel people moving toward us. Whatever. Let them find out that Hana had a lot of growing up to do. That she didn't know how to treat people decently yet.

Besides, I couldn't really control myself.

She took a breath. "Claudia, I don't know why you're doing this, but I—"

"I saw you!" I cut her off. "I saw you last night, okay? You were hooking up with *Christopher* at the volleyball court."

"What are you talking about?" she gasped, but I caught an amber flicker of guilt in her eyes.

"Claudia," Donald said, appearing to my right. "Everything okay?"

Hana's hand went up to her mouth. "Claudia, no, I didn't—"

"Hana." Donald turned and calmly held out a hand. "I saw you there, too. Don't lie."

"*You* don't lie!" she sputtered.

Suddenly, Bee and Ben were there, too. My head reeled. I shouldn't have— This was too much—

"What's going on?" Bee's hands slid to her hips.

"Walk away, Bee." Donald shook his head. "You don't want to hear any of this."

"Like hell I don't!" Bee yelled at him. She glanced at me, then back to her sister. "Hana, what's going on?" Hana went to reply, but suddenly, the other counselors were in on this, too—Connie, John, Rachel, Ellie, Dave, and Doug all hovering around us. Thanks, Bee, that was helpful.

"Guys, calm down," Ben said, his voice low. "Why don't we take a deep breath, and someone can explain what's going on."

Bee ignored him and turned to me. "Why's my sister crying?"

So many times this year I'd been bullied. So many times I'd been blamed. But this one felt worse than all the others. This wasn't my fault. It was never my fault, but especially this.

In an instant, I became stony, hard, cold.

"What's going on," I said, "is that *Hana* was hooking up with *Christopher* without telling me."

Hana flung up her hands. "I would never, ever do that!" she cried.

"That's bullshit," Bee replied quickly. "Utter bullshit. How did you even come up with that?"

My voice and brain replied for me. "I *saw her*. Last night. At the volleyball court."

Bee looked at her sister—*doubt*—but Hana waved her hands around, shouting: "No, no, no, no, no! No, they didn't! I wasn't *there!*"

Bee pulled her in to her side. "There you go, idiots. She wasn't there. Did you even ask before you started accusing?"

Donald and I exchanged a look that the whole group took in.

"I don't want to get into this," he said. "But Hana was there. I saw it too."

"Why are you being an asshole?" Bee asked him.

"Really?" Donald fired back. "*We're* the assholes?"

In one swift motion, he grabbed Hana's cell phone out of her hand.

"Donald, *no!*" Ben yelled.

Too late.

Donald opened it, held it out in the middle of the group for everyone to see. There, in the recent messages—

Christopher.

Total silence. Then Hana: "I . . . We talked, but I didn't *do anything*—"

Hana sobbed and collapsed into Bee's shoulder. I could barely process everything that was happening, but of one thing I was sure: Hana didn't feel the same way about me that I did about her. Hana had been talking to Christopher. Hana had hooked up with Christopher. Hana didn't love me.

My whole body began to shake.

Bee snatched the phone out of Donald's hand and gave it to Hana calmly. Bee cradled her sister for the briefest moment, then looked up again. Her glare blazed like a comet aimed at me and Donald.

"Both of you"—she pointed at us—"stay away from my sister." She pushed past us and ushered Hana down the trail. Hana sobbed into her shoulder.

I immediately went to follow them. My heart still thought I cared about Hana. Donald put a hand on my shoulder and stopped me.

As soon as they disappeared, I took off into the woods.

CHAPTER 44

Bee

I HELPED HANA UP the porch stairs at Big Bat. She hadn't untucked from my armpit—still sobbing quietly, shaking, asking choked questions:

"Bee, you believe me, right?"

"Of course, Hana," I whispered.

"Why did she think I hooked up with him?"

"I don't know."

"Why doesn't she believe me?"

"It's okay; it'll be okay."

Of course, my idea of okay was probably vastly different from Hana's right now. It was relatively early, and when we barged inside, my parents were curled up watching a cheesy horror movie.

"What are you two doing here?" Dad paused the movie. He was slower on the uptake. Mom was already up and crossing the room.

"What happened?" She drew Hana out of my arms into hers. Hana just sobbed, finally wailing at full volume.

"Bee?" Mom looked at me wild-eyed.

I explained that Claudia thought Hana had cheated on her and that Donald had grabbed Hana's phone and shown all the counselors that she'd been talking to Christopher. Dad's eyes almost went black at Christopher's name.

"I *didn't* hook up with him again," Hana insisted, in between sobs, looking at Mom. "I promise Mom, I *didn't.*"

"Okay, okay." Mom smoothed her hair. "I believe you, sweetie." But the glance my way told me otherwise.

"We both do." Dad hovered behind Hana and Mom.

"Good," I said forcefully. "I'm glad we all believe her. So you can fire Claudia and Donald tomorrow."

Mom pursed her lips at me. "Not now, Bee. I'm going to get Hana her pill and get her into bed."

"But—"

"We'll talk later. Stay up, we'll talk."

She directed Hana upstairs. I gave one of Hana's hands a squeeze, and she squeezed back. As I watched them go, Dad's arms wrapped around me for a big Dad hug.

"Hey, Bumblebee," he said, pulling back and resting a hand on my shoulder. "Everything'll be all right."

"Right." I nodded. "If we *fire* them."

"Bee," he sighed. "Like Mom said, we'll talk about that later. But I want to warn you: we don't typically fire people for romantic drama."

I broke away from him. "*Romantic drama?!*" I shouted, throwing up my hands. "Donald showed everyone her phone! That's a violation of privacy!"

"Right, and we'll give him a warning about privacy," Dad said calmly. "But this who-hooked-up-with-who isn't something we want to get into the middle of. Especially—"

"Don't say it." I held up a hand. "I don't want to know how deep in the pocket of King you guys are."

"Bee, that's not—"

"I'm going for a walk."

I stomped to the front door and yanked it open to find Ben there, hand in a fist, poised to knock. I felt tears in my eyes as soon as I saw him.

"Oh, hey!" His hand moved into an awkward wave. "I was just hoping to check on you and Hana. Is she—"

"Come on," I said, purposefully not looking back at my dad. Ben followed me down the porch stairs, onto the trail. We fell into a silent walk, side by side. I led the way to the right, toward Dam.

How could Claudia believe that Hana had cheated on her? I'd always thought she was insecure and whatever, but I didn't know it extended this far. How could she break up with Hana in front of everyone? What kind of person does that?

We reached Dam's veranda, and I sat on the wide bottom step of the stairs. I pulled my knees up to my chest and hugged them. Ben sat down, too, on the other side of the stair. I was vaguely aware that somewhere, far away and overhead, the second round of Messina fireworks were popping.

Boiling, angry tears seared down my cheeks. I had trusted Claudia with Hana's heart. How could she do this? She was *worse* than Christopher.

"Bee? Are you crying?"

"Uh, yup." I didn't look at him. "I'm probably going to be crying for a while."

He scooched closer to me, till our sides were touching. I was too tired and too confused to feel anything special.

"I'm so sorry." He hugged his legs up to his chest, too. "I don't know what happened back there."

I turned and glared at him through half-filled eyes. "Claudia and Donald went asshole rogue. Hana *did not* bring a guy to camp and hook up with him." Only the smallest part of me protested *She might've*, but I threw it in the trash. See, Claudia? Not that hard.

Ben flinched. "Oh I know, I know. I believe Hana. She wouldn't do that."

Relief flooded through me, and I nodded and snuffled a little, wiping at my nose with the back of my hand. I didn't care how gross that was.

"No, she wouldn't." It felt good to say. "And she didn't. And I'm never forgiving Claudia *or* Donald."

Ben scooted just a smidgen closer to me. "I get that."

"I want to fire them. And carve out their hearts with the gardening shears."

Ben laughed, kind of forced.

"I'm not joking."

"I know, it's just . . ." He trailed off.

I sighed, turned away, and stared out into the dark. I didn't care if Ben thought I was ruthless. I wasn't exaggerating. If he didn't get that those people had *hurt* my *sister,* and were therefore *scum,* then—

"Bee, I'm in love with you."

CHAPTER 45

Ben

THE WORDS LEFT MY mouth so effortlessly, I barely registered that I'd said them. Bee froze for, like, *seconds*, so I couldn't even tell if I *had* said them. Just silence, save for some ironic fireworks. If things had gone according to plan, we would've been *underneath* the fireworks when I'd said this, and then maybe she wouldn't be glaring into the night with her forehead perpetually pinched like that.

Finally, she spoke. "What . . ."

I held my breath.

"What the *fuck*, Ben?"

Shit. "Umm . . ." What if Donald and Claudia had been wrong somehow? Crap, crap, crap. "I'm into you, very into you, in like . . . a romantic and, uh . . . sexual way?"

She stood up immediately. "I can't deal with this," she announced. "I have to go." She took off down the trail.

"Wait!" I scrambled up to follow her. She was almost jogging. "Bee, please!"

She suddenly stopped at the waterfront and whipped around. "What do you want?"

I took a step toward her. "To know how you feel. Please."

She stuffed her hands in her shorts pockets. "What, so you can turn around and accuse *me* of being in love with *you*? I don't think so."

"What?" I sputtered.

She rolled her eyes so hard I was sure they'd gone all the way around. "Last summer."

Okay, so we were finally going to talk about this. "Yes."

"*Last summer*, Ben."

"I don't—"

"Do you not remember what happened last summer?!"

WHAT HAPPENED: PART 8

Ben

WHEN I WOKE UP, pain erupted in my back. *Where am I?* Someone asleep, hot and sweaty, was lying on top of me. It was Bee, half-naked, breathing steadily. My shirt was gone, too.

Sunlight poured into Stickleback. Shit. Then the back pain made sense. I'd been lying with Bee on top of me, with crinkled, pointy tarps underneath me, for hours.

I gently shook her. "Bee . . . Bee . . ."

"Mmmm . . ."

"Bee, morning meeting."

Her eyes flew open. "Crap!" She pushed herself off me and up—I looked away—and sprang into action, quicker than I'd ever seen Bee in the morning. She threw my shirt at me, and we both scrambled out the door.

"Have you heard the trumpet yet?" she asked, as we hurried (no running!) down the path.

"Wait." I reached into my pocket and pulled out my phone. It suddenly occurred to me I could check the time. "Oh. It's only six thirty."

We had an hour before we had to wake up the campers.

"God." She heaved a sigh of relief. "I thought—"

"I know."

"We should still hurry back."

"Definitely."

And that was it. We walked in silence along the trail together, and in some nonverbal agreement, back up to Nest. We grabbed the beer cooler and the sparkler bucket and dropped them off down at Dam, buried the beer bottles deep in the recycling.

There, in the grass behind the building, we paused, a few feet away from each other. I needed to go to the right, back to Snowshoe, and Bee would go left, to Little Bat. Disheveled and exhausted, yes, but neither one of us seemed to be able to move.

I felt acutely aware that if we didn't talk about this now, it could all disappear.

"So . . ." I began.

She raised her eyebrows. I almost gulped.

"So . . ." I pushed forward. "Last night?"

"Yeah." Her face went blank.

"I just wanted to say . . . umm . . ." I searched for the words. "Well, I guess what I want to know is . . . do you like me?"

"What?" she snapped.

"I mean, I think you like me?" I said again, glancing at her.

She went quiet for a moment, seemed to decide something, then looked up at me with blazing eyes. What had I done?!

"Yeah, I *like* you," she snapped. "We're friends."

"Just friends . . .?"

"Isn't that all we are?"

"Right." I swallowed. Tactile memories bombarded my brain. Fingers, mouths, tongues, ears, nipples—*friends*?

Bee

I stood there, behind Dam with Ben, furiously processing. It all made stupid sense now. We'd been drunk, it was late, it was after a party. Of course he didn't like me. Neither of us had really meant it. Alcohol and horniness meant it, clearly. And now he accused me of liking him! I could say the same thing! So how dare he pin all of this on me?

I needed to leave. To run the fuck away. I blabbed about us being friends, and then ended it.

"Okay, well, glad we worked that out," I said, cheerfully. "I gotta go."

"Me too . . ."

Strangely, we both went in for a small hug—a hug neither of us probably wanted—and after, he pulled back and did this weird thing. Our faces were close again, and it seemed for just one moment, faster than a second, that he was leaning down toward me. In a kissy way.

But I didn't want to kiss him again if he didn't like me. My hand automatically moved in between us and gently pushed him away.

"No." I half laughed. "No more of that."

"Oh." He laughed too. "Right."

"See you soon."

"Okay."

And with that, I turned and ran the fuck away.

CHAPTER 46

Ben

WAS THAT REALLY HOW it had happened? Bee's side of the story hung in the air, so vivid I could hardly catch my breath.

"And there I was, thinking I was pathetic for liking you, because you didn't like me back," she finished. "And what, now you're *in love* with me?" The pain in her voice screamed.

I tried to process everything I'd just heard.

"Bee." I took a step forward. "I'm sorry. If that's how you . . . I really fucked that up."

"Oh?" She didn't move.

"But I was scared." I scratched my nose. "I didn't know what I was saying . . . or what you were feeling . . . and I should've done what I'm doing now. I should've told you first. I was so scared you didn't feel the same way."

"And now?" she asked.

"Well . . ." I decided it was best *not* to bring up the Donald/ Claudia conversation. That could come later. "Well, it's now or never. I like you. Love you. And if you don't feel that too, I guess tough shit for me."

She laughed, and when she stopped, her smile stayed. My heart leaped. I took another step forward. My sneaker snapped a twig. She stepped forward, too. One step at a time, till my arms were wrapped around her waist, her hands resting on my shoulders. We were at a middle school dance, swaying to "Stairway to Heaven." We were in space, floating between planets.

"Ummm . . ." she whispered, lips so close. "I don't know, okay?"

"What?" I whispered.

"I mean . . ." She looked away. It was physically painful not to be looking into her eyes. She turned back. Thank goodness. "I mean, of course I'm in love with you."

Adrenaline shot through my body, my grip on her tightened ever so slightly.

"But, like, I don't want to . . . I mean, I'm not in love with you, really. I don't even know how to explain this."

I tried not to smile. I must've failed, because she smiled back at me.

And suddenly we were kissing. So much kissing. All the kissing. Memories of kisses combining with current kisses. Pressed into each other, my hands grasping the back of her neck, her hands through my hair. Feeling, feeling, *feeling*. The most intense ten seconds of my life.

We broke away, each springing back a couple feet. I took a moment and caught my breath, tasting night sky and waves. Moment taken, I looked back at Bee. She felt me looking and met my eyes, like a deer in headlights. Crap, was this happening again?

Then she burst out laughing. Loud, magical Bee laughter, and I was afraid she would wake the whole camp.

She paused, wiped tears out of the corners of her eyes. "Ben, what just happened?"

I couldn't help laughing too. It was the most romantic moment of my life so far, with the girl I loved, with Bee Leonato, the greatest girl in the world. But also the girl who got the entire camp to call me Bunny. What even was life?! I kind of wanted to call my mom and ask her.

"Bee, I love you." I said it again, because we could now. "I love you more than anything."

She smiled, rushed forward, and threw her arms around me again. "Do you really?"

"Yes." I went to kiss her again, but when we pulled back a little, and I leaned in again, something broke. A shadow passed over her face. I stopped.

"What's wrong?"

"Ben, I just . . . I can't do this right now." She broke away again and pulled on her hair. "Hana—Hana's so upset."

"Right—I'm sorry." I shook my head. "I didn't mean for this to happen on the same night."

"Well, duh." Bee sighed, staring out at the water. "Who could've guessed Claudia and Donald would turn into assholes for Fourth of July?"

"Tell me about it," I agreed, inching over beside her at the shoreline. "But I'll talk to them in the morning. I'm sure it's just a big misunderstanding. We can work it out."

"Work it out?" Bee turned to me, eyes wide with surprise. "What are you talking about? Those two are dead to me. There's nothing to work out."

CHAPTER 47

Bee

"WHAT?" HE STAYED CLOSE, so close I could feel his breath on my lips when he spoke. *Concentrate.* "What do you mean?"

"Ben, I don't care what kind of misunderstanding this was," I said, feeling my stomach begin to twist in that familiar way it does when I have to set people straight. "Claudia just *dumped* Hana in front of *everyone*, and Donald showed everyone her *private messages*."

Ben winced. That was good. He should wince. "Yeah, I know, that was real bad. He needs to apologize. I don't know what came over him."

"Apologize?" I sputtered. "They both need to leave camp. What they just did was unforgivable."

Ben's eyes got serious in the buzzing lights. They searched mine; I let them. He wasn't going to find what he was looking for.

"Bee, those are our friends, two of my best friends," Ben said, finally, slowly. "They fucked up, but we need to figure this out. We've all known each other for years."

"And?" I growled. "And who the fuck cares? You don't get to hurt people and then explain yourselves. You don't get to just apologize and move past humiliating someone."

He hesitated. *That* was bad. That was all I needed to see.

"We're not talking about this anymore," I explained. "We're done here. I have to go."

"Are you serious?"

I turned and walked away, calling back over my shoulder: "Are *you* serious?"

"Bee, not yet—we need to figure this out first. As friends, right?"

Friends. The word burned in my chest.

"Friends?" I whipped around and pointed at him. "We can't be friends if you're friends with my *enemies*!"

"Are Donald and Claudia your 'enemies'?" Ben demanded. I heard an eye roll in his voice. I hated it.

"Now they are!" I shouted. "They hurt someone I love! You of all people should understand this!"

He brought a hand up over his face. I instantly regretted saying it. I knew what Ben had been through. I knew because he had trusted me last year.

"I'm sorry, I didn't mean . . . I shouldn't have said that." I sighed. "But I'm done talking about this."

"Great," he said, his voice hollow. "Me too."

He stayed; I walked away. What a fucking mess. Maybe this fight was for the best. We didn't make sense. And now I could stop trying to make it make sense.

Now I *knew* this was over, 100 percent. And that was a relief.

CHAPTER 48

Hana

I WOKE UP AN hour after Mom tucked me in. Apparently, Xanax doesn't actually work through your life being *obliterated* in a ten-minute explosion of crap.

I sat up and immediately looked across the room—

Bee's bed was empty.

I grabbed my phone and texted Christopher.

> I hate life. You up?

I waited for half an hour before I gave up on a reply. Fireworks cracked outside my window. Right, it was Fourth of July, and it was only midnight. Christopher would be out partying. He was with someone else.

Text Claudia, my brain automatically proposed. You'll feel so much better.

But that's how it worked before, I thought, tears reemerging. It doesn't work that way now.

I hugged my pillow and screamed into it. I had to. The sadness—the big, angry one—ripped through me. When it was over, my throat felt as raw as the rest of me.

I must've fallen asleep again after that.

CHAPTER 49

Vanessa

"ANYTHING??" SOPHIA WHISPERED. I'd just taken my fourth trip to the bathrooms in Dam. I shook my head. Almost an entire night of bathroom trips and staking out Nest's trail entrance and . . . nothing.

"Maybe we should stop for now, I'm getting tired," I said. Which actually wasn't an excuse—I couldn't stop yawning. Was this what getting old was like?

Sophia sighed in agreement and sat back to watch the movie. We'd done the sparklers earlier, and now we were hanging out in the attic of Luna, the counselor chill spot. They'd abandoned it for the night, so us CITs got to use it to party. And by party I mean eat cheesy popcorn and watch this old movie *Clueless*, which only Wallace had voted against. Wallace explained he was a Jane Austen purist. I don't know what that had to do with Cher, but whatever, the movie was hilarious, and he came around.

Another makeover montage started, and my eyelids began to flutter, my head nodded forward. . . . This beanbag chair was so mushy and if I curled up like a cat . . .

Sophia shook me awake. "Nessa, you gotta go to bed."

"Merrrgh." I batted her hands away. "I'll sleep here."

"You're going to regret that in the morning."

"No, you will." I stuffed my face into the fluffy beanbag cover.

I woke up a few hours later, disoriented. Popcorn crumbs, paper cups. What a mess we'd made. No wonder the counselors didn't like us being up here.

With all my strength, I rolled like a pill bug out of the beanbag chair and pushed myself up. It was chilly. I wanted my sleeping bag now. Why was there so much space between me and my sleeping bag??

I walked back to Moose, too out of it to even swat at the mosquitoes. Okay, mosquitoes, eat me! You win this round!

I reached the cabin, poked my head in. Margo wasn't home, still partying probably, and it felt weird inside without her and the campers. I missed them already, even if they'd chewed me up and spit me out, kind of literally.

I didn't want to go inside yet. I turned around and sat on the little porch steps instead and decided to look wistfully up at the stars.

I missed home, too, wherever that was. Our new apartment, maybe. Camp usually felt like home, but being a CIT was different than I'd thought it would be. And I had to do it for the whole summer. I thought being part of the staff might mean I'd feel insider-y, finally a member of the cool group. But we were still once removed. Or three removed, maybe. The highest up, Ben's group, seemed to glow with royalty—constantly bickering and laughing about things only they could talk about.

I wondered if Sophia, Wallace, and I would ever be those counselors. Siiiiiiiigh.

My eyelids began to flutter again. Maybe I'd grab my sleeping bag and sleep out here. It might be nice to be woken up by the sun. . . .

Instead, whispered voices woke me. I sat up, disoriented, everything dark and blurry. I was still outside. How much time had passed? Instinctually, I lay back down. I didn't know who was there, maybe a serial killer, and I didn't want them to see me.

"I don't know, I feel kind of bad." I knew the voice, but my ears weren't awake enough yet to identify it.

"Like they were going to last anyway," another voice answered. A *pair* of serial killers! "Claudia's an idiot."

Hmm. Serial killers who knew Claudia. Unlikely.

"Ha! Well, that's true. Can you believe how she acted tonight?" Suddenly, I realized: that was Connie. "I just don't get what John sees in her."

"Boobs?" said a boy's voice.

"Maybe," she replied. "But other people have boobs. Do you think Margo's going to out you guys, if she puts it together?"

I peeked over. They were paused on the trail, near the bench.

"I fucking doubt it." Bobby. It was Bobby. "She's totally paranoid someone's going to find out about us this summer. Hook up with me, ignore me in the morning."

"Why do you keep hooking up with her, then?" Connie asked. I was blearily wondering that myself.

"Oh, you know." Bobby's voice sounded sad. " 'Cause I like her. And every year she's funnier, and prettier. . . ."

"All right, I get it." Connie snorted. "I don't need to hear a poem."

"And you know, I get laid. Are you getting laid?" Pause. "Didn't think so."

"You're disgusting."

"That's not what Margo said last night."

I heard a slight shuffle, a thump, and then a yelp.

"Fuck off, Connie!"

"Sorry, you absolutely had to be subdued."

"So, do you actually think this is going to work?"

"What do you mean?"

"Is John going to hook up with Claudia now?"

I held my breath, trying to remember everything. I wished I had my phone to write this down. Did one of the kids leave their dream journals?

"Ehh, I doubt it. Like, highly doubt it. But maybe . . ." Connie didn't sound pleased at the idea. "But maybe if he tries to, and she blows him off, he'll finally get over her."

"Oh, and you're counting on that?"

More shuffling, another louder yelp.

"OUCH! I'm going to bed before you do permanent damage."

"It's not my fault. Quit saying gross stuff."

Jeez, I'm glad I'm not their CIT. When their footsteps and grumbles sounded safely far away, I hopped onto the grass out front to pace. *Think, think, Vanessa!* So John likes . . . Claudia. Connie likes . . . John. But the bigger point: Connie, John, and Bobby had set up Claudia?

With Margo as a pawn? Maybe?

Somebody had to tell her.

I thought about sneaking to Sophia's cabin, but then I realized that waking up to the shock of all of this just might kill her.

CHAPTER 50

Ben

I WASN'T ALWAYS SURE that my mood controlled the weather, but that weekend was proof: Saturday morning rain pelted down. I spent the first few hours in my bed, in my cabin, just listening to the sound. Wallace and Doug both got up for brunch. Wallace asked if I was coming. I mumbled something about catching up on sleep. I hoped my face didn't look obviously puffy from crying. They left.

Fuck everything. Fuck it all to the moon.

My stomach started protesting the whole not-ever-moving-again thing I had going. I pulled myself out of my sleeping bag and shoved into a slicker.

On the weekends, when the kids went home, we usually hung out in Dam too long during meals, messing around, and then chilled upstairs in Luna. Watching movies, playing card or board games. If we had any leftover energy, sometimes we'd do ropes course teams, or go bowling in town.

Not this Saturday. The trails felt like the roads of a ghost town. No campers, no counselors, not even any squirrels or chipmunks. A couple snails. That helped, a little.

I opened the door to Dam quietly, just in case. I didn't want to draw attention to myself. But there was nobody in there, either, except Shane and a few CITs, finishing up pots and pans from brunch.

I grabbed blueberry pancakes and bacon, and sat right in the middle of the room, because why the fuck not? It was usually Donald's seat, but where the fuck was Donald?

My head cleared some after eating. Maple syrup can do that. I took out my phone and texted Donald:

> Hey, where are you guys? In Dam.

> . . . (typing)

> . . . (typing)

Seriously? I thought. It's a simple question.

> We're off campus.

> Where?

I wanted to add *And what the fuck are you thinking?* But also: *Why wasn't I invited?*

> I'm not gonna say, no offense.

I stared at his response. Why even bother texting back if you weren't gonna say. Just don't say anything back at all.

> Look, I need to talk to both of you. What happened last night? This is messed up.

> Not interested, sorry.

Another nothing response. They were freezing me out. I felt like throwing my phone in the harbor. I shut it off and shoved it in my pocket. Returned to my pancakes.

I was starting to get a creeping feeling that Bee was right about Donald and Claudia. And that really shouldn't have been surprising. She was always right.

CHAPTER 51

Vanessa

AS SOON AS I opened my eyes, alarms went off in my brain: *You need to talk to Ben!! And Margo??*

Right. Something totally messed up had gone down last night, and I might've been the only one who knew.

I flumped out of bed—still no Margo; maybe she was in Little Bat? Or maybe she'd been here and had actually gotten out of bed before noon.

I changed clothes, slid into rubber boots and my slicker, and charged through the rain to Dam. Luckily, Ben was in the corner, eating alone. I shook off and ran over to him.

"Ben—"

"You might want to get pancakes before they go cold."

He was correct; I did want that. I grabbed a plate and a mug of tea and squished in my boots back over to the table.

"Ben."

"Nessa."

He looked tired. Nothing new, Ben was tired a lot. But something else. The bags under his eyes were shiny and red. He'd been crying.

Mooooom! I wanted to yell behind me. *Ben's crying! Come help!*

Instead, I pushed the maple syrup toward him. He nodded at me and doused his pancakes again. The rain tapped at the windows. I grabbed an end of my hair and chewed it a little. How to bring this up?

"You excited about the girls coming on Monday?" he said.

"Ben, there's something I need to tell you," I said, at the same time.

He looked up startled. "Okay, Ness, what is it?"

"I overheard this thing, and I just want to know if—"

The door to Dam slammed open, surprising us both. We turned. There stood Sophia, in an orange poncho and rain boots to match.

"Nessa!" she yelled, and squelched over. She slammed down her hands at our table. Ben protectively scooped the small glass syrup pitcher away from her.

"Nessa, you'll *never. be. lieve* this," Sophia said, with huge breaths in between the words. She didn't even wait for me to prompt her, she kept going.

"Last night, at the sparkler party . . ." Did she even see my brother sitting there? Probably not. *"Claudia dumped Hana."*

"What?" I gasped. "That doesn't even make sense!"

"I *know*," she whispered. She didn't know the half of it. The third of it! "I can't believe we missed it! But yeah, turns out Hana was cheating on Claudia with some townie guy. Can you believe that? What a total slu—"

"Wait," Ben said quietly, startling us both. "Where did you hear this?"

Sophia glanced at me, I nodded. "Connie?" she said. "Well, I overheard her talking to Rachel about it this morning in the bathroom."

Ben nodded slowly. He set down his fork. I could tell a grown-up speech was coming.

"Ness, you're better than this," he said. Yup. "This isn't funny, and I don't expect either of you to tell anyone about it. And I don't want to hear gossip anymore." He looked at Sophia. "And I definitely don't want to hear that word you were about to use."

"Sorry," she muttered.

"Sorry, Ben," I added.

Ben shoved away from the table, grabbed his plate and put it away, then disappeared out the side door without another word. Sophia watched all of this silently, but the minute he was definitely gone, she made a face.

"Your brother's kind of a pain."

I smiled at her but felt sick inside, like rotten eggs were scrambling in my stomach. My brother was disappointed in me, and I had this enormous secret. I'd have to go to Margo.

Suddenly, I really, *really* missed being a camper.

CHAPTER 52

Bee

SLEEPING WELL SEEMED LIKE a thing of the past, so hauling myself out of bed for Monday morning when my body screamed at me it needed more sleep just felt totally normal.

Nothing else felt normal.

I poured cereal, milk, coffee like nothing was wrong. I sat down at a table with Margo, who rubbed my back, and continued listening to Ellie overanalyze her feelings for Doug. She knew I didn't want to talk, and I felt super grateful for that.

This weekend was the worst. The worst I could remember for a very, very long time. The cereal wouldn't fit down my throat. Its sharp edges caught and scraped. I let it get soggier.

Pull it together, pull it together, camp is in one hour. There's days when you're gonna have to teach through some bad shit, Bee, I reminded myself. When the president gives another craptastic address, or you actually go through a real breakup, or your dog might die. After you get a dog. And you're still gonna have to teach.

I forced myself to surface, finish my cereal, toss my dishes in the bins, and made my way out for setup. As I was leaving, though, little whispers reached out from tables by the door—

"Can you *believe* that? She brought some townie onto camp grounds."

"Well, if you're the director's daughter, I guess you can get away with anything."

"I just feel bad for Claudia. She was crying so hard."

"I haven't even seen any of them all weekend."

I blinked. Were they talking about . . . ? I turned to look, and both Rachel and Doug immediately shut up. Technically, I'd known there had been other witnesses on Friday, but I'd fled with Hana immediately. I hadn't even thought—I turned and looked out at the dining hall, usually a hubbub of singing and laughter.

Thirty faces looked back, blushing, curious. The face you made when you'd been talking about someone.

I turned and slammed the door behind me. Fuck. *Fuck.*

Even if my mom convinced Hana to get out of bed, she'd now have to deal with *this*? I thought about banging the gong in Dam and announcing that anyone who talked about my sister could fill out their resignation paperwork *immediately*, and I'd be *happy* to help them.

But I'd promised my parents I wouldn't do anything rash about this. I'd promised Hana.

Check-in went fine. How could I care? But I smiled and fist-bumped kids, inquired about their new siblings, their new schools. My heart ached through all of it. And then, two little faces stared up at me, and the sun came out.

"Ava, Layla!" I cried, and bent down to hug them both. They were arguably our cutest campers: *almost* identical—pale; freckly; big brown eyes, like Ben's and Nessa's; dark, shoulder-length hair; and adorable, pointy chins. The only way most people could tell them apart was that Layla had thick red glasses. By the time we'd finished our hug, Ben had appeared, and they both lit up. I tried not to light up too.

"BEN!" Ava threw herself into his gut. "I thought you were DEAD!"

"Well, she tried to convince Mom you were," Layla said, arms crossed, waiting her turn. "So she could have your PlayStation."

Ben scooped up Ava, twirled her around, switched to Layla, and did it again.

"Twice for Layla, since she didn't try to kill me off," he explained to them. Ava stuck out her tongue, grinning. "I missed you munch-kins," he said. And he had. You could tell. His whole being glowed now that they were here. For a moment, I forgot how pissed I was at him.

"Missed you too, Bunny!" Ava cackled.

"He doesn't *like* that." Layla kicked her.

"Hey, babies!" Nessa called out from the lice check. They squealed and sprinted over to her.

Ben's mom, Colleen, appeared, kissed my cheek, and fussed about the weight Ben had lost in the last two weeks. He smiled and took it all good-naturedly, gently asking her how everything was at home, at work. I took a step back so they'd have some privacy.

I glanced at Nessa wrestling Ava into the folding chair while Layla chatted in her ear. Colleen, laughing easily at a joke Ben made. The Rosenthals. Their happy family, free. Tears welled in my eyes.

"I'm gonna go say hi to Nessie," Colleen said with a wave. I waved back, faintly. As she left, there stood Ben across from me. I couldn't hide. Our eyes met.

He registered the tears and quickly closed the distance between us. "Can we talk, later?"

I said nothing back. I had so many feelings, but nothing came before Hana.

"I know, okay?" he whispered. "I promise, I'm on your side."

His eyes flickered back and forth, searching mine. My side. That sounded like an improvement on last night.

"Okay." I gulped. "Later."

He nodded, then went and joined his sisters.

"Bee!" yelled a car pulling in. Three kids tumbled out, and I smiled brightly and showed them where to put their stuff.

CHAPTER 53
John

MONDAY MORNING, WE OFFERED mini activities while the new session's campers settled in. Claudia ran the knots elective again, and I volunteered to help. I found them at the campfire pit, sitting on logs. From the top of the trail, I could see Claudia explaining the basics with her low, calm voice.

But when I walked up and got close, her voice sounded raspy and on edge. She glanced up at me—her face paste pale, purple bags under her eyes like they'd been drawn on with a Magic Marker.

"This is John," she said to the campers. They nodded or said hi quietly. Claudia's mini sessions were always like this: chill as fuck. The kids knew, sensed not to mess with her.

I helped a couple kids through the basics of a fish tail till the session was over. They returned the ropes and then hightailed it to their next activity. The farther from the campfire they got, the louder their voices boomed. Spell broken.

I grabbed the ropes and threw them in the box, then finally looked at Claudia again. She was slumped on a log, staring at her phone.

"Hey, you okay?" I sat down next to her.

Her bronze eyes looked up at me, tears welling on her lower lids. Crap.

"What do you think?" she asked.

Shit.

"Uhh . . . no."

"You get a prize." She looked away again.

I'd meant, I thought—I thought I could maybe bring something up here. Movies this weekend. But her face, her eyes, her shoulders hunched, I didn't . . .

She sighed. "Sorry, but this was the worst weekend ever. Like, ever."

I froze.

She shifted, looking up at the trees above us. "I just feel like, what's the point of me being here anymore?"

"Seriously?" I laughed. "Hana's so . . . young. She was probably just messing around with a girl for fun. You don't need to throw away your summer 'cause of her."

She didn't reply, just stared up at the trees. I checked my watch: we both needed to go.

"I think it's time for—"

"John," Claudia said quietly. "Fuck. Off."

Everything stopped. The waves, the birds, the bugs, the air. I stared into the ashes of the fire pit. She stood up, grabbed the box of ropes from my hands, and walked away. I couldn't have moved if I tried.

How Claudia acted felt so familiar. But it felt familiar because I'd felt like that, acted like that, a hundred times in the last five years, ever since my "family" went public. But this time, it was me. It was my fault.

I'd kind of thought this before, but here it was, knotted in my face: I was an asshole. As big an asshole as my father.

CHAPTER 54

Hana

"IF YOU GO TO work today, we'll talk about whether you have to work tomorrow." My parents broke. "We'll talk" was code for "We'll cave."

"Fine, I'll go." I forced myself out of bed, brushed past them into the hallway to use the bathroom. I turned on the shower, but listened to them whisper about calling Louisa, my therapist, at the door. When I got like this, my family seemed so pathetic. So small in comparison to the wad of dark crap settling into my chest.

I changed into my swimsuit, pulled myself together for the waterfront. Smile, welcome, buddy board, don't let anyone drown. Swim tests, tests, tests. For the first time in a long time, the water felt frigid.

"Hana." Judy looked at me, eyebrows pinching in worry. "Your lips are turning blue. Sit the next one out and go warm up."

I nodded in reply, grabbed my big towel, and shivered into Dam for a snack and coffee. No, coffee made everything worse. But maybe I could talk to Shane into making me cocoa?

Dam bustled with counselors and CITs running in and out, grabbing food or forms from the paperwork corner. No sign of Donald or of . . . her.

I went to the counter to plead my blue-lipped case. Dave and Jen came out of the bathroom, walked by me, I guess not noticing I was there.

"Yeah, Claudia's so messed up about it."

"What a bitch."

"I don't know, man. I was hanging out with this girl last year, and then there was another girl I kind of liked, and so *I* broke up with the first one before I did anything with the second one. . . . It's the right thing to do. . . ."

Their whispers faded the closer they got to the whirring drink machine.

"Hey, Hana." Shane appeared behind the counter. Sweet, professional, older. Didn't know I was a bitch/slut or anything. What a relief. "Can I get you something warm?" he asked.

"Can I just have a packet of instant?"

He smiled and handed me a whole box of cocoa. "Sure thing."

"And can you tell my mom I feel sick and that I needed to go lie down?"

"Sure, but does Judy—"

"Judy knows. Thanks."

"Hana! Are you—"

The side door's slam cut him off. I clutched my box of cocoa and walked barefoot through the needles and ferns back to our house.

CHAPTER 55

Ben

FIRST DAY AGAIN, SPROUTBALL. Outline the rules, hand out a million rainbow squishy balls. And, screaming in three . . . two . . . one . . . go!

Claudia and I both went down fairly quickly, because half the fun of Sproutball was being tagged as a seed and getting to throw balls at people (both maniacally and helpfully). Claudia and I made a big pile in the middle of the field and crouched down.

"Hey. We need to talk after this," I whispered, tossing a few to Maddie. Session 2, she was vicious.

"No thanks." She lobbed one across the field that hit Ilse in the butt.

The freezing out continued all morning. When we finished our last session, Claudia disappeared with the final group, leaving me to put away the giant bag of sproutballs and cones by myself. Cool.

I'd now given both Donald and Claudia opportunities to explain their shitty-ass behavior. But neither one of them was interested. Which meant . . . I had no way forward to fix this.

"ARGH!" I said out loud on the field, to no one in particular. "Just ARGH!" And then: "I *told you* so!"

It wasn't that satisfying. *Whatever, Ben. Get to lunch, talk to Bee about what you heard at breakfast.* She'd know what to do.

But lunch was a nightmare.

If Camp Dogberry had a gossip magazine, then Claudia and Hana would've been on the front page. In line, Sophia and Wallace talked about Hana's mystery guy (guess she really took my outburst to heart). I passed Ellie, Dave, and Rachel whispering in hushed tones about Claudia's broken heart. Gossip happened at camp, but something about this seemed especially off.

This gossip had a slant: Claudia wronged, Hana the wronger. Amid the bustling, in the corner, Donald and Claudia sat at a table, purposefully not looking my way. A couple younger counselors and CITs surrounded them, talking in excited, hushed tones.

Those. Assholes.

They were doing this. They were not only feeding the gossip flame, but putting their own spin on it so that Hana was the bad guy.

The screen doors slammed open and in walked Bee and Margo, escorting a group of campers. They showed their kids where to get food, where to sit. Bee's single-minded concentration on the campers shouted her anger loud and clear. Margo looked around nervously, glancing at the evil table in the corner.

I tried to get near Bee, to warn her, but she artfully avoided me by offering to replenish the napkin baskets. I sat down with my sisters instead, for the Layla and Ava recap of life at home.

"And that's why Mom won't let us make a fourth cat elevator." Layla sighed.

"How are we going to be engineers?" Ava demanded. "Where's the support for the sciences in our house?"

Nessie jabbed a thumb at me. "Mom's paying for Ben to go to

doctor college, doofuses. Stop almost killing the cat and you'll get support."

I laughed; she shot me a small smile. I hoped she understood what I'd said earlier. I wasn't mad at her, I just didn't want her to forget that gossip could *hurt* people.

Lunch ended. I ran outside without staying to help clean up. There was too much on the line—I waited at the side entrance, nearest Luna, where like magic, Bee appeared, slamming open the door.

"Hey!"

"What!" she yelled, then saw it was me. "Fudge nuggets, Ben, what are you *doing*?"

"Can we talk now?"

"I need to get to class."

"Please?" I knew she was early. She was always early.

She sighed and threw up her hands. I motioned for her to follow me, toward the back of the building where we'd have some privacy. As soon as we got there, I realized this was the spot where everything had gone wrong between us last summer. *Don't let it happen again.*

Standing across from her, I saw she didn't look much better than I did. Sleepy eyelids, braids hastily bunched, no earrings. Not exactly typical Bee.

"Look, you were right," I explained. "Claudia and Donald shut me out all weekend, they're *still* shutting me out, and I think—"

"This isn't about you, Ben."

"Can you let me finish?"

"Fine." She crossed her arms. Clearly she was still skeptical.

"*Everyone* knows," I said, lowering my voice. "I've heard it all morning, all through lunch. The story's that Hana cheated on

Claudia, and Claudia's heartbroken, and Hana's an asshole. And *I'm* not telling them that, and I'm assuming *you* aren't."

Bee sighed a sigh so large I swear it blew my hair back. "I know . . . I heard some of it this morning." She paused, then raised her eyebrows at me. "But wait, aren't they your *friends?*"

"Not if they're doing this!" I tried not to yell. I gestured at Dam, at the general camp. "This is—*crap*. It's unforgivable."

"It's socially and morally reprehensible," she spat out in agreement.

The mutual anger brought us a step toward each other. Up closer, I saw in her eyes that something else was wrong.

Her face softened, her arms went from crossed to lightly intertwined. She started talking, on her own this time. "I've spent all weekend messed up about it. It feels like everything's . . ." She sighed. "Everything's fallen apart."

She looked so vacant, so tired. I wanted to hug her so badly. Turns out, she did, too, because suddenly she was pressed up against me, and my arms circled around her.

"I didn't want to write you off," she whispered.

"Please don't," I said, squeezing her. "I promise I'm on your side."

"Her side."

"Her side." As I said, I realized the thing I'd seen in her eyes, the other thing that was wrong. I pulled back. "Bee, where's Hana?"

Her chin quivered. "Emergency therapy session."

"Shit," I whispered. "I'm sorry. Those crapheads, if they had any idea—"

"Don't you dare say anything," she fired back.

"Of course not," I said, quietly. I felt my chin quivering back. "I'm just, I'm so sorry–"

"I have to get to class," she said, squeezed my hand, wiped her eyes, and took off.

⚬

That evening, after evening games, for the first time, I used my activity leader privileges to skip the nighttime sing-along. I sprawled out in Luna, with a camp map and a notepad, planning out Wednesday's event. For a couple years, I'd had a secret idea for how to win Capture the Flag. It was dirty, it wasn't nice, and it didn't follow most of the rules. When last year was my *last year*, I'd put the idea away forever.

But plans change.

And Claudia was going down.

CHAPTER 56

Hana

TUESDAY MORNING SHONE THROUGH the window of my cabin. Mom had talked me into sleeping there. I know she thought I'd get up with everyone else, change, go down to the water early. I didn't. I slept in, and then I watched the campers get up with Bee, go to the shower, come back, grab their things. I couldn't imagine doing all of that, going to Dam, hearing their voices again.

"Hana cheated on Claudia." "Claudia's better off without her." "Thought she was nicer than that."

It sounded just like school.

"Do you actually think Chris was into her?" "It's just kind of pathetic and sad." "I didn't want to say anything but . . ."

It was back; it was back; it was back.

The sun warmed the cabin and soon the air became thick and stuffy. I sweated through my sleeping bag. Kamile, a CIT, came to find me—I knew I was missing my first class. I pretended to be asleep. She said my name a few times, loudly, but didn't have the guts to shake me. She left.

I fell half-asleep. The gray in-between sleep.

"Hana?"

I opened my eyes. Bee's face hovered so close to mine, I groaned.

"Let's go to the house, okay, sweets?"

I tugged sweats and a T-shirt on over my clammy skin. I felt like the third day of a terrible cold. Bee walked me around back, through the woods to get to Big Bat. I guess I wasn't fit for the campers' innocent eyes. I took some sick pleasure in that—*See, Mom? I can't go back to work.*

At the house, Bee led me up the stairs to the shower and handed me a towel.

This was all so familiar.

This time I actually showered, I think. I was wet, then I was slightly less wet, then I was back in my sweats and my Messina Squids swim team shirt.

I wandered downstairs, paused on the last step, around the corner from the living room.

"You *have to* fire them!" Bee's voice hissed.

"What I *have* to do is take care of your sister." Mom's voice, much calmer. "She needs to see Louisa again today."

"Yes, definitely," Bee replied. "*And* you have to fire Claudia and Donald."

"We've talked about this." They had? "I can't fire people over a romantic dispute, Bee. Especially if it happened at a nonexistent party."

"But, Mom, they're bullying her. They've got the whole camp talking about her. It's the Chris thing all over again."

"Sometimes people talk about you—"

"Preaching to the irate choir, here, Mom."

"—and then they stop. It'll pass. You know that, Hana knows that. Like you said, she's been through this before. Everyone'll get bored by the new session."

"She didn't get out of bed this morning."

"It's a breakup, Bee, that's kind of normal."

"It's *not* normal!"

"I know you're scared, but we'll get Hana in to see Louisa again this afternoon, and we'll talk to her about getting back on the water tomorrow."

Yeah, right.

"Aren't you even worried about what happened last time?"

I bit my fist to keep from screaming. I was causing so many problems. Again.

"Bee! That's enough! I think you know I love Hana, and I'm concerned for her."

They must've moved to a different room, because the conversation morphed into angry muffles. I tiptoed back to my room, pushed in earplugs, climbed into bed, and hoped I would dream of kissing Claudia.

CHAPTER 57

Vanessa

"VANESSA! HAVE YOU DECIDED?" Sophia demanded, as we deposited compost. "Are you Team Claudia or Team Hana?"

"Don't be gross!" I insisted, dumping oatmeal-french-fry-mayo mush onto the pile.

"I'm Team Claudia," she said. "Hana was such a jerk the other day about the party. She totally blew us off."

"But—"

"And if she cheated on Claudia, that's *super* crappy."

"Yeah," Wallace agreed.

Had she? I wanted to ask How did we know that for sure?

Ben's comment had hit me hard. And I hadn't told anyone about that weird conversation I'd overheard on Friday night/Saturday morning. How many people might hate me if I did?

For once, this didn't seem like any of my business. Especially since I was just starting to get a handle on my CIT life. Get up ten minutes earlier than you want to, always keep extra Band-Aids in your pockets, and never let them see you flustered. My seven-year-olds felt a lot more manageable this week, which was good, because

Margo was super out to lunch. Like, more than usual. I felt like I was running our group without her.

I snuck up behind Layla and Ava on the way to campfire. Layla screamed, and Ava turned and hugged me. I'd missed them so much, the stinkers. This was a much better week.

On the way back to our cabins, though, I heard two girls from Connie's group, the eleven-year-olds, talking.

"Can you believe that?" one asked the other.

"At camp?" the other gasped.

"On the *volleyball court*."

"Wow, what a slut."

My mouth dropped open. I turned around and fell back with the little kids, grabbing the hands of the two who were already home-sick. My heart pounded in my ears, I barely heard them singing "There Was a Great Big Moose." I felt my voice echo their verses, while my thoughts were decidedly un-mooselike.

A slut?

Really?

Campers knew about this???

The littles brushed their teeth, which was a massacre, we tucked them in, and Margo sang to them. Then we went out onto the porch, like usual, me with my book, and Margo with her phone. But I couldn't read.

Was it gossiping if you just went straight to the source?

"Margo?" I bit my lip.

"Mmm?" Margo asked, eyes glued to her screen.

"Can I talk to you about something?" I whispered.

"Give me a sec, darlin'. . . ." She sent another text and then looked up and smiled at me. "What's up?" Was I imagining things, or was her smile not reaching the freckles on her cheeks?

"I, umm, I heard a camp rumor."

"Okay, Nessa." Margo laughed. "You need to be a little more specific."

I must've looked stricken, because she gave me a pat on the knee. "Spill, sweetie!"

"I heard this thing about Hana."

Margo sighed as big as the moon. "Oh, that, yeah—don't listen to that. Hana's not a slut, or whatever. *Slut* is actually a not-real word, because women should be allowed to express their sexuality, too."

"Okay, thanks," I said quickly. "But what I need to tell you is that I overheard Bobby and Connie talking on Friday night."

Margo's head tilted.

"About that night?" I said. "They said a lot of things, but they kind of made it seem like . . . like they'd tricked people into thinking it was Hana and some guy on the volleyball court."

"The volleyball court."

"Yeah. They said that you and Bobby had been down there." I winced saying the words. "And I think that maybe John told Claudia it was Hana and someone else? Or something?"

Margo set her phone down. She paused. I held my breath, waiting for her to explain this.

"That's not true," she said, finally. "None of that is true. You must've heard wrong."

"But they said that John liked Claudia." I was determined to get it all out. "And he does, doesn't he? That's what Rachel said that Connie said last summer."

Margo's face went so pale, her freckles disappeared. "I need to go to the bathroom." She stood up and hopped off the porch. Then she turned back. "Just don't . . . don't repeat this, okay? I'll take care of it."

I paused, then nodded.

"Great." She turned back to her phone, her fingers moving like lightning across the screen.

I had done it. I'd told someone. Someone who could do something. But I didn't feel any better.

CHAPTER 58

Ben

I THOUGHT I KNEW what Ilana was feeling. Well, not exactly, because nobody can exactly be in someone else's shoes. But I remembered feeling that stuck, and dark, and hopeless.

That January night that my mom took us all to Camp Dogberry wasn't the first time I'd gone there that year. My mom didn't know this, but I'd run away a few months earlier, Thanksgiving night two years ago. Tim's family came over—they're terrible, even compared to him—and they stressed him out so badly he roared at Ava at the dinner table, and the twins both burst into tears. Ava'd interrupted grace, or something stupid like that. I started to snap back, but my rotten "grandmother" said, *"Can't you just stop?"* Like it was my fault—like I had been the one who'd started this. But my mom caught my eye from across the table, and I knew whatever I did was going to make it worse for her. Head pounding, I'd apologized. The kids made it through dinner silently, and none of us stuck around for dessert.

It was late. I told my mom I'd take my sisters for a drive so they'd fall asleep. All the girls had been car babies, and the hum of the road could still conk them out. I whispered I had my phone with me. She clearly had her hands full with our charming extended Tim family.

I had a secret thought, though. What if I took them and drove away and never came back?

The girls blinked tears as Nessa and I wrestled them into their pj's and coats. I grabbed all our toothbrushes, just in case. I tucked the girls in the back seat of the car, and we pulled out of the driveway. After a couple rounds of camp songs, the twins fell asleep, and twenty minute later, Nessa fitfully drifted off to an audio book. And then I jumped on the highway.

I only stopped once, for gas—paid to fill the tank. A few hours later, we took the Messina exit, followed the brown signs with jaunty white lettering, and let the road slowly give way to dirt and gravel.

Camp Dogberry's parking lot looked strange in the off-season. Empty, no check-in tent. It didn't matter, though. The minute I pulled in, a sense of calm washed over me.

I thought about driving through and up to the main house, but seeing Bee felt like way too much. And though it would be great to see Nik and Andy, I couldn't have explained why we were there without someone getting suspicious, or getting in touch with my mom.

And it's Thanksgiving, duh. They might not even be there.

The parking lot it was, then. The girls were still fast asleep. I left the heat on and braced myself for the cold outside.

The air bit but didn't feel so bad. I jogged over and sat down on the ground, right where the white tent would have stood. Where I checked kids in and out every summer; where I got checked in and out every summer.

What if we just stayed here? Vanessa, Ava, Layla, and I could learn to adapt to the winter camp temperatures. We could grow long white hairs all over our bodies, sturdy paws, thick black noses, slowly transform into polar bears. Maybe my mom could, too, if she ever actually left Tim.

Tim couldn't turn into a polar bear. You knew just looking at him.

The water on my eyeballs got hard and sticky. I blinked. Was it really that cold? I tried to move my fingers; they creaked in protest.

But the block of ice in my chest had started melting. It didn't feel great, but it felt better than before. Despite the sharp air, I could breathe.

Eventually, I stood up and went back to the car. I turned around and drove straight home. Nessa and I carried in the little girls, tucked them in their beds. Tim yelled at me for being gone for so long. Once he finished and stormed off to watch TV, my mom thanked me and kissed me goodnight.

I'd gone to bed that night feeling something more than despair. Hope. Summer was only six months away. Surely we could exist until then.

CHAPTER 59

Bee

THIS WAS THE MOST dysfunctional week of camp, ever. Half our staff wouldn't speak to one another anymore. I had to squash a newsletter poll of "Team Hana or Team Claudia." I kept sending CITs to Monarch or Turtle instead of going myself. Claudia and Donald probably thought I was scared of them, but really, I was scared of my parents. I knew that they would kill me if I blew up.

They already wanted to kill me.

I woke up Wednesday morning: Capture the Flag. The air stuck to my skin. Scorcher in the making. I wrapped my blue bandanna over my braids and slipped out to Big Bat to check on Hana.

I walked in on a confrontation in the living room, my little sister in her sweats, snuggled defensively on the couch. Not dressed, curly hair matted. This was off to a good start.

"I'm leaving," she said, with the force of someone who's repeated themselves again and again.

"Pumpkin," Dad sighed, "I don't even know if Aunt Beth *can* take you for a whole summer."

"And you need to work," Mom reminded her.

"So I'll get a job at a café in Portland," Hana said, flapping her right hand. "None of this is a problem."

"It's a problem for me that you wouldn't be here," Mom said. "I'd need to hire a new instructor—"

"Call the Y."

"You're leaving?" I said.

Everyone turned and looked at me. Hana's normally warm brown eyes looked dusky and cold. I slid onto the couch next to her.

"I can't be here with her," she said softly. "Please tell them to let me go."

I stared up at my parents. They looked helpless. I didn't blame them, really. Hana like this was like . . . parallel-universe Hana. Angry, bitter, always sad.

Still, she was Hana. I smoothed her hair. "I just want you to feel better."

"I can't." Tears started. "Not here."

I hugged my sister and looked past her at my mom, who threw up her hands. I shook my head, just a little.

"Want to play Capture the Flag?" I asked Hana, just in case.

"No."

"Okay. I'll grab you some paper from the art building."

"Don't bother. I threw out all the stars this morning."

I gulped. None of this was good. "Okay. I'll see you later, sweetie." I stood up off the couch, and Mom took my place. Dad followed me to the entryway.

"She dumped out all her water vases too," he said, voice low, eyebrows furrowed together.

My poor dad. I hugged him.

My poor Hana.

CHAPTER 60

Ben

I WOKE UP AT five a.m. Wednesday morning. *Capture. The. Flag.*

I grabbed an orange and got out on the field before anyone else, map and pen in hand. Time to *get ruthless.*

The breezy, blue, warm day didn't feel very ruthless, but instead of clouds, there was *doom for my enemies* hanging in the sky.

Around eight a.m., the counselors shuffled the entire camp onto the field. Claudia and Donald, talking mostly to each other. Bee and Raph arrived in the same manner—no sign of Hana. My heart hurt. No Margo, either. Eventually, Claudia wordlessly helped me take out the two boxes of red and blue bandannas. Thanks so much, sports assistant.

We divided up the camp into colors. I picked all the new counselors. I made sure I got Vanessa this time, and that the twins got split down the middle. Nik came out on the field with her whistle and explained the rules:

- Capture the Flag would last until noon, lunchtime.
- Each side had a flag to hide somewhere in camp.
- Each team had to appoint at least one guard for the flag.

• Each team had a "caught zone" where they would guard the other team's captured players.

• No touching except for tagging, no inappropriate language, and everyone needed to wear closed-toe shoes.

• Nik and Andy would be walking around camp keeping an eye on things, so if anyone needed help, they could find them.

"Finally," Nik said. "Listen to your counselors. Except when their plan isn't a good one—then, I'd advise you to stage a mutiny."

A great cheer went up from the campers, and I smiled for real for the first time all day. It felt good.

I led the blues to our base camp: the garden/compost bin. It smelled, but there was no way to approach without someone seeing you. I would normally turn to Bee as my right hand, but she looked exhausted.

I grabbed Rachel instead, and we passed out the blue bandannas. Then I sat everyone down and laid out the plan. Layla giggled, Jay's face lit up, Nessa whooped, and everyone was generally super enthusiastic. Only Bee eyed me with a little bit of scorn, but I'd known she wouldn't like parts of it. I reminded everyone that, *technically*, trickery was in the rule book for Capture the Flag. She conceded.

I broke it down for the group.

"All right, here's how it's going to go." I laid out a camp map in front of them. It was a brochure, and kind of inaccurate, but I'd scribbled on it with red and blue markers, which got the team very excited.

"Ava is a double agent. Layla swaps out for her and grabs the flag, while you guys create a diversion—a fake base, on the island."

Giggles and gasps broke out. A few campers asked if this was allowed.

"You're on Team Ben now." I pointed at the map. "I run sports. Everything I say is allowed."

That got a big laugh. I broke everyone up into patrol, scout, and special ops groups. Then I assigned counselors and CITs.

"Hey," I whispered to Bee. "Do you just wanna guard?"

"Sure. Thanks."

I assigned the other guard positions to a handful of less adventurous campers. Then I grabbed special ops 1, led by Raph (I really liked that Raph always showed up for Capture the Flag).

"Head to the island, noisily, with a blue T-shirt," I explained. "You'll need to be good actors, though, because you have to pretend you're trying to be sneaky going out there, and you *have to* make sure someone from the red team sees you doing it."

"We got this," Raph assured me. He had football black stripes under his eyes. "Right, y'all?"

"And it's very possible," I continued, "that you'll get put in the caught zone, so you have to be okay with that."

"We're team players," Meredith replied.

"Excellent. Go around the back of the island, to the west end dock," I instructed. "And remember: pretend you're *trying* to be inconspicuous."

"We're the worst spies ever!" Raph clarified. *"Got it!"*

We all put our hands in the middle. "Go BLUE!"

Bee and company set up the base with our actual flag. Rachel, Dave, Vanessa, and Doug went on their scouting patrols. I took special ops 2 to get some cereal, because Layla hadn't eaten breakfast.

"It was too early," she complained. "My stomach hurts when I eat that early."

"I know," I said quickly. I loved the kid, but her voice was screechy and I was worried someone on red would hear. "But we can't have you, our star player, running around on an empty stomach."

I coaxed her into eating with Shane's secret stash of marshmallow cereal.

"So what do I have to do?" she asked, mouth full.

"Now, we wait for intel."

I didn't like the waiting part of the plan. It made me antsy, and then I had time to think. Like about how my enemies in this game were actually my enemies. And about how Bee's eyes seemed permanently lined with tears now.

Luckily, Vanessa's group returned quickly, handed off the info, and it was just as I'd hoped—

Ava had weaseled her way on to the red guard team.

"Let's move out, special ops two."

❦

Ah, classic. Team Red had hidden their flag on the hill behind the art building. The hill was always a great pick. Normally, it would mean it would be impossible to get there without strenuous activity.

My sister and I stayed low, approached the building from the right corner. They didn't have anyone guarding around the side, because the entrance was so narrow; they could tag anyone on our team the second they came through.

But I wasn't sending someone through from our team.

There they were: waiting for us, a flash of red hidden under a pile of leaves under the building's drain spot. Ava'd come through.

"You ready? You remember where to meet?"

"I got it."

I saluted. "Godspeed, shortcake."

Ava put on Layla's glasses, grinned, and went in.

Ten minutes later, red flag in hand, we were running for our lives.

☙

Halfway back to base, off trail, I heard leaves rustling. I knew two things.

"Layla," I whispered, and handed her the flag. "You need to run. Quietly. *Now.*"

Her eyes went wide, and she took off. I ran to the right, making a big effort to crash and stomp through big piles of underbrush. Soon, I was apprehended by a snickering Maddie. Sometimes you have to take one for the team.

She led me down to the waterfront, where they'd set up their caught zone. Waterfront was smart, because you'd have to somehow swim to get in and tag your caught teammates. Pathetic but unsurprising, I was the only one captured there.

"Where's the rest of your team?" I asked the guard, Claudia. Talk about hiding with her head in the sand.

"The island," Claudia said. "And out looking for our flag. We probably have yours by now."

"Thrilling," I said. And it was, but mostly because they'd fallen for the whole thing. We were minutes away from winning, I was sure.

"So the mastermind is caught!" Donald sauntered over. To Claudia, he said, "We got the flag." Then to me: "Didn't think I'd see you here, Rosenthal."

"Well, perhaps I'm still masterminding, *King.*" I stood up.

Claudia stood up too. "Hey, you're not allowed off the dock—"

"We need to talk."

Donald glanced at Claudia, then back at me. Claudia looked at her feet.

Maybe they felt guilty. Maybe I could actually get through to them.

I pulled off my bandanna and raked my fingers through my hair, pushing it back. So sweaty. The water actually looked pretty good right now, and running the length of the dock, jumping in, and swimming away and never returning would solve a lot of my problems.

But Hana was more important.

"Okay, look," I said finally. They both did. "Why haven't either of you actually asked Hana about that night?"

"I saw it," Claudia said simply. Her face was blank.

"I did, too." Donald sighed. "Look, Hana's a great kid"—I saw Claudia flinch—"but she was a real jerk. You can't blame Claudia for dumping her."

"No, I can't!" I said. "You can dump whoever you want. But why are you being such an asshole about it? Why not have a conversation with her?"

"I tried to!" Claudia fired back. "But then I saw her phone." She glanced at Donald, who looked at the ground. "She was using me, okay? She probably just wanted to make Christopher jealous. Or maybe I was, like, that girl fling everyone has, I don't know."

"Something's screwy here." I gestured at the general everything. "You know Hana's not the kind of person who would do this."

"I *thought* I knew her!" Claudia said.

"It was really bad," Donald said. "They were hooking up right out in the open."

"Fine." I threw my hands down. "Fine, but even if you think she did this, what excuse do you have for telling people about it? Why make everyone hate her?"

"Back off." Donald stepped forward, in front of Claudia. "Ben, buddy," he said, weirdly slowly. "Don't you think your judgment is kind of clouded on this one?"

I crossed my arms. "Meaning?"

He looked back at Claudia, then at me again. "Did Bee put you up to this?"

I was so taken aback, I couldn't reply. Donald sighed and nodded, taking this as an admission, which I guess it kind of was. But this wasn't *just* because of Bee.

"Seriously, Ben?" Donald rolled his eyes. "You spend all this time harping on people for 'creating drama' when they like someone, and it happens to you, and you do the same thing?"

"I'm not being dramatic."

"Then how do you explain this: you taking her side, just because you like her?" he asked. "You didn't even check to see if Claudia was okay on Friday. What happened to friends coming first?"

I looked at Claudia. She met my eyes briefly, then stared at her shoes.

Too many ideas flooded my head. Was that what I was doing? What was going on right now? I closed my eyes, and I immediately saw Hana's face, tears running down her cheeks. I saw her helping my sisters learn to swim, holding the nervous kids in her lap during campfire. This wasn't about Bee. Or it was, because she was right.

It had only been an instant, but it was clear now. I opened my eyes to Donald's.

I stared at him, and replied: "Bee *is* my friend."

"Are you serious?! After she totally screwed you up last summer?" Donald fumed. "Don't pretend she didn't!"

"I—"

"Besides," Donald fumed, "she didn't even *say* any of that stuff. We just—"

A cheer went up from somewhere over by Dam, then the victory horn. My team had done it. These two had lost. They were going to keep losing. Just then, one of our little windjammer sailboats pulled around the corner, Bee at the bow, my knight in shining armor.

"I think that's my cue." I backed up, pointing up toward my base. The look of disbelief on both of their faces, in the beautiful sunlight, was just completely priceless. I wished I had a camera so I could take a picture and commission Donald to make a mosaic of it later.

At the end of the dock, Bee held out a hand and steadied me onto the boat. Immediately, I felt nauseous, but I didn't really care.

"Ready to sail in to victory?" She smiled.

"In every way possible." I turned back, briefly, and called out: "You guys are being fucking douchebags! We're done! Got it?"

"Fuck you, Ben!" Donald called back.

On that melodious note, Bee sailed us around the beach, then into the old west dock. And I only puked once in the whole five minutes.

Victory.

CHAPTER 61

John

THE GOOD NEWS WAS, if you went to enough pointless, enormous events, you recognized them for what they were: opportunities. You could either make a scene and piss everyone off, *or* you could wait an hour and slip away, without anyone noticing.

CHAPTER 62

Bee

"I LOVE WINNING." Raph sighed happily. "It just makes me feel warm and fuzzy all over. It's the opposite of losing. Losing's the worst."

"That's an excellent example to set." I snorted. We'd taken our Jell-O and whipped cream desserts—and snuck away to the parking lot to sit under the white tent.

Not particularly comfortable, but outside, away from everyone else. Whenever I spent time in the dining hall this week, I'd come out reeling and internally swearing. Especially the last two days, without Hana.

"Hey, aren't we always telling kids to be themselves?" Raph quipped, smiling with a spoon between his teeth. "I'm just insanely competitive."

"Thank goodness you're not a gym teacher."

"Honey, improv *is* gym. Or at least, I sweat so much during class that it would be weird if it wasn't."

I snorted with laughter this time. "All right, all right. You really kicked butt today. You're the whole reason we won, and winning's the best."

"I wasn't fishing for compliments, but I'm not mad I caught some."

"Hey, Bee! I was looking for you."

I looked up. In the after-dinner Jell-O twilight stood the shadowy, stocky figure of Ben.

"Hey, you found me," I said, and smiled.

"That's my cue to exit," said Raph, standing up.

"Pursued by bears?" I asked.

Ben shuddered. I'd almost forgotten about his history with bears.

"I sure hope so!" Raph toasted at us with his Jell-O. "See you in the morning, Queen Bee." As he walked past Ben, he turned to wiggle his eyebrows at me. I tried not to make a face, but I think I failed, because Ben turned to look—by then, Raph was halfway to his car.

"Can I sit?" Ben asked.

I looked dubiously at the dirt patch beside me. "If you really want to," I said. "We could also go somewhere else?"

"Nah." Ben dropped down next to me. Raph's car started. The light blinded me for a moment. "This is one of my favorite spots at camp."

I laughed. "The dirt parking lot?"

"Yep." Ben looked across the lot, wistfully, as Raph's car pulled out, like we were standing on a cliff beholding the roaring ocean. "I love it here. Under this tent."

"You're kind of weird."

"You kind of like it."

"I thought we weren't accusing me of liking you anymore?" I fired back, straining my voice to sound lighter by the end of the sentence. Ha-ha-ha, just kidding, just kidding.

"But I've already said *I like you* now," Ben reasoned. "Isn't it official?"

I thought for a moment. "Well, I think I'd need it in writing." Then I had an idea: "Hey, can I see your phone?"

He handed it to me. I opened a text message, sent it off, and handed it back. He checked out the message, and then laughed and held out his hand. I gave him my phone. He typed, sent, handed it back.

Done. Official.

"So we're good?"

"We're good." I nodded, taking another spoonful of Jell-O.

"But for the record, again, you're right." Ben turned to me, his face closer to mine, looking me in the eyes. The light from our one parking lot lamp bounced back and forth between us. "I'm sorry. I won't accuse you at all, I promise. I like *you*, and I hope you like me, even if I'm weird."

I'd asked for honesty, I'd gotten honesty, and I felt like I might pee myself from it.

"So," he continued. "During Capture the Flag today, I had a few moments alone with the red team captains."

Donald and Claudia. They'd been sore losers. Aching losers. Throbbing losers. I'd have found the whole thing hysterical if it hadn't been so surreal, if Hana had been there laughing with me.

"Yeah, I think I barged in on that." I smiled.

"That was *the best*." He smiled, then sighed, ran a hand down his face. "It was a special conversation. I tried to talk it through with them, and ask them why they didn't just talk to Hana. And why they were telling everyone about it."

"And?"

"And they said a bunch of bullshit. Like that they hadn't told everyone, and they really . . . I don't know. They've cracked. They think they're right, and they're being dicks about it."

"Couldn't agree more," I said, wishing with every bone in my body we weren't talking about our friends right now.

"Yeah." Ben sighed again. "So you know how that ended. I told them they were being douchebags and that I was done with them."

"It was colorful." I nodded. "And very definitive."

He barely heard me. "I just don't get it. I tried to talk to them reasonably, and they just wanted to trash Hana. Something's wrong with them."

My calm, listening demeanor evaporated instantly. The Jell-O in my stomach turned into liquid fire. *Trash Hana.* Those losers. Those complete and absolute fuckers. I *would* tear out their hearts and eat them in the dining hall. I would—

"Hey." A hand rested on my knee. My bare knee. "I'm sorry, I didn't mean to upset you. I just want you to know I'm on your side, here, Bee."

My eyes followed his hand up to his wrist, his elbow, his T-shirt line, his neck, his face. His eyes.

"Our side," I corrected. "Hana's side."

"Hana's side," he said. "How is she?"

My nose immediately wrinkled in an effort not to sob. "Bad," I said, my throat choking. "She's really bad."

"Oh no."

"Yes." I preemptively wiped under my eyes. "It seems like this Claudia thing brought back her depression full force."

"I'm so sorry."

"She wants to leave camp and go stay with my aunt in Portland, but my parents don't love that idea."

"Why not?"

"They want her to stick it out." I bit my lip. "And they want to be able to keep track of where Hana's at."

"That kind of makes sense?"

"But the real solution is super clear to me," I said. "Hana shouldn't go, Claudia and Donald should."

Ben didn't hesitate this time. "I wish they would."

"She's sinking, Ben." I looked at him again. "She's sinking, and I don't know what to do—"

Without warning, for either of us, I ducked my head onto his shoulder. His arm went around me. I scrunched my face up really tight, trying to squeeze out tears and keep them in all at once. Ben smelled strangely refreshing and tropical.

"It'll be okay," he whispered, his voice touching my ear, sending shivers down my spine. "I promise, it'll be okay. She'll be okay."

I pulled my head up. A few stray tears fell from my eyes, but I didn't care—I pushed my lips into his. Then away, then back again. For a few moments, I only felt the kissing, the warm and fuzzies racing through all parts of me. This was better than winning.

We broke for air, and the pause became a halt. Ben's hands grasped my face, my hand lay on his stomach. We breathed like that, staring at each other, for maybe a whole minute.

I got up first, fighting the urge to rip his clothes off. Ugh. How could I be feeling so many things at once?

We walked back to the head of the entrance trail. Our hands found each other, intertwined. We hesitated at the opening.

"Maybe there's some way you can show her?" Ben said suddenly.

"What?"

"Maybe there's a way to show Hana you don't want her to go," he said.

"Like what?"

"I don't know. There must be something."

I closed my eyes, took a deep breath, and tried to imagine the big gesture. What would get through to Hana. How could I make her see?

The frogs peeped. The stars danced.

And an idea came to me.

WHAT ELSE HAPPENED

Bee

I KISSED BEN FOR the first time two years ago.

One night in January, Ben's mom brought him and his sisters over. It was after dinner, I remember, because it wasn't a normal time to have people over. That was confusing. There was something hushed about the whole thing, too.

Knowing what I know now, Mom was probably giving Colleen advice or help. Mom had gotten out of a bad relationship a long time ago that she sometimes talked about. Maybe Ben's mom was thinking about leaving his stepdad then.

So yeah, Maine, January, freezing, always snowing. Suddenly, Mom told us the Rosenthals were coming over. I remember running upstairs and changing into my favorite shirt at the time—my long-sleeved Ethiopian pro soccer shirt, striped green and yellow with red trim. I don't know why I thought wearing my favorite shirt was important.

They'd shown up a few minutes later. Colleen and Ben carried in the twins, both asleep in their big girl car seats. Nessa insisted we play a board game, so Hana and I set up Monopoly in the living room, while our parents "had coffee" in the kitchen. Ben kept getting up to check on the twins. I remember thinking it was so weird to see him in winter clothes—plaid flannel bottoms and this dorky argyle sweater.

All through the night I tried not to look at him. Eventually, Nessa ran out of steam, and Dad asked us to tuck her into Hana's bed. I remember exchanging an awkward glance with Ben, like we were thinking the same thing:

Were they really not going home yet?

After we settled Nessa, Hana said she was ready for bed, too, and went to sleep in my room. Ben and I wandered into the kitchen. Our parents were huddled around our small wooden kitchen table, heads bent forward. I got one brief look at Colleen's face, and I turned around and pushed Ben back with me, before he could see.

But my mom saw us and brightly asked if Ben and I would go get firewood.

Phew. Something to do.

We both grunted a yes, bundled up, and went out into the snow, neither of us saying a word. Which was a miracle in retrospect, because my hat was covered in pom-poms, and his pointy blue hat made him look an elf.

The air didn't nip—it *bit* at our cheeks. We stomped a trail through the crunchy snow, around the side of the house, grabbed a few logs, and shuffled back to the front door and set them down. We'd done our task, but for some reason, it seemed like we weren't going inside right away.

We looked at each other. Ben's cheeks were bright red, his nose had started to run. When looking at each other got too awkward, I glanced up.

There's nothing more beautiful than a Maine sky at night. You can see every single star, big or small, bright or fading. I loved it, and Ben was looking at it like he loved it too. For the first time that night, I let myself feel excited he was here, and that I got to see him in the middle of winter, like magic. I felt my heart rise up, up into the starry black sky. It floated up there, gently bouncing between the lights.

I glanced over at him; he was already looking at me. His kind, twinkly eyes, strands of floppy brown hair swooshed over his forehead, squished under his elf hat.

Suddenly, we were a foot apart. I pursed my lips. Kissing, right?

He reached out a hand, grabbed mine.

I fell closer, and our lips met. One second, one kiss: floating, starry.

When we drew back, I looked at him and quickly said, "Um, this never happened, okay?"

CHAPTER 63

Bee

I SAT WITH RACHEL and Ellie at evening campfire, with dozing littles in our laps. Apparently, Margo had been in Black Bear for a headache and was now asleep.

I tried not to enjoy seeing Ben across the flames too much.

Later, past bedtime, on my way back from another visit to the parking lot, I felt someone hovering behind me on the trail.

"Hey!" I called softly. "Do you need a buddy?"

Claudia stepped forward, out of the shadows.

"Ugh, not you," I said. "You've already got one." I turned around and started to march toward my cabin.

"Wait!" Claudia called out.

"I'll pass!" I called back.

"No, seriously, Bee—"

She caught up with me, face-to-face. I always forgot Claudia was taller than me. The bags under her eyes were as dark as squished blueberries. She wore boxer shorts and a black T-shirt. I crossed my arms over my chest.

"I don't want to talk to you," I said.

"Same," Claudia said quickly.

"Great." I went to turn around—

"But I want to know how Hana's doing?"

I turned back. Her face looked hopeful, in the way Claudia's face can. Not quite as serious, eyebrows slightly arched instead of a terrifying straight line across. What did Hana see in this asshole?

"Maybe you want to know that," I said slowly. "But you don't *get* to."

Her lips quivered ever so slightly. "I know, but . . . I heard she's leaving."

Ha! The Dogberry rumor mill. Hana hadn't shown up to work in three days, so I guessed that made sense. What did this girl want me to do, though? Tell her the location of the person she'd beaten up on? How dare she?

"Yeah, she's gone." I spat it out. "She left, because *you* made her life here miserable. You made up a shitty rumor, and she fell apart, and now she's gone. Are you happy?" The lie came out fast, and I didn't care that it wasn't all true. It was only not true *yet*.

"I—"

"You gigantic bully," I said, stabbing a finger at her. She winced and stepped back. "Do you get off on making other people feel bad?"

"Bully?" she sputtered. "I know all about bullying, believe me. The kids at my school—"

"Boo-hoo," I snapped. "So school's rough sometimes. You think it wasn't for me?"

"Umm, no, but—"

"So shut up!" I heard my voice getting too loud. "If you take it out on other people, you're just like them."

"That's not what I'm doing!" Claudia's voice almost matched mine. "Your sister cheated on me, Bee!"

I shook my head. "Bullshit. I hope all of this was worth it. And I hope you don't miss her. Because now she's gone, and she's going to miss the entire summer at camp, our last summer before I leave. So good on you for taking that away from her." I was done. I turned around and stomped away. When I got to my cabin, I glanced back—Claudia was sitting on the side of the trail, her face buried in her hands.

Fuck you, I thought.

And then I quietly burst into tears.

I zagged and went home to Big Bat. Rachel was in my cabin for the night, she could handle it.

CHAPTER 64

Hana

WAKING UP FROM MY dream—

I'm in her arms.

I'm touching her.

And then I'm drowning, gasping for air, choking on sharp gulps of water, the sunlight tries to reach me, but I'm already too deep—

My bed. The sheets, wrinkled and damp from sweat. It took me moments to understand where I was, who I was, why I was here.

"What can you do to help yourself feel better, Hana?" Louisa had asked me earlier, in our session.

"I can sleep," I'd said. "And pretend this never happened."

"What about work?" Louisa pressed. "You love swimming, teaching."

"It's a little hard to swim when your body feels like lead," I explained patiently.

It hadn't been the worst session. But I hadn't felt a whole lot better leaving it. She must've talked to my parents, because she didn't want me to leave camp, either. Why didn't they get it was killing me to stay?

I have to go. Now, I realized. *I can't wait. If I see her one more time, I'll drown.*

I had never been so miserable before. Well, in months. Being this miserable was impossible.

It was late. Really late. No one to keep tabs on me.

I changed into jeans and a sweatshirt and sneakers. I don't need to visit Aunt Beth, I thought. I can go somewhere else.

Christopher. Christopher wouldn't turn me away, if I showed up at his house. Christopher understands miserable. He would let me crash. Or we'd drive somewhere. And maybe he'd kiss me. . . .

My hands grabbed the car keys. I closed the front door quietly behind me.

It felt like ten miles to get to the parking lot, but I finally reached the blue hatchback. Dad's new car. I jumped in the passenger's seat, before realizing I was on the wrong side.

I settled behind the wheel, moving the seat up a few inches so my foot could safely reach the pedals. I was only just learning to drive, but I didn't intend to get pulled over. And if I did, what was the worst that would happen? I'd get arrested? The thought made me laugh inside, just a little.

I rotated the key carefully, feeling the engine wake up. I realized I needed to plug my phone in—I knew how to get to Christopher's, but I'd never driven there myself before. I flipped on the overhead lights and rummaged around for the phone charger in the glove compartment, but it wasn't there. I turned to check the back.

There, on the seat, was a pile of gear.

At first I sighed, thinking I would need to sneakily drop this off back at camp before I could go, in case they needed it tomorrow.

But then I saw whose gear it was: mine.

My old purple backpack with the daisies on it, monogrammed with my initials. The orange two-person tent my parents got us when we were little so Bee and I could camp out together. My mess kit and mini cooler, with my name written in all caps in black Sharpie: *HANA*.

I picked up the backpack and plunked it in the space between the front seats. Inside were a change of clothes, a pair of pajamas, a bathing suit, bug spray, sunscreen, a small thing of dry shampoo, and a toothbrush kit, all the kind we sell in the camp store. There was even a plastic bag with scissors and origami paper.

Only one person could've put this backpack together.

Heart pounding, I realized who it was.

Slowly, I unzipped the tiny top pocket, the one that didn't really fit anything. Except a small piece of paper, with a message, written in sloppy Magic Marker:

Hana. I love you. Please don't go. ♥

Under the overhead car lights, I reread the note four times, then folded it up and held it in my lap.

I could go. I could put the car in reverse, and back up, and follow the dirt road to the highway. I could go to Christopher's, where he'd probably make out with me. Or I could pull over on the highway instead, and sit in the dirty highway grass, and cry and cry and cry, and when I was soaked with tears, I could go find a river and wash it off.

But I loved Camp Dogberry. In a way, this note was from this place too.

But it was mostly from Bee.

I turned off the car. My feet found their way—down the dirt trail, up the front porch steps, up the stairs.

Bee was in her bedroom, waiting up, reading. She smiled when I came in.

"Hey, baby."

I crawled up into the bed, in between her and the window. I fell asleep with my back pressed against her.

CHAPTER 65

Vanessa

THURSDAY. WE'D ALMOST MADE it through another week. I was actually pretty sad to see this group go home. My silly, cranky peanuts.

They had even sort of distracted me from the terrible secret that had been taking over my brain, and from that terrible conversation with Margo. And now she was sick and MIA?

Sophia and I had our break at the same time Thursday morning, when we dropped the kids off at swim, right after breakfast. I helped them use the buddy board (most of them got it by now), moved their towels far enough away from the shoreline, and waved good-bye.

"Come hang out with me in Luna!" Sophia grabbed my arm. She'd been kind of obsessed with hanging out in the "counselor room" ever since Fourth of July. I didn't love how hot it got up there, but there were some video games, sooo . . .

As we walked away, I looked back one more time. No Hana, again. Just Judy with the sub instructor. I felt the creeping secret again. I turned and followed Sophia.

Luna's loft was empty. We fell back onto the couches, took out the old Nintendo console.

I'm usually awesome at the racing games. Ben made me learn

when I was little so he'd have competition at home. But the third time I came in last, Sophia paused the game.

"Okay." She shifted on the couch, bouncing to face me. She wore lime green today. "*What* is wrong with you?"

"What do you mean?"

"Why have you been weird all week?" she said. "You won't be on Team Claudia with us, you mope around, you spend all your free time with your campers—you're hardly taking breaks unless I make you!"

"I'm trying to get hired next year," I reminded her.

"It's not just that, though," Sophia insisted. "You're more lethargic than Gustavo."

"Can you not compare me to the camp turtle?" I asked. "And hey, Doc gave him some medicine. I think he's doing a lot better."

"Fine. So you're *more* lethargic than Gustavo!"

She waited for me to laugh. I managed a weak smile.

"Tell me what's wrong."

I bit my lip. "I can't?"

She grabbed my arm. "Now you're freaking me out, Nessa! You have to tell me!"

"I'm not freaking you out!" I complained. "You've done that to yourself!"

"Fine! So help me and tell me! What's the worst that could happen?"

You'll tell everyone, I said to myself. Then I realized: maybe that wasn't such a bad thing? But Margo might hate me forever. I liked *hearing* rumors. I didn't *start* them . . . but if I didn't tell someone, would that creeping sensation ever go away? It would feel so good to be done with it. . . .

"Hey." Wallace appeared over the railing, at the top of the stairs. "So I heard something, at Capture the Flag."

Sophia and I looked at each other. Wallace sat down and methodically explained the conversation he'd heard between Ben and Claudia and Donald. When he'd finished, my head was stuffed in a beanbag chair again.

"Okay," I groaned into the fabric, then sat up. "My turn."

And then I spilled my guts. I watched Sophia's jaw drop farther and farther. I almost stopped to laugh, but it felt so good to tell her, both of them. When I finished with Margo's reaction, she smacked her forehead.

"Nessa, why would you tell Margo?"

"I don't know!" I said. "It was about her?"

"She's obviously in the middle of this." Sophia shook her head. "You know who you need to tell."

"My brother."

"Yup. We've got lunch plans."

CHAPTER 66

Bee

HANA DIDN'T GO TO work on Thursday. But she didn't insist on leaving, either, so that was a win. Meanwhile, both my parents were pissed at me.

"Do you know anything about this?" Mom shook her phone in my direction.

"Yes, I can show you how to use a smartphone," I replied calmly. "But honestly, I'd ask Hana before me."

"Nooo." Mom shook the phone again. "I got a *call* from Senator King last night. John's back in New York City. As in, not at camp."

"Why would I know anything about that?"

Mom raised her brow at me. That brow, tho.

I held up my hands. "I seriously have no idea, Mom. Is someone covering for him?"

"Doug," she huffed. Then she grumbled something about camp drama, like she had any idea. She was living in a blissful bubble.

Hana left for therapy again around lunchtime. Which ended up working out well, because lunchtime, oh lunchtime, imploded in a way I'd never thought possible of lunch.

"Bee?" Ben approached my table, mid-conversation with Kamile and a few older campers.

"Ben?" I asked dramatically. The girls giggled. Ben turned red, which was satisfying.

"Can I talk to you?" he asked. I nodded, ignoring my table's escalating giggles.

He led me down the center of Dam, past all the tables. I felt Claudia and Donald watching us.

"Where are we—"

There, at the flagpole, stood Sophia, Vanessa, and Wallace, shifting and whispering to one another.

"What's going on? Do we need to get my mom?" I whispered on our way over to them.

"Not just yet," Ben said. "Hear this first."

ॐ

"Hey. How's your headache?"

Margo looked up. She was sitting on the little bench she'd put in the goat pen. Her phone sat next to her. The four kids crowded around her knees.

"Hey, Bee," she said. The goats turned and stared at me with their weird eyes. I eased into the pen, reached into the bucket, and scattered a handful of feed to clear a path to Margo.

I sat down on the bench next to her. "We need to talk."

"Are you breaking up with me?" she joked. But she wouldn't meet my eyes. It was only when I put my hand on her hand on the bench that she looked up at me.

"Never," I said. "But I do need to ask you something—have you been hooking up with Bobby this summer?"

Tears formed in her perfect twinkly eyes. "Bee, I promise, I didn't know."

"At the volleyball court?"

She nodded. "Bobby and I have been meeting up there."

"And so . . ."

"And I think Donald and Claudia must've seen us."

"Why didn't you say anything?"

"I didn't know what they were talking about that night!" she cried. "I thought they were talking about Christopher. And then I thought they meant that Hana had been hooking up with him at the volleyball court, too."

I raised my eyebrows.

Margo blushed. "Okay, but Hana *was* still texting him," she protested. "And with how things went last fall, I thought it might be a possibility. . . ."

Mushroom Fairy tried to eat the end of my shirt. I brushed him away.

"I only found out the other night what had actually happened, for sure," Margo admitted. "Vanessa told me that John had set me up, and Bobby had been in on it."

"Vanessa told Ben, who told me."

"Makes sense." Margo shrugged. "I knew she probably would. I just freaked out. I couldn't believe that I'd . . . That Hana had stopped coming to work . . . That this was all my fault."

"Not all your fault," I said quickly.

"Hugely my fault." Margo sniffed. "If I had been honest and

told you. Or if I'd been less pathetic, and just gotten over Max, or Donald . . ."

"Donald?" I gaped.

"Oh my God, you prude." Margo rolled her eyes. "Yes, I like Donald. And he asked *you* out."

"But he didn't really—"

"Darlin', you need to stop pretending people don't feel things." Margo stood up. "Camp is complicated, and we all feel stuff about it. Including you. That's part of why we like camp."

I crossed my arms and stared at the goat poop. Maybe she was right.

"But I *do* have an idea," she continued. "About a way we could fix this."

"That seems impossible." I sighed. "We're too far into it."

"It's only second session." She smiled. "Summer's only just started."

CHAPTER 67

Bee

I TOLD HANA ABOUT the misunderstanding, and about Margo's idea. Her whole face lit up for the first time in a week. After a quick conference with Raph, Margo released the news the next morning.

Kangaroo Court that evening, after camper pickup. Counselor and CIT–only edition.

Thus, camper pickup buzzed with tension. Yes, yes, here, take your child, right now, please. They had a good time, but we have a ton of shit to sort out.

Raph, Margo, and I walked over to Luna together, conferring on the stage directions.

Luna felt especially packed with all the adult-size people. Everyone was murmuring, and the crowd's eyes widened when I walked in.

No Bobby in sight. Connie sat at the front of the room with Ellie and Rachel.

At first, I didn't see Donald and Claudia, but Ben pointed out Claudia in one corner, and Donald in another, no longer united in their assholery. I nodded at Ben, walked to the back of the room, opened a window, and then sat down at the defense table. Ben sat down next to me, and Raph took his place front and center.

"Welcome to another round of Kangaroo Court," he announced. The room hushed. "Today, I present to you a personal case. We won't be needing a jury, no offense."

Ben called out: "Also, we're gonna have a dance party afterward."

A few tentative giggles from the crowd. "Yes, that too," Raph agreed. "Dance party in the dining hall after we're done here." He banged the gavel before continuing. "No doubt you have all heard rumors," Raph said, raising his voice slightly higher than the whispering, and they were quiet once more. "That our beloved Hana viciously betrayed Claudia." Audible gasps. Were we really going to address that *here*? "Bee, please present the rest of this case."

You bet we were. I tried to see Claudia's face in the back, but it was hidden in shadow.

I stood. "I don't know how many of you believed this absolute and total falsehood, but let me set the record straight: my sister did no such thing. She did not deserve your glares or gossip, and she left, humiliated, determined to spend the summer somewhere other than Camp Dogberry, for the first time *in ten years!*"

My crowd delivered a reaction with an appropriate amount of terror and excitement. I turned to look at Ben, whose face clearly said to me: Oh, Bee, *come on.*

Okay, okay.

"All right, so I want to clear the air here for Hana. This week—"

"Wait, Bee!" Margo stood up.

"Oh right, your turn."

Margo marched to the front of the room and stood where the witness usually stands.

Raph smiled and gestured at her. "Ms. Margo, you have the floor."

"Thank you." Margo nodded back. Her purple hair flew out in

all directions. She glanced around the room until her eyes landed on me. I smiled at her, and she lifted her chin.

"I need to apologize," she said. "For what's happened here. Donald and Claudia made this assumption because they saw two people on the volleyball court . . . together."

The room murmured.

"I know you've all heard about that," Margo said, raising her hands up. "But what you didn't know was that was Bobby and me."

Gasps. But I couldn't take my eyes off Claudia, who flinched so hard it looked like she'd been punched.

"I didn't realize what had happened until it felt too late to tell the truth," she explained. Raph nodded encouragingly, Santa beard bobbing. "But Vanessa did, and she convinced me to do the right thing."

All eyes turned to Vanessa, whose cheeks flushed pink. She gave a small wave.

"And here's the thing: this was just an *enormous* waste of time!" Margo smiled, a little unconvincingly, but the room felt lighter when she did. "And really, the problem is: people need to stop making out at the volleyball court. It's not camp appropriate."

Everyone laughed, even Donald.

"I highly recommend any romantic endeavors happening in a less public spot." Margo shrugged, finishing the last line of her statement. "And I'm sorry for any part I played in this."

The audience murmured in what sounded like disapproval. But at the exact right moment—

"I forgive you!" Hana's beaming face appeared in the open window.

"She's aliiiiiive!" Margo shouted.

All the counselors burst out laughing and started shouting. Hana ran around the front, and walked through the door to an enormous cheer. Everyone crowded around her, hugging her, yelling their apologies. She hugged everyone and smiled. The laughter in the room sounded relieved, and my heart panged.

Hana pushed forward to me and slid under my arm, and the audience began to clap, but then another person took the stage, one who was definitely not included in my carefully planned script. Bobby had jumped up toward the front of the room, over by Raph.

"Hey, so, umm . . ." The happy action immediately paused. When did he get here? "Yeah." He sighed. "I need to come clean. John was really into Claudia—" He gestured at Claudia, who looked like she might dissolve instantly into bug juice. "And he thought they were gonna, um, go out. So he got really upset when he heard about her and Hana, and we planned this thing, and then things got out of hand. . . . I'm sorry, Margo."

The whole room went silent. I quickly looked at Ben, then Margo, who looked like she might stab Bobby with an improv'd knife. I wouldn't have blamed her at all.

"And to be fair"—he turned to Claudia and Donald—"*we* were the ones who helped spread all that Team Claudia stuff. I'm sorry about that, too."

"You're fired," I said firmly. I totally didn't have the authority to do that, but in that moment, it didn't matter to me at all. I was sure what he'd done crossed professional lines.

Bobby shrugged. "Yeah, that makes sense." And he hightailed it out of the room. Nobody had any idea what to make of all of this, so I went into teacher mode.

"Another lesson needs to be learned here—we need to be careful with gossip at this camp."

I was met with dubious stares.

"Look at where these rumors got us!" I gestured at Hana. "It's one thing to buzz for fun, another to believe everything we hear and pass it along as if it's truth."

The room was absolutely silent, but then Connie raised a fist in the air. "Yeah!"

"Hear, hear!" called out Raph, banging his gavel. The crowd began to disperse, in a giant, rumbling cloud of excitement. "Dance party in Dam!" Raph shouted over everyone, and began leading the staff out the door, still wearing his puffy white beard. He turned and winked at me. Thank goodness for Raph.

Hana turned to give me a full-on hug. I was so happy to have her back from the edge that I almost starting crying right there. Then I saw someone approach from the corner of my eye. It was Connie, with Donald and Claudia hovering behind. I nudged Hana and she released me.

"I'm sorry," Connie said. "I knew what John was doing, and I didn't stop him." Her eyes were watery, too. She looked genuinely ashamed.

"That's okay," Hana said. "We all get confused sometimes." My benevolent sister pulled her in for a hug.

"But, um . . ." Connie glanced between us nervously. "Do you know where John is? I haven't seen him."

"John's left camp," Donald cut in, his voice flat. "My dad's gonna be so pleased."

Connie smiled tightly. "Thanks. Good to know." She turned and caught up with Rachel and Ellie on her way out. Donald, after shooting Ben and me a rueful, apologetic glance, followed.

But Claudia stayed, eyes locked on one person.

CHAPTER 68

Hana

CLAUDIA GLOWED FAINTLY, LIKE the sorriest star in the sky. She walked toward me, past Bee and Margo, as if right out of a dream. I walked toward her, and we met in the middle of the room.

"I'm sorry," she whispered. "I can't believe I thought—"

"It's okay. You were tricked," I said. "This whole thing was unreal."

Tears were falling on the floor, pattering quickly, like rain.

She took my face in her hands. "I'm so sorry. I'm so, so, sorry."

"I'm sorry, too." I gently reached out for her waist. "I'm sorry that I texted Christopher back, and that I didn't tell you." When I said this, her gaze never faltered. "I wasn't hooking up with him," I explained, my voice low. "He just messaged me a couple times, and I messaged him back . . . and then realized I needed to shut it down. I promise, I'm done with him."

It's you forever and forever.

"I believe you," she said, so seriously I almost laughed, but I didn't. "I shouldn't have assumed. I was just afraid, I just thought—I thought you didn't love me like I love you."

I blinked, then smiled. "I think I love you exactly like that."

CHAPTER 69

Ben

CLAUDIA RAN OFF AS soon as the group got to Dam. She made Hana wait outside on the porch while she sprinted to her cabin and inside the dining hall. About fifteen awkward minutes later, Hana was allowed to enter.

Strung in the entryway, across rows and rows of garlands, were a million little paper stars.

"I got them out of the compost," Claudia explained. "The less gross ones, anyway. I was going to apologize, but then you left, and now . . . Here." She gestured, spastically, romantically, above her head. "I'm sorry."

Hana cried, and they kissed. It was pretty freakin' cute.

And then the dance party finally started. Raph had dimmed the lights, moved the table, and happily DJed from the kitchen counter.

It felt like a fog had finally lifted from camp. Nessa talked and laughed with her friends. Rachel, Ellie, Connie, Jen, and Margo led the Macarena and Electric Slide. Maybe the drama had just exploded early in the summer, and we'd be done now!

One could only fucking hope.

Eventually, a slow song came on. Couples immediately formed, pulling each other out on the floor. Bee and I automatically didn't look at each other. No matter how much I wanted to sweep her into the music, I wanted her to be comfortable. And she clearly wasn't.

I offered her a baby carrot instead. She smiled, like she knew the carrot was really a dance.

Suddenly, a shout from our left startled me.

"Ben, Bee!" Donald stepped forward. "Aren't you two going to dance?"

Suddenly, we'd attracted our entire group's attention. Even Hana and Claudia wandered over.

"Oh yeah," Margo chimed in. "I think they really should."

"What?!" Bee shouted, looking like a deer in headlights again.

Everyone burst out laughing. I leaned over and whispered, "Umm, maybe they know?"

"They can't know anything—we have nothing to tell them!" she hissed back.

Maybe before that would've hurt, but I knew Bee now in a way I didn't before. I squeezed her hand again. "Bee—"

"Okay, listen up." Donald laughed. "It's time for us to reveal our plot."

"Yes!" Margo squealed. "It's the best thing we've done all summer."

"By far." Claudia rolled her eyes. Hana kissed her cheek.

"What?" Bee demanded.

"Cupid Donald's plan," Margo explained. "Hana and I—"

"And Claudia and I—"

"Set you two up!" Margo finished proudly. "We tricked you into liking each other!"

I thought back to what had started this—the conversation in Dam, Claudia and Donald saying she liked me. It all dawned on me at once.

They must've have seen that on my face, because everyone burst out laughing.

Bee looked at me, in a mix of emotions I'd never quite seen on her before. She was half laughing, watching everyone shout, half crying, for, like, four thousand reasons, and one part of her looked at me in the way I wished for every second I was awake, and in every dream I had.

Bee

Did everyone seriously know? Was this entire camp shipping us the whole time?

My knees shook forcefully, knocking and rubbing together under the table. I looked at Ben—he seemed okay, smiling, laughing at their reactions. Why couldn't I be so relaxed?

And yeah, I was happy we'd all united again, in the name of humiliating me. I felt anger bubble up inside me, and then the truth along with it—

"You didn't trick us," I said, my voice cutting like the adult scissors in the art building. "We're—we're not—"

"Before you say anything," Ben said, "can I see your phone?"

What? But I pulled it out of my pocket and handed it to him.

"Ahh, yes, here it is. Here's mine." He handed it back to me. "Open up the texts from me."

I did and immediately burst out laughing.

> Hey, girl. I like you so much. I'm actually in love with you. I worship the ground you walk on. I think you're funny and fiery and gorgeous and ambitious. Please go to college prom with me

Ben showed me the text on his phone that I'd apparently written.

> Hey, I like you so much Ben. Really, I love you. You're super hot, and hilarious, and you're premed, which is devastatingly attractive, and I think it's really sexy that you sleep in late

"In writing, remember?" Ben said gently. My heart warbled, and then sang out long, clear notes.

And then we both cracked up, but nobody knew what we were cracking up about. When I finally recovered, I replied to their amused stares.

"Fine, fine," I said. "You didn't trick us, because Ben and I have liked each other for *years*."

That sent up a big cheer from all of our friends.

Including Ben. He grinned. "Years and years."

"And I'll have you know—"

"Bee." Hana put an arm on my shoulder. "Babe, just dance with Ben, okay?"

I looked at her in disbelief. My baby sister had never condescended to me, ever. I was going to say that, when Ben grabbed both of my hands and placed them around his neck. I heard a whistle from the back. *Raph.*

I'd fantasized about bringing Ben to every school dance. About everyone watching us. About his laughing eyes meeting mine as we swayed to some cheesy love song. And now that was exactly what we were doing.

We danced far enough apart, on purpose, so we could stare at each other. Disgusting but true, and it felt so good.

After a minute, Ben pulled me closer and leaned to whisper in my ear, "Bee, I'm in love with you."

My vision got blurry. My heart tripped up its beat.

"But aren't we just friends?" I whispered back.

∽

After the dance was over, we flew out of Dam—*flew*—down to the trail, to the water. He pulled me so close, while the waves lapped. And just like that, I forgot everything else, the last few weeks, the last year. We kissed, again and again and again, and it all made perfect sense.

CHAPTER 70
John

SUMMER IN NEW YORK CITY smelled like hot dogs and pigeon poop, but man, oh man, had I missed it. My mom had a million questions, and I'd felt bad she'd looked so worried when I'd shown up. I told her not to answer her phone if King called—I'd handle it. And I did, by ignoring him. Maybe he'd cut me off. Maybe Yale wouldn't take me back. I didn't care anymore. I watered the plants and got back my old job at the café down the street. I smoked and wandered blocks at night with friends who knew me.

A few weeks after I'd ditched Dogberry, Bobby came to visit for a night. I had to hand it to him—I didn't think that kid could hang in the city with my friends here. But they liked him, and I didn't mind having him around.

After a couple beers at a friend's house party, I finally got the balls to ask, "So, what happened with Claudia?"

Bobby smiled, and popped the collar on his terrible acid-washed jean jacket. "I knew you'd ask, eventually."

"And?"

"It's all good. She and Hana got back together."

That night, under the lights, on the road behind camp, their hands in each other's hair, flashed in my mind.

"Okay, good."

"Good?"

"Yeah." I finished my beer. "I'm glad."

Bobby cackled and shook his head. "Seriously? You pull all this crap, and then you're just, like, 'Good'?"

I shook my head. "You don't get it."

Bobby shrugged. "Nah, I don't. But the whole thing got me fired."

I got him another beer.

WHAT HAPPENED NEXT

Ben

THE SKY IN MAINE has the best stars, and everyone knows that, but Boston's streetlamps were beginning to look more beautiful every day. And while snow in Maine fell in sparkling, trustworthy heaps, these city-scattered flakes had their own look about them. I could barely remember what it felt like to hate living here. Especially when a figure hustled toward me from the subway stop, and when she got close enough, her smile beamed as bright as any summer star. She wore her Dogberry-green beanie all slouchy and perfect.

"Can you believe this?" She laughed, holding up a mittened hand. "It's not even Thanksgiving! Isn't Massachusetts supposed to be warmer?"

"It's still New England." I grinned, reaching for her other hand to pull her closer. Our lips touched. "That's the second time we've kissed in the snow," I whispered, when we pulled back.

She only rolled her eyes a little, which was how I knew she loved me.

We grabbed coffees and started our usual routine—loops and loops around Boston Common, catching up. We were both so busy with classes, and Bee's part in *West Side Story*, that sometimes we only saw each other once a week.

"So, what's the news on Hana and Claudia?" I asked.

"Back together." Bee sighed. "That's three times since this summer."

"That's ridiculous," I sputtered. "Can you imagine if we broke up and got back together that many times?"

She laughed, lighting up the snowflakes. "Yeah, because we kind of did."

"Oh, right."

Bee

Ben's hand in mine felt like the sun—constant, even in the cold. I couldn't imagine a time when we wouldn't be together. Although I never told him that. Some secrets you keep to yourself. They make you glow inside.

Ben was talking about class, the snow was falling, his eyes were twinkling in the fading, hazy city lights. When I was with Ben, I felt . . . myself. Relaxed. At home. My dorm, my classes, and rehearsals—my new life was exhilarating, and sometimes confusing and overwhelming. A kind of free fall.

But with Ben, I felt like I was standing on solid ground. Our hands, together, made sense.

"Hey, did you know it's our three-month-and-three-day anniversary?"

I looked up from our hands—his eyes smiling at me from behind his hair smooshed on his forehead from his dorky elf winter hat.

"I did know that!" I said. "I have it marked on my calendar, next to *remind Ben to get a hobby*."

"So since it's our anniversary," he continued, "I was wondering if you'd tell me: When did you first fall in love with me?"

I tried to tell my EBU friends that my boyfriend was a sap, but they just didn't get to what extent. I pulled him down to sit on a bench, just in case I was going to pass out from his cheesiness.

"Well, it had to be when you puked at the lobster fest," I reasoned. "When we were nine."

"Yeah, that must've been pretty attractive." Ben nodded, "I remember feeling very bold, throwing up right there in the middle of the sing-along."

"Exactly." I nodded back. "When did you first fall in love with me?"

"Same." He shrugged. "When I was puking."

We both cracked up, and he reached over and wrapped a glove around my neck and pulled me in for a kiss. And then another.

"You're so weird," I whispered.

"Mmmm," he countered, nuzzling my nose with his.

"But the world is full of weird things," I continued, my lips touching his to form the words.

"Yeah?"

"And you're my favorite," I said.

He pulled back, his eyes twinkling into mine. "I'm your favorite?"

"Yeah." I smiled, pushing his hat back. "You're my favorite weird thing in the world."

ACKNOWLEDGMENTS

Book two! Here we go! I have so many people to thank, again. I swore it'd be shorter this time, but . . .

Thank you, Gus, Nellie, Tory, and Jenny, for being such wonderful, witty siblings. Thank you, Mom, Vicki Horton, for believing in me and believing in yourself. And happy sixtieth birthday!! Thank you, Aunt Lynn, for all of your help and for Suzie.

Thank you to my agent, Alex Slater, for your keen eye and never-ending enthusiasm. Brainstorming with you is like the best kind of summer camp. Thank you, everyone at Trident Media Group, for believing in and supporting my career.

Thank you to my editor, Kieran Viola, for, oh gosh, everything. But a lot for infusing power and friendship in everything we do, and for sharing my vision of this Much Ado. Thank you, Cassie McGinty, and every lovely person at Hyperion I've had the pleasure of working with.

Thank you to Shadae Mallory for your thoughtful feedback.

Thank you, Girl Scouts, specifically Camp Runels in New Hampshire and Camp Pennacook in Massachusetts, for making me love summer camp. Thank you, Camp Blueberry Cove in Maine, for the inspiration, especially for Counselor Hunt and Sproutball.

Thank you to Deborah Cooper and Samrawit Silva for sharing with me your adoption stories.

Thank you, Tower counselors: Rachel Gianatasio, Jen Locke, Shane Mulcahy, Doug Pass, Sam Stratton, David Thibodeau, and Nellie Booth (again, it's fine, it bears repeating). Thank you, CITs: Ilana DeAngelo, Nick Hurley, Eric Krouss, Joe McKeever, Liam Norton, Chris Shepard, Nate Shepard, Danielle Shiloh, and Matthew Wallace. Obviously also, big thank-yous to Judy Locke, Ginny Morton, and Janine.

Thank you, Elisabeth Joffe, for being you and helping me be me.

Thank you, Rosie Kahan, for listening to me cry, cry, cry, and for being *Saving Hamlet*'s bookstore champion. Thank you, Jen Locke (Jewelry Ken), for being there when no one else could and also for playing Buckbeak in Video Production at camp. Thank you, Megan Reed, for our friendship, which includes clarification on split infinitives and many doggo Snapchat messages. Thank you, Ellie Roark, for endless Gchats and love.

Thank you, Julia Perlowski, the Beatrice to my Beatrice. Thank you, Brian Mooney and Vaune Trachtman—you two make me feel like I can do anything. Congratulations, Geraldine Pittman de Batlle and T. Wilson, on years of extraordinary teaching at Marlboro College.

Thank you, Betsy Klimasmith and the University of Massachusetts Boston, for a new, lovely academic home.

Thank you, Bridget Hodder and Dana Langer—your friendship got this book written.

Thank you to Doug and Lise Pass for being so supportive of my books. You truly make this world a better place.

Thank you, All the World's a Stage Players, for renewing my love of theatre and Shakespeare. Thank you especially to Jenny, for helping me create Margo.

Thank you, Lin-Manuel Miranda. Thank you, Griffin and Rachel McElroy. Thank you, Tegan and Sara.

Thank you, Paul Nelsen, for taking me to the Globe, and for showing me Shakespeare's Globe's *Much Ado About Nothing*, my most favorite production. Thank you, Eve Best and Charles Edwards, for your glorious performances that so much inspired Bee and Ben.

Thank you, Harriet and Suzie. You don't know why I stare at a screen so much, but you accept me and love me anyway, and trust that I'll come out of my trance and feed/walk/pet you soon.

Thank you to past me, summer 2016. I don't know how you wrote this book. From now on, when I doubt that I'm a writer, I'll look to you, and this book, as proof.

Thank you, William Shakespeare, for Don John, Don Pedro, Margaret, Claudio, Hero, and Benedick, whom I love so much and felt inspired to explore.

But most of all, thank you for Beatrice, forever dancing in the stars of my heart.